# ALSO BY MICHAEL PEARCE

## The Mamur Zapt Series

## The Dmitri Kameron Series

## The Seymour of Special Branch Series

# MICHAEL PEARCE

# A COLD TOUCH OF ICE

HarperCollins*Publishers*

HarperCollins*Publishers* Ltd
1 London Bridge Street,
London SE1 9GF

www.harpercollins.co.uk

First published in Great Britain by
HarperCollins*Publishers* 2000

This paperback edition 2017
1

A catalogue record for this book is
available from the British Library

ISBN: 978-0-00-825947-1

# 1

A man pushed his way through the crowd and arrived at the bar beside Owen.

'Wahid whisky-soda!' he instructed the bartender. 'No, make that a double. After all,' he said, turning to the company, 'it's not every day that one gets a death threat in the mail.'

'Yes, it is,' objected the man on his other side. 'I get one every morning.'

'Ah, but that's just from colleagues or from the Finance Department. Mine,' said the man, pulling out a piece of paper from his pocket and waving it with a flourish, 'is the Real Thing.'

'Can I have a look?' Owen stretched out his hand. 'Yes,' he said, 'it's the same handwriting.'

'Same as what?'

'The one I got.'

Someone peered over his shoulder.

'It's just an ordinary bazaar letter-writer!' he said disgustedly. 'That doesn't count!'

'Just because you haven't got one, Patterson!'

'How many other people have had one?' asked Owen.

Several other people put up their hands.

'You see!' said the first man. 'It's just people who are important. Sorry about that, Patterson!'

Some had their letters with them.

'I was going to have mine framed, so that my grandchildren will see that once upon a time I was a man to be taken seriously.'

They passed them to Owen.

'It's all the same handwriting,' said Owen.

'You mean it's only one man? Well, that is a relief. I thought it was everybody that wanted to kill us.'

'It's just some nut? Well, I do feel let down!'

'Don't worry prematurely,' counselled Owen. 'Perhaps he means it.'

There was no doubt, thought Owen, as he sat in a meeting later that afternoon, that the British were unpopular in Egypt. The letter-writer was not an isolated case. Since the war had started, there had been a number of such expressions of hostility. Stones had been thrown, British-owned premises vandalized and solitary soldiers attacked on their way back to barracks.

And yet, for once, it was not Britain's fault. When, a few months before, Italy had invaded Tripolitania, and Turkey, to whom Tripolitania belonged, had retaliated by declaring war, Britain sought to stay neutral. Unfortunately, that was not what most Egyptians wanted. Egypt was still, at least in theory, part of the Ottoman Empire and Egyptian sympathies were heavily with Turkey.

'Egypt is, after all,' Ismet Bey, the Turkish representative at the meeting, was saying now, 'our country.'

Well, yes and no. Yes, it was true, Egypt was still formally part of the Ottoman Empire and the Khedive, Egypt's ruler, owed allegiance to the Sultan at Istanbul. But in practice the Egyptian Khedives had been virtually independent for the best part of a century now, and for the last thirty years, in any case, the real rulers of Egypt had been the British, who had come in 'by invitation' to help the Khedive sort his finances out, come in and then, well, as it happened, stayed.

'All we are asking,' said Ismet Bey, 'is that we should be able to move our troops from one part of His Highness's domains – Palestine – to another – Tripolitania – through a third: Egypt.'

'I do see your point,' conceded Owen's friend, Paul, who was chairing the meeting.

'Well, that is something.'

'However –'

2

However, thought Owen, there wasn't a cat's chance in hell of Britain agreeing to let a Turkish army march through Egypt. Who knows, they might even step aside to assert Ottoman rights in other respects.

'Shouldn't Egypt herself have a voice in this?' asked the Khedive's representative.

'Egypt's is the point of view that I am expressing,' said Paul.

'No, it's not. Yours is the view of the British Administration. We Egyptians strongly condemn Italy's action as Western aggression and would wish to do everything we could to help Turkey repel its foreign invaders.'

'Have you thought,' asked Paul, 'that if you take too active a part, you could yourselves become the object of aggression?'

'We would take care of that,' said Ismet Bey.

The British Commander-in-Chief coughed modestly.

'I think,' he said, 'that the presence of a British army in Egypt is all the guarantee that you need against foreign invasion.'

Ismet Bey sighed. They had been here before in the last few months: many times.

'At least,' he said desperately, 'allow us to move supplies.'

'Medical supplies, certainly,' said Paul. 'As you know, the Consul-General is anxious to provide whatever humanitarian help he can.'

'Arms?'

'I'm not sure that counts as humanitarian.'

'You always used to allow passage.'

'Limited passage. To allow unrestricted passage would be to prejudice our position of neutrality.'

'It's not even limited now,' protested the Bey. 'You've stopped passage altogether.'

'That's because you were sending so much.'

'But –'

'If we include what you've been smuggling.'

'Smuggling?' cried Ismet Bey. 'How can we be smuggling when it's our country?'

3

'Exactly!' said the Khedive's representative. 'And if it's not his country, then it's certainly ours!'

There was a long pause.

'I'll tell you what,' said Paul conciliatorily: 'there's clearly a problem here, and it seems to me that it can best be resolved by appointing someone to regulate the arms traffic whom we can all trust.'

'Well, that sounds very reasonable,' said the Bey, surprised.

'The Mamur Zapt.'

'What?' said Owen, waking up.

'Mamur Zapt?' said the Khedive's representative.

'Yes. A faithful servant of the Khedive.'

'But he's a faithful servant of the British too!' cried the Bey.

'Oh dear, Ismet Bey!' said Paul, beginning to gather up his papers. 'What a shocking suggestion!'

There was, alas, some truth in what Ismet Bey had said. One of the first things the British had done when they arrived was to install their own man as Mamur Zapt, Head of the Khedive's Secret Police, the man ultimately responsible for political security in Cairo. Successive Mamur Zapts had therefore found themselves serving two masters; something which had hitherto not presented much of a problem to Owen, the present incumbent, since he had happily played off one against the other. Lately, however, that had been getting more difficult. Since the new Consul-General had taken over, relations with the Khedive had become strained and the two were often now pulling in different directions.

This evening, though, he was putting such difficulties behind him. An Egyptian colleague had invited him round for coffee. Owen was pleased, because although he had known Mahmoud for nearly four years now, this was the first time he had actually been invited into his house.

The reason for this was partly, he knew, that Mahmoud didn't really have a home of his own. Although he was now in his thirties, he still lived with his mother. Mahmoud's father, a lawyer like himself, had died young and Mahmoud had taken over responsibility for the family. Being the man he was, he had probably taken it too seriously, as he tended to do with his work at the Ministry of Justice. Owen doubted if he ever got home much before midnight. He seemed to have very little life apart from his work.

Mahmoud was, in any case, as Owen had learned over the years, an intensely private individual. Owen was certainly his closest, perhaps his only, friend, but in some respects he felt he had never got to know him. He was delighted now that one of Mahmoud's defensive walls seemed at last to be coming down.

The house was a tall, thin, three-storey building just off the Sharia-el-Nahhasin. Across its roof, surprisingly near, he could see the minarets of the Barquk and, yes, that other one was probably the Qu'alun. The street was towards the edge of the old city, balanced precariously between the new Europeanized quarters to the west and the bazaars to the east.

There was a servant but Mahmoud himself came impatiently to the door and led Owen upstairs to the living room on the first floor. It was a large, sparely furnished room with box windows at both ends, one looking down into an inner courtyard, the other out on to the street. There were fine, rather faded, rugs on the floor and one on the wall, and three low divans, arranged round a brazier, on which a pot of coffee was warming. On the little table next to it were three cups.

'The third is for my father-in-law,' said Mahmoud.

'What?' said Owen, stunned. This was the first he had ever heard about Mahmoud being married.

'My father-in-law to be,' Mahmoud amended.

He seemed a little embarrassed.

'You are getting married?'

Mahmoud nodded.

Owen had never expected this. He had always taken Mahmoud to be one of nature's celibates. In all the time Owen had known him, he had never shown the slightest sexual interest in any woman they had met.

Owen pulled himself together.

5

'Congratulations! Well, this is a surprise!'

'It is to me, too,' Mahmoud admitted. 'But my mother felt the time had come.'

'I see. Yes.' Owen couldn't think what to say. 'Have you known each other for long?' he ventured tentatively.

'About a week. Of course, our families have known each other for much longer.'

'I see.'

'She lives locally so I must have seen her about in the street. But I can't say I ever noticed her.'

'Well, you wouldn't.'

Not in a veil, and covered from head to foot in black.

'But I must have seen her going to school.'

'Going to school?'

'She's just finished at the Sanieh.'

How old could she be? Fifteen? The Sanieh, though, was something. It was probably the best girls' school in Cairo.

'I said she had to be educated.'

'Quite right. Companionship, and all that.'

'She seemed very sensible.'

'Oh, good. You have – you have met her, then?'

'Oh, yes. Once. After my mother had made the contract. She seems very suitable.'

'Oh, good.'

'You'll like her father. I know him quite well.'

'Well, that's important, isn't it?'

'Yes. As a matter of fact, that's partly why I invited you. I wanted him to meet family. I know that, strictly speaking, you're not family, but . . . Well, the fact is, we don't actually *have* many male relatives . . .'

'Glad to do what I can –'

It was no business of his. Mahmoud was old enough to arrange his own life; or, rather, to decide to let others arrange it for him. And if that was the custom of the country –

All the same, he felt bothered. In a way it *was* his business. Mahmoud was a friend of his and he didn't want him to get hurt. As a matter of fact, he didn't want *her* to get hurt, either, a mere schoolgirl. But what could he do about it? And who was he to interfere, anyway? Jesus, he couldn't even sort out his own life, the way things were between him and Zeinab –

When the prospective father-in-law arrived, he felt a little better. Ibrahim Buktari was plainly such a nice man. He was short and wiry, with close-cropped grey hair and an open, intelligent face. They embraced warmly in the Arab fashion.

'You have something in common,' said Mahmoud, pouring out the coffee.

'Oh, yes?'

'You were both soldiers.'

Ibrahim Buktari's face lit up.

'You were?'

'Well,' said Owen, 'briefly.'

'I was with Al-Lurd,' said Ibrahim, 'in the Sudan.'

'With Kitchener?'

'That was before he was a lord,' said Mahmoud.

'And now he returns to Egypt!' said Ibrahim. He shrugged. 'Well, at least we have as Consul-General a man who knows something about Egypt.'

'He knows it only as it was twelve years ago,' said Mahmoud.

That was something that all the Egyptian newspapers had said when the appointment was announced. Especially the Nationalist ones. When Kitchener had been here before, Egyptian nationalism had been in its infancy. But a lot of things had changed since then and among them was that there was now a Nationalist movement which touched almost all parts of the population, especially the young professionals. Like Mahmoud.

How would Kitchener handle it? Would he try to work with it, as his predecessor, Gorst, had done? Or would he – and this was what was feared in Egypt, given his recent record against the equally Nationalist Boers in South Africa – try to suppress it? Was that the point of putting a general into what had hitherto been a civilian post? Was that why Kitchener had been made Consul-General?

When Kitchener had been here before, at the time of his conquest of the Sudan, Owen had been just a junior subaltern on his way out to India to take up his first posting.

'India?'

Ibrahim began to question Owen eagerly about campaigning conditions in the North West Frontier. Seeing them getting along well together, Mahmoud, who had in truth been slightly apprehensive about his prospective father-in-law's visit, sat back happily and let them talk.

The conversation was still in full flow when the door opened suddenly and an elderly woman came into the room. She was very agitated and wasn't even wearing a veil.

'Mahmoud!' she said. 'You are needed. Sidi Morelli has collapsed.'

Mahmoud sprang up and hurried out of the door.

'Sidi Morelli?' said Ibrahim, standing up too. 'Perhaps we can help,' he said to Owen.

'It was in the coffee house,' said Mahmoud's mother, lighting them down the stairs.

Owen had noticed the café as he had turned into Mahmoud's street. Indeed, he could hardly help noticing it, for its tables and chairs spread out right across the street and into the Nahhasin also. Now there was a large crowd gathered at the corner, their faces all strange in the light from the café's vapour lamps. He could see Mahmoud bending over a man lying among the tables.

'Has anyone sent for an ambulance?' asked Ibrahim Buktari.

'We have, Ibrahim, we have,' said someone. 'But it is taking a long time coming.'

'All the ambulances are at the front,' said someone, 'because of the war.'

'A hakim, then?'

Mahmoud looked up.

'There is no need for a hakim,' he said.

Someone in the crowd gasped.

Mahmoud straightened up.

'Cover him,' he said.

Several people at once stripped off their long outer gowns and laid them over the body.

Mahmoud glanced round.

'It didn't happen here,' he said.

'It happened over there, Mahmoud. Just round the corner!'

8

Some of the men took him by the arm and led him a little way along the Nahhasin to where an alley snicked off among the houses.

'It was here, Mahmoud. I found him here,' said one of the men, distressed. 'I nearly fell over him. I didn't see him, it was so dark.'

'And then I called for help, Mahmoud,' said another man, 'and we carried him back to the coffee house.'

'We laid him down,' said someone else, 'and then we saw – saw that it was Sidi Morelli.'

'Sidi Morelli!' Some in the crowd had clearly not realized previously who it was.

'But he had been here!' said the *patron* of the café, bewildered, 'only the moment before!'

He pointed to a table at which three elderly men were sitting, stunned.

From further along the street there came the sound of a bell and then a moment later someone crying: 'Make way!' A covered cart, drawn by two mules, was trying to work through the crowd.

'Make way for the ambulance!'

Somehow it forced its way through the mass of people and drew up alongside the coffee house. A short, thickset, youngish man, Egyptian, but dressed in a suit not a galabeah, began organizing things.

'It is good that you are here, Kamal,' Mahmoud said affectionately.

'I had just got here. I was still shaking hands –'

He seemed, for all his efficiency, bewildered.

The body was lifted, passed over the heads of the crowd and laid in the back of the ambulance.

'To the death-house,' instructed Mahmoud. 'Not to the hospital.'

The crowd watched sombrely. Many of them were weeping. Owen was surprised; not at the crowd, for if there was anything that drew a crowd in Cairo, it was an accident or a fatality, but at the extent, and sincerity, of the feeling.

'Sidi Morelli, Ibrahim!' The man beside them shook his head as if in disbelief.

9

Everyone here, thought Owen, appeared to know everyone else.

Ibrahim Buktari seemed suddenly to have aged.

'I shall go home, I think. Excuse me!'

He shook hands with Owen.

The efficient young man whom Owen had noticed earlier appeared beside them. He put his arm round Ibrahim Buktari's shoulders and led him gently away.

Mahmoud touched Owen's arm.

'I am sorry,' he said. 'We shall have to end our evening early. Another time, perhaps.'

'Of course!'

The crowd was breaking up.

'I have work to do,' said Mahmoud.

'Work!'

'He did not collapse. He was strangled.'

In Cairo at that time investigating a crime was not the responsibility of the police. Nor, most definitely – with the exception of political crime – was it the responsibility of the Mamur Zapt. When a crime was suspected, it was reported to the Department of Prosecutions of the Ministry of Justice, the Parquet, as it was known, and the Parquet would appoint one of its lawyers to conduct an investigation. Ordinarily the appointment would come first. Mahmoud being Mahmoud, however, he had seen a responsibility waiting to be taken and had been unable to resist taking it, with the result that by the time – the following afternoon – that he was actually appointed to the case, he had already been pursuing his inquiries for some hours.

A bearer had brought Owen a message from him about midway through the morning asking him to come to the Morelli house. Owen had been a little surprised, for it was not normally the habit of the strongly Nationalist Parquet to involve the Mamur Zapt in its investigations, and this was particularly true of Mahmoud, who, despite their friendship, did not believe that there should be a Secret Police at all, let alone that it be headed by an Englishman. However, Owen knew that he wouldn't have sent for him unless it was

10

important and, as there was nothing particularly to detain him in his office, set out almost at once.

When he arrived at the house Mahmoud was somewhere else in the building and he was received by the dead man's widow, Signora Morelli; and this was another surprise, for he had not realized, the evening before, that the dead man was Italian.

'Italian?' said Signora Morelli. 'Of course we're Italian! And Egyptian, too. We've lived in this country for forty years. In Cairo for thirty. In this very house! Everyone knows us here. Our children grew up here. This is the place they look upon as home. We, too. We have made our lives here, we were happy here –

'And now this! How can it be? How can they do this to us? He was their friend, everybody knew him. Everybody loved him. He used to go there every night, to that café, and play dominoes with Hamdan and Abd al Jawad and Fahmy Salim. Every night! For years and years. They were inseparable. People made a joke of it. They were the four corners of the house, people said. Take one away, and the coffee house would fall down. That's what they said. And now – now they have taken one away.'

She poured it all out.

'And it is all because of this stupid war. It must be! There can't be any other reason. He never did anyone an injury.

'This stupid war! But it's not our fault. We were against it from the start, we were appalled, like they were. And they said: "No, no, Sidi," – that is what they called him, Sidi – "you cannot be blamed. The politicians are mad. They always are. They are mad here, too. No, no, Sidi, you are one of us."

'And he thought he was one of them, too; I thought I was. This is our home, this is our country. Why should it turn on us? We have loved it, we have worked for it. We thought we were Egyptian too.

'And now this. How can it be? How can they turn on him? What harm has he ever done them? What harm has he ever done anybody? Why should they turn on him, their friend, the man who has lived among them for years? How can people be like that?'

Mahmoud had come in and was standing by the door expressionlessly. He caught Owen's eye and Owen followed him out.

'I see,' said Owen. 'So that's why you called me.'

'No,' said Mahmoud. 'We don't know yet that it was a political crime.'

'Then –?'

He led him off through the house. It was tall and thin, rather like Mahmoud's own, and, like that one, had an inner courtyard. They went across the courtyard and out through a door on the other side. It led them into a great, cavernous, hall-like building which seemed to serve as a warehouse. It contained a bewildering diversity of goods: divans, tables, rugs, great copper-and-silver trays, a lot of brassware – there was a whole corner of the elegant brass ewers called *ibreek* which the Arabs use for pouring water over the hands, along with the *tisht*, the quaint basins and water-strainers that went with them. There were, too, oddly, piles of clothes: finely embroidered shirts which might have belonged to sheiks, lovely old Persian shawls, hand-worked as close as if they were woven, filmy rainbow-coloured veils worn by dancing girls.

Mahmoud led him across to a huge stack of bales of raw cotton. The stuff of one of the bales had been torn, probably in transit, and through the tear there appeared the gleam of something black. Mahmoud pulled more of the cotton aside, put in his hand and tugged. Even before it came out, Owen knew what it was: the barrel of a gun.

# 2

Only four of the bales had guns concealed in them. When they had opened them all, they found a total of fifteen rifles and six revolvers; numbers which Owen found puzzling. Gun-running or gun-using? The numbers were too small for the former and large for the latter – there were assassination attempts all the time, but they seldom involved more than two or three people.

And then there was another puzzle: where they had been found. In the house of an Italian. Gun-running in Egypt at the moment was from the Sinai peninsula to Tripolitania, from the Turks to their allies fighting *against* the Italians. What sort of Italian was it who would be arming enemies against his own kind? He could think of plenty of people who might for one reason or another, for profit or for patriotism, be running guns; but the one national group that wouldn't be, just at the moment, was the Italians.

But then, neither would they be smuggling guns in order to prepare for some armed raid or assassination attempt. It wasn't from foreign nationals that such attempts came; it was from nationalistically-minded Egyptians.

One thing, however, was clear.

'It looks,' he said to Mahmoud, 'as if I'll be joining you in your investigations.'

Sidi Morelli had been an auctioneer. For some reason that Owen could not fathom, many of the auctioneers in Cairo and Alexandria were Italian. The counting at auctions was often done in Italian: *uno, due* . . . Strangely, that was not always so at the auctions conducted by Sidi Morelli himself, whose business included both an up-market end, based upon hired premises in the Europeanized Ismailiya Quarter, and a down-market end held in a tented enclosure close to the Market of the Afternoon, where proceedings were conducted totally in Arabic.

When Owen went there the following day he found a few people poking round the various lots stacked at one end of the enclosure while the sundry Levantines who normally assisted Sidi Morelli stood about uncertainly. An auction had been scheduled for that morning but then, since instructions had been lacking, had been abandoned.

'No, I don't know when it will be held,' one of the Levantines was saying to a rather crumpled-looking Greek. 'Yes, I know you're looking for cotton, and, yes, we do have some in our warehouse, but the Parquet are crawling all over it and I don't know when they'll be finished.'

'It's raw cotton, is it?' said the Greek.

'Yes.'

'And slightly damaged? That's what the man told me last week.'

'Yes, it's slightly damaged. That's why we've got it and why it's not going to the cotton market.'

'Do you think I could go to your warehouse and take a look at it?'

'I wouldn't if I were you. Not just at the moment. As I said, the Parquet are all over the place –'

'The Parquet? What are they doing there?'

'I *told* you. Our boss has just died and –'

'Do you think there's any chance of a reduction?'

'For the cotton? Look –'

'Yes. You know, to get rid of it. Not have it hanging about on your hands. While they're working out the estate.'

'Look, he's only just died!'

'Yes, but –'

'No!' said the Levantine in a fury. 'No!'

The Greek moved away.

'These bloody Greeks!' the Levantine said to Owen. 'They're so bloody sharp, they cut themselves!'

An Arab dressed in a dirty blue galabeah came in under the awning.

14

'Louis,' he said to the Levantine, 'is there any chance of the *angrib*?'

He pointed to a rope bed in one of the lots.

'Sidi said I could have it if you didn't sell it this time, and I've got a customer waiting.'

'I don't see why not,' said the Levantine. 'If it's not gone twice there's no reason to suppose it would go the third time.'

'Thanks.'

The Arab called a porter, who picked up the bed and walked out with it across his shoulders.

The Arab hesitated.

'If I sell it, you know —'

'That's all right,' said Louis.

'I wouldn't like the Signora —'

'That's all right.'

'We let the stallholders have the stuff we can't sell,' the Levantine said to Owen.

The Greek returned.

'I'm looking for a baby-chair, too,' he said.

'Baby-chair!'

'You know, one of those high chairs that kids can sit in.'

'We don't have any baby-chairs.'

'It's for when they get big enough to sit up at table.'

'Yes, I know what a baby-chair is. But we don't have any. Not here. We wouldn't have any. People around here sit on the floor. Babies too.'

'Oh!'

The Greek seemed cast down.

'Maybe our other place —' said the Levantine, relenting.

'Other place?'

'We've got a place up in the Ismailiya. That's where we put the better-quality stuff. It's brassware, antiques, mostly, but occasionally we get some European furniture. You could try there.'

'Thanks,' said the Greek gratefully. He hesitated. 'You don't think they'd have any cotton?'

'No!' The Levantine almost shouted. 'It's only the better-quality goods. Everything else comes *here*. Cotton comes *here*.'

'Yes, I see. And when –?'

'Look,' began the Levantine again, desperately.

Owen went out into the huge square beneath the Citadel in which the Market of the Afternoon was held. All round the edges of the square camels were lying and among the camels were great cakes compounded equally of dates and dirt. The Market itself was up on a raised platform. You climbed the steps and found yourself in a kind of giant village market, where the stalls were often mere pitches, with the owner sitting on the ground and all his goods spread round him in the dust. Potential customers would crouch down and finger the goods; and the dust came in handy for writing out the bills.

The goods in the Market of the Afternoon were different from those in the bazaars. They were for the most part copper or brass and almost entirely second-hand, the copper pots often worn with the use of generations. Everything here was for use, although the use was sometimes a little strange: the manacles for the punishment of harem women, for instance. Yet among the worn and battered goods you could occasionally find things of value, brass bowls inscribed with Persian hunting scenes, finely wrought candlesticks for standing on the ground, intricately chased scriveners' pots, one of which had been acquired here once by none other than the Mamur Zapt.

In the centre of the Market was a restaurant area, the restaurants consisting often merely of large trays on the ground, with meat and pickles in the middle. Customers sat round on the ground and dipped their hands in.

It was at one of these that Owen found the Arab who had collected the *angrib* from the auction room.

'Sold it yet, then?'

The Arab pointed out beyond the stalls to where a man was loading a donkey. The donkey already had panniers hanging down on either side but now the man put the bed across its back; and then he climbed up on top himself.

'I'll let the Signora have the five per cent,' the Arab said to Owen.

16

'The Signora? You reckon she'll be taking it on?' asked the man crouched next to him.

'Her or someone else.'

'They won't be like Sidi Morelli,' said his neighbour definitely.

'No. He was one of us.'

It was a phrase that recurred whenever people spoke of Sidi Morelli. Owen heard it again that evening when he returned with Mahmoud to the coffee house at the end of Mahmoud's street, the one to which Sidi Morelli had been carried when he died, and where he had been in the habit of going every evening, punctually at six, to play dominoes with his friends.

They were sitting there now at their usual table, the table that Owen had seen them at that evening. The dominoes had been spread out on the table but they weren't really playing.

Mahmoud made straight towards them. They seemed to know him and stood up to shake hands. Mahmoud introduced Owen, first as a friend, and then, scrupulously, feeling that they should know, as the Mamur Zapt. They looked at him curiously but acceptingly. To be someone's friend was sufficient to invoke the traditional Arab code of hospitality.

Sidi Morelli had been a friend, a long-standing one. The four of them had first started meeting, they explained, ten years before.

'Hamdan and I were sitting here –'

'With the dominoes.'

'– when he came across and asked if he could join us.'

'The dominoes were all in use, you see.'

'Well, of course we said yes.'

'But that was only three. However, just at that moment Fahmy came in –'

'Whom he seemed to know –'

'He used to come to me for ice,' Fahmy explained.

'And so then there were four of us and there have been four ever since.'

There was a little, awkward silence.

17

The *patron* came across, carrying two water-pipes. Behind him his small son struggled with a third. They put the bowls down on the floor beside the three men. The patron looked enquiringly at Mahmoud and Owen. They shook their heads.

'He never smoked either,' said Abd al Jawad sombrely.

The *patron* touched him commiseratingly on the shoulder, then went off for the coffee pot.

'How can it be?' said Fahmy suddenly, plainly still distressed. 'Doesn't God look down?'

'He looks down,' Hamdan chided him, 'but he does not always interfere.'

'He sees further than we do,' said the third man.

Hamdan and Abd al Jawad were, it transpired, shopkeepers. Fahmy kept an ice house just round the corner. They all lived and worked within three hundred yards of the coffee shop.

'Have you been to the Signora?' Hamdan asked Abd al Jawad.

'Yes. I said that we would wish to do what we could. Of course, it will be in the Italian church.'

Fahmy picked up one of the dominoes. He put it down again, however, aimlessly.

'It's not the same,' he said.

'No.'

'You know no reason?' asked Mahmoud.

They shook their heads.

'He had no enemies,' said Abd al Jawad.

'People always say that, but –'

'He had no enemies,' Abd al Jawad insisted stubbornly.

Mahmoud let it rest.

'He was no different that night?'

'No different.'

'Tell me how it was.'

'Well, he came, and sat down as usual, and we played –'

'What did you talk of?'

'Fahmy's nephew, and would he marry.'

'It happens, you know, Mahmoud,' said Abd al Jawad, with an attempt at humour.

'He has just returned to Cairo,' Fahmy explained.

'Where had he been?'

'In the Sudan. He is a soldier.'

'Fahmy was worried that he might marry someone unsuitable while he was there.'

'We told him that he was much more likely to marry someone unsuitable back here in Cairo.'

'And that the only thing to do was to get him properly married beforehand.'

'Yes,' said Hamdan. 'In case he was sent away.'

'Fahmy's worried that he might be posted.'

'Well,' said Fahmy defensively, 'it could happen, couldn't it? Especially these days.'

'Egypt's not going to get involved in the war. The British will see to that.'

'I wouldn't want him to go to the war,' said Fahmy.

'Then you can look on the British as a blessing,' said Hamdan wryly, but with a quick look at Owen.

Owen laughed.

'That is not how we are usually seen,' he acknowledged.

The slight note of tension that had crept in seemed to ease.

Mahmoud brought it back again.

'Sidi Morelli was Italian,' he observed, as if casually.

'He was one of us,' said Abd al Jawad quickly, almost reprovingly.

Afterwards, Mahmoud took him to the spot where Sidi Morelli had been found lying. It was no more than twenty yards from the coffee house, but around the corner and along the Nahhasin. The Nahhasin was quiet at that point and almost deserted. There was a group of shops further along but here there were only houses, and they were the old, traditional ones which presented a blank wall at ground level containing only a door. The windows were higher up, at the level of the first storey, and tonight, at any rate, they were without lights. The street was dark and Owen could quite see how someone might have stumbled over Sidi Morelli.

He suddenly realized that that was the point of them being

here. Mahmoud had wanted to see it as it had been the evening before, at the time when Sidi Morelli had been killed. It wasn't exactly a reconstruction, although Mahmoud, trained, like the Parquet as a whole, in French methods of investigation, favoured reconstructions. It did, though, enable him to see it as it had been, and to check on one or two things: the witness's story, for example, of how he had come to find the body.

Times, too. Owen guessed that they had retraced Sidi Morelli's movements pretty exactly. Their arrival at the table might had been arranged to coincide with the moment when Sidi Morelli had reached it the previous night. Similarly, their departure might well have coincided with his. He had got up and left the table, shaking hands, as was the Arabic custom, with everyone else in the coffee house and then set off round the corner and along the Nahhasin towards his house.

And exactly here, where a little, dark alleyway ran off between the houses, someone must have been waiting for him. They had probably been standing in the darkness of the alleyway and then, as he had passed, reached out and pulled him into the shadow and strangled him; so quickly and efficiently that he had not had time to utter a cry or make a sound loud enough to catch the attention of those seated in the coffee house not twenty yards away. And then they had fled, almost certainly up the alleyway.

'Well, yes,' said Mahmoud. 'Except that there were some porters further along the alleyway hauling up a bed and they claim that no one passed them.'

He led Owen down the alley. At its far end the blank walls of the big houses of the Nahhasin gave way to tenements. From some of the upper storeys came the weak light of oil lamps. They could see the window through which the bed had been hauled. Its frame was still out and beneath it, on the ground, there were still some bulky objects awaiting their turn to be lifted.

'There would have been a lamp up there,' said Mahmoud, 'and possibly one on the ground, where they were working.'

'Pretty dark,' said Owen, looking round, 'even so.'

'But narrow,' said Mahmoud. 'They are sure they would have seen him. Still, I think it more likely that he escaped along here than that he went down the Nahhasin. I asked the men who found the body and they were positive that they had met no one coming away from where Morelli had been killed. The alleyway seems somehow much more likely.'

They retraced their steps.

'It all happened in about five minutes,' said Mahmoud. 'From the time he left the coffee house to the time they found him.'

'How was he killed?'

'Strangled.'

'Not garotted?'

'No.'

'Quick, then.'

'No money was taken,' said Mahmoud.

'No money? But then –?'

'He was killed for some other reason.'

Owen didn't like the sound of that. He hoped that Mahmoud would soon find a reason, some private, personal motive, rooted in family, perhaps, or in business. The alternative opened up too many disquieting possibilities. 'One of us' Morelli may have been; but had he been 'one of us' enough, at a time when war was placing such a new, heavy stress on old identities and relationships?

There was a reception at the Abdin Palace that evening and Owen, as one of the Khedive's senior servants, was bidden to be there. Although there were plenty of other Englishmen in the Khedive's service – the whole British Administration, nominally, for a start – he was, in fact, one of very few Englishmen present, an indication of the chill that had come over the relationship between the Khedive and the new British Consul-General. The absence was all the more marked because the reception was for someone who was to all intents and purposes an honorary Englishman.

Slatin Pasha had entered the Khedivial service some thirty years before and had been appointed governor of a province in the Sudan. During the Sudan uprising he had been taken prisoner and had been a slave of the Khalifa for eleven years. His famous escape, made with the help of the British Intelligence, had led to him becoming the darling of the British public. He had paid many visits to Windsor and been showered with honours by the Queen, including a knighthood. He was just the man you would have expected the Consulate to turn out for; and yet no one was there.

Slatin was very keen on honours and the reception was in recognition of him collecting yet another one a short time before, this time from Austria. Slatin was himself an Austrian and had naturally been pleased. All the same, he was not entirely happy about this evening.

'It won't do, Owen, it won't do,' he said, looking around him. 'It's bad if His Lordship wasn't invited to something like this.'

'Perhaps he was invited and just didn't come.'

'Then that's bad, too. Countries should come together in Egypt even if they have their differences elsewhere.'

'Not always easy,' said Owen.

Slatin looked at him in his sharp, bird-like way.

'Especially it is not easy for people like you and me,' he said.

Owen suddenly wondered about Slatin. He was the most Anglophile of Anglophiles; and yet he was also Austrian. If the two sides started pulling apart, how would he react? Which would he choose?

'Dilemmas, dear boy, dilemmas!' said Slatin, and scurried away.

And how far would their common service to the Khedive, to Egypt, that most cosmopolitan of countries, containing so many different nationalities, be able to hold the strain?

Across the room he saw Ismet Bey talking to – this was surprising, you hardly ever saw a woman on an occasion like this – a tall, blonde woman, about thirty. No veil, either; she must be foreign.

Later in the evening, one of the German attachés caught him by the arm.

'Come over, Owen. There's someone I'd like you to meet.'

It was the girl.

'Fräulein von Ramsberg; the Mamur Zapt.'

'Ah, the Mamur Zapt!' said the girl, as if she knew about Mamur Zapts.

'Fräulein von Ramsberg has just completed a crossing of the Sinai desert. On camel.'

'Good heavens!' said Owen.

'But you yourself, who have lived so long in this part of the world, have no doubt made similar journeys?' she suggested.

'I'm afraid not.'

'No?'

'I do occasionally go out of Cairo. Reluctantly,' said Owen.

The girl laughed.

'You are a city man. Well, there are different sorts of Arabists. I am a desert one.'

'I do admire people like yourself who make these long, arduous journeys.'

This wasn't entirely true. In fact, it wasn't true at all. He thought they were crazy. He had done some camel-riding, which he had found most uncomfortable, and quite a lot of horse-riding, especially in India; but on the whole he preferred sitting in cafés.

'Fräulein von Ramsberg has a request to make,' said the attaché.

'I wish to make a journey, and I wondered if you would give me a *firman*.'

A *firman* was a kind of permit.

'Where are you going?'

'I want to go west out of Cairo and then drop down to the top of the Old Salt Road.'

'That's quite a journey!'

She laughed.

'That's the kind of journey that I like.'

Her English was very good.

'Well, rather you than me.'

'You wouldn't like to come with me?'

'No, thanks!'

'A pity. Just the *firman*, then.'

'Actually, you don't need a permit to go there.'

'Nevertheless, a letter of some kind from you would, I am sure, be of great help.'

'If you wish. But I don't think it will help much down there.'

'Does not the word of the Mamur Zapt strike terror into men's hearts in even the most remote parts of Egypt?'

'I very much doubt it. When are you setting out?'

'At the end of the week.'

'Well, I'll get it to you before then. And perhaps in return you would like to accompany me on one of my sorts of expedition?'

'I very much would,' said Miss von Ramsberg.


'You great dope!' said his friend, Paul.

'Dope? Why?'

'Agreeing to give her a letter of recommendation.'

'It's just a letter!'

'It will have your name on it, won't it?'

'Yes, but it's not even a *firman*!'

'That's something we ought to think about introducing,' said Paul. 'A *firman* for people like her.'

'People like her?'

'What do you think she wants to travel in Egypt for?'

'She likes travelling. She's just crossed the Sinai peninsula –'

'Yes, I know. Another of these great camel-riders. Pain in the ass, all of them. They upset the local tribes, get killed or kidnapped, and then you've got to spend a lot of time – and money! – looking for them.'

'She seems to have managed it all right without any of those things happening.'

'Oh, sure! Competent, too. Well, if she's so competent, how come she lost her way?'

'Lost her way? I didn't know that.'

'The Sinai is one of those areas which, being a border region, *does* require a *firman*. When she applied for hers she had to specify a route. Which she then did not follow.'

'Well, hell, all kinds of things –'

'She didn't make any attempt to follow it. She didn't go anywhere near it. Instead she followed the route that Saladin took against the Crusaders.'

'Yes, but –'

'Which is likely to be the route if anyone else was invading Egypt.'

'Invading!'

'It would take the Turks a matter of days to get to the border.'

'She's not a Turk, she's –'

'A German. Yes, I know. And the Germans are building the railways which are going to help them get to the border.'

'Paul, you don't mean –?'

'Yes, I do.'

The Mamur Zapt's remit was confined to Egypt and he did not follow very closely what was happening beyond its borders. He thought, however, that Paul was making too much of this. It was unlike him to be so alarmist; but perhaps now that he was working so closely with Kitchener, as his Oriental Secretary, some of Kitchener's own alarmism with respect to anything beyond his borders was rubbing off on him.

'We can't be sure, of course,' Paul said now, softening slightly, 'but just in case she is, we oughtn't to go out of our way to encourage her!'

'It's just a letter!'

'Can you write it in such a way as to lead to information coming back as to where exactly she is?'

'I'll try.'

'She's in Cairo for the best part of a week. It would be interesting to know what she's up to while she's here.'

'Well, as a matter of fact –'

He had given her a choice of two places: the Semiramis, which had a dining room with a romantic view over the river, and the Mirabelle, which was a French restaurant in the noisy Arab Mouski. She chose the Semiramis; Owen would have chosen the Mirabelle.

'But then I *am* romantic,' she protested.

25

'Is that what brought you out to these parts?'

'Yes. But not in the way that you think. There are two sides to being a romantic, the side that gets you bowled over by the moon on the water, and the rebellious side. It was that other side that led to me coming out here.'

'Who or what were you rebelling against?'

'My family. The life they were charting for me – the life of a rich woman in Germany. My family are' – she grimaced – 'respectable. We have an estate. The men for generations have been soldiers, the women, soldiers' wives. Which means you spend your whole life in boring garrison towns. And then you retire to your boring estate. And it is all so predictable.

'My brothers knew from the start that they would be soldiers. For a long time I thought I would be a soldier, too, and joined them in their horse-riding. But then they went off and it suddenly became apparent that all there was for me was marriage to some absolutely dreadful man.

'I bought time. I said I wanted to travel. Some relations took me out with them to the Bosphorus. And then I looked around.'

'And took up camel-riding instead of horse-riding?'

She laughed.

'It looks like that,' she admitted. 'And maybe there's some truth in it. I sometimes think I took it up only in order to outdo my brothers. They are both great riders, horse-riders. I wanted to be not only a better rider, I wanted to be a different one.'

'At any rate, to ride to a different tune.'

'That is so. That is exactly so.'

'It is hard, though, especially out here,' he said, thinking of Zeinab, 'to be a woman and to be independent.'

'Less hard than you think, if you're a foreigner. There are no people from home to order me around and the locals don't know what to make of me.'

'But on your travels –'

She shrugged.

'I carry a gun. In fact, though, the Bedu have never bothered me. It's only in the towns that there has ever been any trouble. And then it's usually been only from

26

interfering officials. In the desert, at least you can get away from all that. There's space, there's freedom. You can choose your own route.'

'As you evidently did in the Sinai.'

She gave him a sharp look.

'You do do your homework,' she said. 'You have been making inquiries?'

'No. I just heard.'

'Well, it is not important. Is it important to you?'

'Not to me. To the authorities, perhaps.'

'The authorities!' she said contemptuously.

They went out on to the verandah and stood looking down at the river. While they had been dining, the moon had risen. The leaves of the palm trees along the bank had turned silver and immediately below them the water was full of silver sparkles, too, where some men had waded out into the river to fill their water-bags. As they watched, the wind stirred the palm leaves and a long silver ripple ran out from the shore right across the river.

'Let us go for a walk along the bank,' she said. And, later:

'It is a pity you are not coming with me,' she said.

# 3

---

'Effendi,' said the warehouse foreman, almost weeping, 'on my oath, I did not know. Am I a genie, to see what lies hidden inside the bales?'

'Did not they seem heavy? Heavier than usual?'

'If they did, Effendi, the camels did not tell me.'

'The porters, then; did not they remark on it?'

The foreman looked at the warehouse porters, great, bull-necked men, who would think nothing of carrying a piano single-handed.

'They remark on much, Effendi. Too much. But they did not remark on this.'

Owen thought it likely that they wouldn't even have noticed.

'Where did the bales come from?'

'Sennar, Effendi.'

'Sennar? That is a long way.'

'It is. But, Effendi, on their way they pass through Assuan, and there they are sorted into different lots. Most go on to the cotton markets, but some are rejected, and it is those which come to us.'

'So the guns could have been put in either at Sennar or at Assuan?'

'They could, Effendi. They would not have been put in during the march, for the camel men would not have it. But –'

'Yes?'

'Effendi, *why* were they put in? And why,' he said, distressed, 'were they sent to us?'

'That is what has to be looked into.'

Owen asked for the names of the firm's agents at Assuan. The foreman gave them to him.

'But, Effendi, they may know nothing about it. Do you know the great traders' market at Assuan? It is by the river. The caravans come in and camp and unload their goods. The bales would have stood as unloaded, waiting for another caravan, one of ours, to pick them up and carry them on. There are many people in the camp, Effendi, hundreds, if not thousands, and they walk around freely. Anyone might have come to the bales in the night.'

Owen nodded.

'The bales were brought here, then, from Assuan. How long would they have stayed in your warehouse before they were opened?'

'They would not have been opened. We would have auctioned them as they stood.'

'But surely buyers wish to examine the goods before bidding?'

'The goods are taken up to our place near the Market of the Afternoon on the day before the auction. Then anyone can come in and see them.'

'Would they open the bales?'

'Not usually. They come and feel the cotton, Effendi, that is all they need.'

'So that if someone knew that the goods were arriving, they would break in either to your warehouse or to your place near the Market of the Afternoon and take the guns?'

'They could, Effendi. But our warehouse is safe. We have an interest in making it so. And at our place near the Market of the Afternoon we have a watchman.'

Owen had his own theories about the efficacy of watchmen; especially near the Market of the Afternoon.

'But, have you thought, Effendi,' said the foreman, 'there is no need to break into either; provided you are prepared to pay the highest price at the auction.'

'I really don't think –' began Owen.

'I think you should,' said Paul.

'Appointment of a librarian? Look, I've got important things to do –'

'Not as important as this,' said Paul.

Paul, now, as Kitchener's right-hand man, was in a position to insist, so, grumbling, Owen went.

When he entered the room he was staggered by the status of the people present. There was Paul, of course, and his opposite numbers from the principal Consulates. There was the Turkish representative, Ismet Bey. And there was one of the Khedive's senior cabinet ministers. That was, possibly, explicable since the appointment was to the Khedive's Library. Even so, they were only appointing a librarian, which was hardly the stuff of international disputes.

Except that it appeared to be.

'But I *am* a scholar!' said the German representative, beaming.

'A very distinguished one,' said Ismet Bey.

'One who, moreover, enjoys the full confidence of the Khedive,' declared the cabinet minister.

'No, you're not; you're Number Two at the German Consulate,' said Paul.

'In Germany, that does not preclude scholarship,' said the German representative easily.

Stung, Paul retorted:

'No, but it ought to preclude taking up a sensitive senior post in His Highness's service!'

'Sensitive?' murmured Ismet Bey.

'Senior?' said a representative of one of the other Consulates doubtfully.

'A key post,' declared Paul, 'and one that has hitherto been occupied only by distinguished scholars of independent standing.'

'A tradition I hope to maintain,' murmured the German representative.

'But you are not independent. You are –'

'German?' suggested Ismet Bey. 'The post has always been occupied by a German.'

'On scholarly grounds,' put in the German representative.

'There is, of course, an argument for appointing an Egyptian –' began the cabinet minister.

'– at some time in the future,' said Ismet Bey, 'though at the moment –'

'On scholarly grounds,' murmured the German representative.

'Britain accepts that in the past the post of Khedive's Librarian has always been reserved to German nationals. However, –'

However, thought Owen, that was all right when the incumbent was someone as unworldly as old Holmweg, the man who had just retired. He was beginning to pick up the hidden agenda now. For some reason Paul, and, presumably, the British government, were set against having someone as politically astute as Paul's opposite number in the post. But why? It was, after all, only a librarian.

'– my government could not accept the appointment to the post of someone who would give it a different character.'

He turned to the German representative.

'Not, of course, that we wish to cast any reflection upon Dr Beckmann. Nor upon his scholarship. It is just that we feel that his qualities, great though they are, are not ones entirely suited to the post, at least for the immediate future. No, gentlemen, I am sorry: I am afraid we will have to cast our net wider.'

He gathered up his papers.

'Cheeky bastards!' he fumed, as he and Owen walked away together. 'Do they think we're daft, trying something like that on?'

'But, Paul, does it really matter?'

Paul stared at him.

'Matter? Of course it matters. It means that he'd be able to carry on even if the Consulate went!'

The whole community turned out to watch the funeral procession. Both sides of the street were lined with people and that was so all the way from the Nahhasin to the Italian church. They bowed their heads and beat upon their chests. Many were openly crying. Used as he was to the extravagance of Arab protestations of grief, Owen could not help being moved. For this was not one of their own that they were mourning but a foreigner.

Since the funeral was that of a foreigner, there was a hearse. With Arab funerals there was no hearse; the body was carried upon a bier. Usually there was a kind of horn at one end, on which the turban was hung. The whole was often covered with a rich cashmere shawl. The bier was borne by the dead man's friends, often, it seemed to Owen, precariously, for the feeling was intense and grief-stricken mourners would pluck at the bier, threatening to overturn it. Even today at times they pressed in on the hearse, touching the sides as if it was only through touch that they could communicate the strength of their feelings. Communicate or demonstrate? To Westerners there often seemed something histrionic in the affectation of grief. Owen knew, however, that there was nothing false about this. They were mourning someone dear to them.

Sidi Morelli was a Roman Catholic and the funeral service was being held in the Catholic church used by the Italian community. Sidi Morelli's neighbours, as Muslims, would not go in. This public demonstration of grief and affection was therefore their way of participating. Some were no doubt there merely because they enjoyed a good funeral; but Owen was struck by how many in this most conservative of neighbourhoods were prepared to come out and display their feeling for an infidel.

Beside him, outside the warehouse, while the hearse was waiting, were Sidi Morelli's three domino-playing friends.

The coffin was brought out of the house and laid in the hearse.

'We ought to have been carrying that,' said Fahmy.

'Let each man die in his own way,' said Hamdan pacifically.

'Perhaps it is as well,' said Abd al Jawad. 'For it is a long way to the church and he is a heavy man.'

'There would have been many to assist,' said Fahmy.

The hearse moved forward a few paces and another carriage drew up outside the house. Signora Morelli and members of her family got in. As she came out of the house she saw the

32

three friends and came across to them and said something. The men were openly moved.

The carriages advanced. The road filled up behind them. Hamdan, Abd al Jawad and Fahmy put themselves formally at the head of the procession.

As the ranks passed in front of him, Owen suddenly saw among them the alert figure of Ibrahim Buktari, Mahmoud's prospective father-in-law. He was talking animatedly to the efficient young Egyptian whom Owen had noticed at the coffee house. He waved an arm when he saw Owen and Owen fell in beside them.

'This is Kamal,' said Ibrahim Buktari; 'and this,' he said to the young Egyptian, 'is a friend of Mahmoud El Zaki's. A soldier, like yourself.'

'Soldier?' said the young Egyptian, surprised. 'I wouldn't have thought Mahmoud would have had any friends who were –'

He stopped, embarrassed.

'Soldiers?'

'British soldiers.'

'A hundred years ago,' said Owen. 'I'm not a soldier now.'

'Once a soldier, always a soldier,' said Ibrahim Buktari.

'Where are you stationed?' asked Owen.

'At the Abdin Barracks, at the moment. I've just got back from the Sudan.'

'Ah,' said Owen. 'Have I met your uncle? Wasn't he one of Sidi Morelli's domino-playing friends?'

'That's him up there,' said Ibrahim Buktari.

'Fahmy Salim?'

'That's right,' said the young Egyptian.

'He was worried about your being sent to the front.'

'What front?' said Kamal bitterly. 'The British are keeping us away from any front.'

Ibrahim Buktari clicked his tongue reprovingly.

'You'll get your chance,' he said.

'But when?' asked the young man. 'And who against? It's not the Sudanese that I want to be fighting.'

'It doesn't matter who it's against,' said Ibrahim Buktari.

'The important thing, for a young soldier, is to be fighting.'

Kamal laughed and laid his hand on Ibrahim's arm affectionately.

'You're a fine friend for my uncle to have!' he said. 'I'll tell him what you said!'

'Tell him! And then I'll tell him that the one thing a young officer wants is war. That's the way to quick promotion.'

'Yes, I know. That's what they all say. But that's not the only thing, you know. You need to be fighting on the right side.'

'Nonsense!' cried Ibrahim Buktari, greatly enjoying himself. 'There is no such thing as the right side. Not here in Egypt, there isn't. Sides are all over the place, and the only thing that counts is to be on the winning side!'

'Shocking!' cried Kamal. 'To have respectable elders leading young men astray! What is the country coming to!'

They embraced each other, laughing. This was obviously a continuing pretend argument between them.

Then they sobered up and the young Egyptian excused himself.

'I must go and walk beside my uncle. It is a long way in the heat and he is much stricken by Sidi Morelli's death. He may need help before the end. And perhaps,' he said to Owen, 'you can talk some sense into this old firebrand. The only people he listens to are the British!'

'Outrageous!' shouted Ibrahim Buktari. But the young Egyptian was gone.

'He's all right,' Ibrahim Buktari said to Owen. 'I've known him since he was a boy. Full of wrong ideas, of course. But then, the young always have been.'

That evening Owen went round to see Zeinab. She lived in the fashionable Ismailiya Quarter, and had an *appartement* of her own. This was unusual for a single Egyptian woman; but then Zeinab was unusual in many respects.

She was the daughter of a Pasha, which explained how she could afford to own an *appartement* but which did not account for the audacity of maintaining a separate establishment itself. Most Pasha's daughters were as harem-bound as other Egyptian women and spent their lives at home with their families until they could be suitably married. The circumstances of Zeinab's birth and upbringing were, however, mildly out of the ordinary, even by Egyptian standards.

Her mother had been one of Cairo's most famous courtesans and the young Nuri Pasha had been desperately in love with her, to such an extent, indeed, that he had scandalized Cairo society by proposing marriage. To his surprise, and the even greater surprise of society, she had turned him down, preferring to keep her independence. This had endeared her to Nuri – who liked a bit of spirit in his women – even more, and the two had lived happily together until, tragically, Zeinab's mother had died giving birth to Zeinab.

The shattered Nuri had clutched at the baby as representing all that was left of the great passion of his life, acknowledging Zeinab as his daughter and bringing her up as, in his view, a Pasha's daughter should be brought up.

This was not quite, however, as other Pashas' daughters were reared. Like most of the old Egyptian ruling class, Nuri looked to France for his culture, and had brought Zeinab up to share that culture. Being Nuri, however, he had rather overdone it, with the result that Zeinab was as much a Frenchwoman as she was an Egyptian. She spoke French more naturally than she spoke Arabic.

Consistent with this approach, the doting Nuri had throughout her childhood allowed her considerably more licence than her peers enjoyed, rejoicing, indeed, in every expression of independence as reflecting something of the spirit of her mother.

True, still, to his enthusiasm for things French, especially women, he had encouraged her, as she approached womanhood, to assume the *ton* of the young Parisienne. Basing himself, however, largely on the latest magazines that he had received from Paris, he had tended to confuse the current normal with less widely shared notions of the New Woman, which, admittedly, he interpreted as merely the adding of a piquant new flavour to the more traditional ones of sexual attraction. The upshot of all this was that by the time she was eighteen Zeinab had come to take for granted a degree of freedom unusual among Muslim women; and what Nuri was reluctant to grant, she took.

Zeinab, too, was enthusiastic about French culture, although her interests were more aesthetic. The Cairo art world, where she found most of her friends, was heavily French in tone, and had the additional advantage of taking a more relaxed view of women than the rest of Egyptian society. She was able, therefore, to pursue her interests in painting and music more or less in peace, and sometimes thought that one day she might establish a *salon* along the lines of that of the great Parisian ladies.

First, however, she would have to get married, and this presented a problem, since the only man she could contemplate was someone who shared her views on personal freedom, and there appeared to be no rich young Egyptian men in that category. That only left Owen; and he, alas, was English.

Meanwhile, she was just coming up to thirty.

'Mahmoud? Married?' she said now, raising herself upon her elbows. She seemed disconcerted. 'I wouldn't have thought he was the marrying kind.'

'I think it was a bit of a surprise to him, too.'

He told her about the evening.

'School?' said Zeinab. 'She must be about fourteen.'

'I think she's left school now.'

'Well, that, I suppose, is something.'

'I met her father. He seems all right.'

'The trouble is,' said Zeinab, 'that Mahmoud is not marrying the father.'

'I know. It does seem strange. But there you are. Time passes.'

'Yes,' said Zeinab.

'Owen, I've had a letter this morning –'

It was McPhee, the Deputy Commandant of the Cairo Police.

'Everyone's had them,' said Owen.

'Not just me, then.'

McPhee seemed pleased. He turned to go. Then he came back.

'I've had them before,' he said.

'The same writing?'

'It's a letter-writer's hand,' said McPhee, who, despite his eccentricity, knew his Egypt.

'Got one?'

McPhee laid it before him.

'It's the same as mine,' said Owen. 'And the same as everyone else's. Whoever it is always used the same writer.'

'We could look out for him, I suppose,' said McPhee. 'Though there are dozens of letter-writers in the city.'

'The ones to you, and to the Mamur Zapt,' said Nikos, the Secrets Clerk, 'were both posted in the Box.'

Fastened to the wall outside the Governorate was an old wooden box in which from time immemorial it had been the habit of the citizens of Cairo to deposit petitions, complaints about the price of bread, denunciations of their neighbours and accusations against their neighbours' wives, together with sundry informations which were thought might be of interest to the Mamur Zapt. And some of them were.

McPhee had told him once – McPhee was a fount of such curious knowledge – that it was like the 'Bocca del Leone' at Venice, a letterbox decorated with a lion's head, into which Venetians could drop communications which they wished to bring to the attention of the authorities. In Venice the communications had to be signed. In Cairo the informant could remain anonymous, but Owen, who liked the custom, felt that didn't matter. In principle it was a way of giving every citizen a chance to communicate with the highest in the land; although these days the Mamur Zapt was not, as he once had been, the right-hand man of the Sultan, the most powerful of all his Viziers.

'The point is,' said Nikos, whose duty it was to unlock the

Box every morning and bring its contents to Owen, 'we could have the Box watched.'

Neither Owen nor McPhee liked the idea. To McPhee it was an affront to the spirit of the city. Owen was uncomfortable with the idea too, though he rationalized his discomfort away on the utilitarian grounds that once the anonymity of the Box was breached, its value as a democratic means of communication would be lost.

Nikos, the ever-realistic Copt, shrugged. He wasn't, after all, the one who had been receiving the death threats.

For some days now the weather in Cairo had been unusually hot. Fans were whirring overhead in all the offices. The green shutters on the windows were kept closed. The windows themselves hung open and a little air, and a thin sunlight, came through the slats. In Owen's, as in all Cairo offices, a vessel of drinking water stood in the window where the incoming air might cool it. Not today, however; the water was lukewarm. Owen summoned the office orderly and asked for some ice.

The orderly spread his hands.

'Effendi, there is none in the ice box. There has been a run on it this week. Everyone else has thought the same as you; only they have thought of it first.'

Owen looked at his watch. It was a bit early to go to the Sporting Club.

'However,' said the orderly cheerfully, 'the ice man comes this morning and when he comes I will bring some ice along for you.'

He still hadn't come by lunchtime, but when Owen went down into the yard he saw the donkey with its great heavy bags on either side coming in at the gate.

'No, Effendi, I am *not* late,' protested the ice man. 'I am very busy, that's all. *All* the offices want ice, but I've only got one donkey, haven't I?'

'Well, have you?' said Owen. 'I would have thought there were other donkeys that might be called on. And other ice men, too, at a time like this when you need help.'

'Effendi, they are as I am: working themselves to death.

38

In this heat everyone wants ice. The palace wants ice, the hotels want ice, all the barracks want ice. So they cannot help me when I do the government offices. And the government offices want ice most of all. Fortunately I am a man of diligence and resource and so they get ice. Eventually.'

He fished in one of the saddlebags and produced a loadshaped block of ice wrapped in sacking.

'You want ice, Effendi? You have it. So what are you complaining of?'

Once the funeral was over, the Signora assumed control of the business. The auctions started again.

'I thought you said there was some cotton?' said the crumpled Greek.

'There is,' said the Levantine wearily, 'but it's still in the warehouse. As I told you, the Parquet's interested in it.'

'Still?' said the Greek, aghast.

'Still.'

'You don't know when –?'

The Greek thought for a moment.

'Presumably you've got loads coming into your warehouse all the time?'

'That's right.'

'With cotton?'

'Sometimes.'

'Any coming in soon?'

'There is, I believe,' said the Levantine coldly, 'a load coming up from the Delta sometime.'

'Ah, the Delta?' The Greek seemed interested; indeed, strangely, cheered.

'It'll be coming in next month.'

'Alexandria,' said the Greek with satisfaction. 'I like the sound of that.'

'What?' said the Levantine.

'Alexandria. The Delta. That's much better than Sennar.'

'Sennar? What's that got to do with it?'

'It's a hell of a place.'

'The cotton's the same' said the Levantine, puzzled.

39

'Ah!' said the Greek, laying his finger alongside his nose.

'Perhaps it's different to people who know,' said the Levantine, impressed.

'It's not the cotton, it's the place,' said the Greek.

The Levantine looked puzzled, then shrugged his shoulders and moved away.

The Greek went on poking round the lots that were coming up for auction.

After a while he went up to the Levantine again.

'Yes?' said the Levantine reluctantly, over his shoulder.

'This load that you've got in your warehouse at the moment, the bales that the Parquet are so interested in: it will be coming through at some time?'

'Yes,' said the Levantine.

The Greek pinched his fingers, as if feeling a crisp note.

'I wonder – is anyone else interested in it, do you know? Not the Parquet, I mean. Another dealer?'

'I don't think so.'

'I mean, you do have cotton from time to time, don't you? So there will be people who know. Perhaps they'll have bought from you before.'

'Well, I don't know that I'd call them regular customers –'

'But they know, don't they? They know about the cotton. I was just wondering if any of them were particularly interested this time?'

'Not as far as I know.'

The Greek pinched his fingers again and winked.

'You know,' he said, 'it could be of great help to me to know their names.'

He pinched his fingers.

'Well,' said the Levantine, weakening. 'All right.'

'And anyone else,' said the Greek, smiling encouragingly, 'who shows an interest.'

The Greek wandered out of the showroom, sauntered along the edge of the Market of the Afternoon, and then dived into one of the little streets beneath the Citadel. He came to rest in a little, dark, almost subterranean coffee house.

Owen followed him in.

'You're going to have to buy that cotton if you're not careful,' he said.

The Greek settled himself comfortably on the stone slab and sipped his coffee.

'At the last moment,' he said, 'I shall feel the cotton and look disappointed. Then I shall ask him if he's got any more coming in.'

'They get cotton from both the north and south,' said Owen. 'The lot with the guns in comes from the south.'

'I know,' said the Greek. 'Sennar. Then Assuan. A pity.'

'Pity? Why?'

The Greek looked slightly embarrassed. 'I thought you might want to send me – I was hoping it would be Alexandria.'

'Alexandria?'

'I thought I might take Rosa. She's been looking a bit peaky lately.' The Greek looked down at his coffee. 'It's the baby, you know.'

'Baby!'

'Due in the summer. July.'

'Baby!'

Rosa was about fourteen. At least – Owen began to calculate, time passed more quickly than you thought – maybe she was a bit more than that now. Sixteen? Seventeen?

'Congratulations! To both of you. Tell Rosa I'm delighted.'

'Thanks. I will.'

'July, you say?'

'Yes.'

'And she's looking a bit peaky?'

'It's the heat. She gets tired.'

'So you thought a holiday would do her good?'

'That's right.'

'Seems a good idea to me. Take her with you . . . But, hey, you're not going to Alexandria! The guns came up from Assuan!'

'It just seemed a good idea . . . Two birds with one stone . . .'

'But it's *not* two birds with one stone! You're not going to Alexandria. There's no reason why you *should* go to Alexandria! Assuan, the guns came from Assuan!'

'All right, all right.'

'You can take a holiday after!'

Baby! The shocks were raining in fast. First Mahmoud getting married, now Rosa having a baby. He would have to tell Zeinab.

On second thoughts, perhaps he wouldn't tell Zeinab.

# 4

The warehouse this morning was buzzing with activity. Strapping, bulging-armed porters were carrying things to and fro, the harassed warehouse foreman ran about chiding everybody, and the Signora herself, black-dressed, arms folded, stood firm at the centre of the maelstrom.

Two carts were being loaded, one bound for the Ismailiya showrooms, the other for the premises near the Market of the Afternoon. Now that the Signora had taken over the management of the business, the auctions were beginning again.

Among the goods being put on the Market of the Afternoon cart were the bales of cotton. Owen had decided that there was no need to hold them longer, now that the arms had been extracted. The arms themselves were piled in a corner, black and leaden, looking oddly at home among the bric-a-brac that surrounded them.

The cart Owen had sent for them was arriving now. The two warehouse carts were occupying all the space in front of the warehouse doors and there was an altercation. The foreman hurried out.

'Put it there!' he said, pointing to just the other side of the carts. It would block the street entirely: but then, Cairo traffic was used to that. Not that the camel drivers, donkey men and carts would accept it lightly.

'Can't we put it closer?' pleaded the policemen with the cart.

'Oh, you poor things!' said the porters. 'Why don't you get your wives to give you a hand? Come to that, why don't you send them round anyway.'

Affronted, one of the policemen, a giant of a man, jumped

43

off, stalked into the warehouse and picked up a bundle of guns. They were heavier than he had thought and he had to hitch them up with his hip to get them into the cart.

The porters laughed. One of them went across to the guns and picked up two bundles, one under each arm, and then put them up into the cart with ease.

The big policeman went back into the warehouse, half bent to pick up the guns as the porter had done, considered, and then considered again.

'Come on, you idle sods!' he bellowed to his colleagues still on the cart. 'Do I have to do all the work?'

Reluctantly, the policemen fell to. The porters watched them and laughed.

The big policeman walked across to his rival and patted him gently on the head.

'There are more things to strength, little flower,' he said, 'than being able to pick up pianos.'

'Come on, Selim,' said Owen hastily. 'Get on with it!'

It did not, in fact, take the policemen very long, but even so, in the intense heat, by the time they had finished, they were running with sweat and glad to collapse into the shade beside the cart.

By this time, of course, the street was totally jammed in both directions and there were angry shouts. Selim stood for a moment contemplating the furious, gesticulating crowd, then lay down deliberately in a shady part of the street, stretched out and put his arms behind his head.

'Selim! Selim!' came an agitated cry.

Selim levered himself up on to one elbow.

'Why,' he said, 'it's Mustapha, the ice man!'

'Selim, let me through!'

'Certainly,' said Selim. 'We could do with some ice.'

The ice man and his donkey pushed through the crowd.

'Selim,' said the ice man hesitantly, 'the fact is, I've run out of ice. I am just going back to the ice house for some more.'

'Then you're no good to us,' said Selim, lying down again. 'You'd better stay there.'

'Selim, the ice house is just round the corner –'

'You'd never get through.'

'I could send Amina.'

'Amina?' said Selim, levering himself up. 'Who's Amina?'

The ice man pushed a small girl forward. She was about twelve or thirteen, dressed in rags and had arms and legs like matchsticks.

'All right,' said Selim, 'she can go and fetch us some ice.'

'Sod off!' said the girl.

'What?' said Selim, astonished.

'Sod off!' said the girl defiantly.

'You'd better watch out,' said Selim, 'or I'll put you across my knee!'

'You'd have to catch me first,' said the girl.

Selim began to stand up.

'You leave our Amina alone!' came a warning cry from among the porters.

There were other cries from among the crowd of blocked bystanders. The girl seemed to have a following.

Selim, who although robust in his approach to mankind wasn't stupid, changed tack.

'Amina, my darling,' he said. 'Light of my eyes. Pearl of the deep seas. Rose of roses. You are like the smell of jasmine, the taste of honey –'

'Go on,' said the girl.

'Your breasts are like the breasts of doves. Or will be,' said Selim, who on things like this was inclined to be accurate.

'Go on.'

'Your smile is like the sunrise breaking across the water, your words like the fall of distant fountains –'

'All right,' said the girl, 'I'll get some.'

'I like a girl of spirit,' said Selim, watching her go.

'You like any girl,' said Owen. 'Now come on, get the street unblocked!'

'Get back to work!' cried the Signora.

'Yes, that's right,' said the foreman. 'Get a move on with these carts. We haven't got all day.'

Owen had arranged to meet Mahmoud afterwards but when he turned into the street where Mahmoud lived, he stopped, stunned.

The street had been transformed. A great yellow-and-red-striped awning covered the entire street. Palm trees in pots had suddenly sprouted along both sides. At one end men were working on a dais, above which a massive yellow silk canopy curled down; and other men were laying a red-and-blue carpet directly across the street itself.

Further down the street he saw Mahmoud talking to some of the workmen. Mahmoud suddenly noticed him and came hurrying towards him.

'What's all this?'

Mahmoud looked embarrassed.

'It's the wedding,' he said.

'Already? But, surely –'

'It's going to be next week,' said Mahmoud. 'It has to be,' he said soberly. 'Aisha's mother has cancer. She wants to see her daughter safely married. So everything's been brought forward. He touched Owen pleadingly on the arm. 'You will come?'

'Of course.'

'There are no male relatives, you see.'

'Don't worry. I'll be there.'

They walked down the street together. At every four paces Mahmoud stopped to shake someone's hand and exchange embraces. People even came out of their houses. Owen suddenly realized. He was in Mahmoud heartland. Mahmoud was the local boy made good.

A shopkeeper hurried out of his shop and came towards them. Owen recognized him. It was Hamdan, one of Sidi Morelli's domino-playing friends. He embraced Mahmoud and shook Owen's hand warmly.

'What do you think of this?' he asked, waving at the carpets. Another one was appearing now, behind the dais, hanging down upright from poles across the top of the tent.

Mahmoud flinched.

The shopkeeper laughed and clapped him on the shoulder. 'Don't worry, Mahmoud,' he said. 'It'll soon be over.'

He insisted that they come into his shop for coffee. It was a grocer's shop, smelling of spices and raisins and the rich kinds of soaps that Egyptians loved. At the back of the shop was a low counter, on which they all sat. Hamdan clapped his hands and an assistant brought coffee in brass, thimble-like cups.

'It is good to see you here, Mahmoud. Although I suppose it is not to see the wedding arrangements that you have come.'

'No,' said Mahmoud.

The shopkeeper sighed.

'It is four days now,' he said, 'and I still can't get used to it. We meet every evening as before and set out the dominoes as before: but the gap gets bigger, not smaller.'

Mahmoud laid his hand on his arm. 'I know, Hamdan,' he said sympathetically.

'That someone could do this! For a trifle. A purse, a few coins –'

'It was not for money, Hamdan,' said Mahmoud quietly. 'His money was not taken.'

The shopkeeper stared at him.

'Then why –?'

'I do not know, Hamdan. But perhaps you do.'

'I?'

'You knew Sidi Morelli. He spoke to you. Often.'

'Of course. But –'

'Has he ever spoken to you recently about something that was troubling him?'

'I do not think so.'

'You were close. He might have spoken.'

'But he has not spoken, Mahmoud. I am sure. We would have noticed it.'

'He had not appeared troubled?'

'No. The reverse. In fact, we made a joke of it. "There is Fahmy," we said, "with all his worries about his nephew; and there is Sidi with not a care in the world!"'

'You see, Hamdan, if it was not money, then it must have been something else. A grudge, perhaps, someone who felt that Sidi had done them a wrong.'

'But no one could feel like that!' cried the shopkeeper. 'Not about Sidi! He was not like that. He was generous, Mahmoud, kind. Mahmoud, you do not know – because he would not speak of it, or let us speak of it – the things he has done for people round here. The Koran entreats us to charity, but – I have said it to the Sheik himself – there are few Muslims who have given as much as he!'

'But a man with a grudge does not look at the all, he remembers only the one thing.'

'Mahmoud. I –' The shopkeeper stopped. 'Mahmoud, I really cannot believe it!'

'You look for the reasonable, Hamdan. But the attack on Sidi was not reasonable.'

'Mahmoud, I am sure this must be some criminal. Perhaps he was surprised and so ran away without taking the money –'

'He was not surprised. If he had been, someone would have told us. And, besides, Hamdan –'

'Mahmoud?'

'I do not think this was a professional criminal.'

'Why not, Mahmoud?'

Mahmoud hesitated.

'Hamdan, I do not wish to add to your distress –'

'Mahmoud, please!'

'Sidi was strangled.'

'I do not understand, Mahmoud.'

'He was strangled, not garotted. I am sorry, Hamdan.'

The shopkeeper held up his hand.

'Please, Mahmoud. Why does that make a difference?'

'Usually, when a professional wishes to kill, he garottes. At least, in Cairo. It is quicker. Strangling is slow, and it requires much strength. There is more risk of the victim breaking free. I am sorry to have to tell you these things, but they are things I know from my work. Add that to the fact that no money was taken and you will see why I do not think it was a professional criminal.'

There was a long silence.

'It must be some madman!'

'That is possible. Although, again, I do not think so. For madmen do not usually plan, and this was planned. The killer knew, I think, that Sidi would be passing at that time and stationed himself where he could first kill and then escape.'

The shopkeeper was silent again. Then he said:

'Mahmoud, you say that the killer knew that Sidi would be passing at that time?'

'That is so.'

'Then he must have known how Sidi spent his evenings – he must have known about us.'

'That is so, I'm afraid.'

'Many people knew about us. But they knew about us only if they lived in this neighbourhood.'

'That is so.'

The shopkeeper shook his head.

'I find that hard to believe, Mahmoud. We are not like that.'


Since Sidi Morelli had been an Italian national, the Italian Consulate had asked to be kept informed. Politically wise, Mahmoud took the precaution of asking Owen to go with him to the meeting.

'So,' said the consular official eventually, 'you haven't got very far.'

'It takes time,' said Mahmoud.

'I appreciate that. However, in the present circumstances, with the war on, I think it would be unfortunate if it took too much time. My country might feel that the investigation was not being taken seriously.'

'It is being taken seriously,' said Mahmoud.

'I am sure. And the presence of the Mamur Zapt is a helpful guarantee of that. In the circumstances. But the Consul would feel more comfortable if he could see some progress.'

'It is still very early –' objected Owen.

'Yes. But, you see, my country feels that if speedy action is not taken, there could be other attacks.'

'Well, that is always true –'

'But especially true in this case, don't you think?'

'You are afraid that there might be other attacks on Italian nationals?'

'Yes.'

'There is no reason as yet to suppose that the attack on

Signor Morelli was made because of his nationality,' said Mahmoud.

'I am glad to hear it. But then, what was it made for? It appears,' said the official, glancing down at his notes, 'that he was not robbed?'

'No.'

'Perhaps your inquiries have turned up some other possible motive?'

'Not so far.'

'Then how can Mr Zaki be sure that the attack was not because he was an Italian?'

'Signor Morelli was a very respected figure in the local community,' said Owen.

'I am glad to hear it. However, don't you think that makes it even more likely that he was attacked because of his nationality? He was an Italian whom everyone knew.'

The Consulate was in the Ismailiya so Owen called in afterwards to see Zeinab. A little unexpectedly, for Nuri seldom called on his daughter, her father was there. This didn't matter, since Nuri regarded himself as largely free from the strict conventions of Egyptian society and didn't mind Owen seeing his daughter alone. He knew about their relationship and, indeed, regarded it as entirely normal. Ordinarily Owen got along with him very well. This morning, though, he sensed a slight coolness in Nuri's greeting.

He wondered if he had come at the wrong time, and after a moment or two made to go.

'No, no,' protested Nuri. 'I am just on my way.'

He picked up his tarboosh and made for the door. At the last moment he turned and said to Zeinab: 'You will think about what I said, my dear, won't you?'

'No,' said Zeinab. 'In France women are nurses.'

'But the women who are are very low creatures. Believe me. I know.'

'Not always. And it is the same in England. There was a great lady there. I have been reading about her in the newspapers, she has just died. She was a nurse and had the ear of the king!'

'Women have always had the ear of the sovereign,' said Nuri, unimpressed.

'Not in that way. This lady was a great lady in her own right. And she was a nurse.'

'That's true, actually,' Owen put in, guessing that she was talking about Florence Nightingale. 'She was rather like' – he fished around for a comparison which would make sense to Nuri – 'Caldicott Bey.'

Caldicott Bey was the British Adviser on Health.

'Really?' said Nuri, astounded.

'Yes. She was a bit more than a nurse, though,' he said to Zeinab. 'More of a manager. She managed nurses. And hospitals too.'

'That is what I wish to do,' said Zeinab.

'Yes, but I'm not sure you can start there.'

'I can't start anywhere,' said Zeinab bitterly, 'the way things are.'

He'd got it now. When the war had begun next door between Italy and Tripolitania, Egypt had been gripped by sympathetic patriotic fever. Forbidden by the British Administration from more active engagement, Egyptians had poured their energies into medical help. Cairo had dispatched all its ambulances to the front (they probably hadn't got there yet, since they were all horse-drawn) and a fund had been set up to purchase more.

Zeinab, identifying passionately with the Ottoman cause, had at once thrown herself into raising money. Clearly, however, that had not been enough for her and she must have volunteered to go with the ambulances as a nurse. (Owen thought it quite possible that she had offered herself as a soldier first.) Here, though, she would have come into collision with the great masculine forces of Egyptian society: all Egyptian nurses were men.

'I do not,' said Nuri, 'usually complain. But you must remember you are a Pasha's daughter. Having lovers is one thing; being a camp follower is quite another. And female nurses are just camp followers.'

'Not in France,' said Zeinab, looking daggers. 'Nor in England.'

'I absolutely forbid it,' said Nuri. 'Remember you are a Pasha's daughter. There is no need to be quite so disreputable.'

It took Owen a little time to work out who the people at the auction were. Not the ordinary poor of the city nor the villagers from outside. They went to the Market of the Afternoon and did their buying and selling quietly with the stallholders. Not for them the publicness and formality of the auction. Nor the wealthy professionals or the foreign dealers. They went to the showrooms in the Ismailiya. It was, rather, traders of the lower to middling sort, men who made their turn in the morning and then for relaxation came along here in the late afternoon to see if they could make another turn. For the most part they were not Arabs but Levantines, sometimes distinguishable into their original national types, the Greeks, the Italians, the Montenegrins, the Albanians, more often part of that cosmopolitan Mediterranean mix that went by the general name of Levantine. They browsed expertly among the lots, often touching, sometimes sniffing, but somehow giving the impression that the goods were always in some way inferior, slightly dubious; and Owen thought that there was this truth in the impression, that the goods themselves were genuinely of lesser interest to them than the prospect of the bargain.

Some of the Greeks had brought their wives and children with them. The difficult Greek, whom the Levantine auctioneer was already eyeing malevolently, had brought his wife. Here, too, though, it was very evidently only a question of time before a child would be accompanying them. The Greeks, thought Owen, seemed to go in for families.

Today Georgiades seemed to have no interest whatsoever in the cotton; indeed, he seemed to be interested in everything but the cotton. The Levantine, used to this form of buying behaviour, settled back satisfied.

Rosa detached herself from Georgiades and came across to Owen. She had always had a soft spot for him and sometimes thought that if Georgiades ever fell under an arabeah she would make a bid for Owen; that was, if Zeinab should also fall under the arabeah. Rosa, like Zeinab, divided the world up into female power zones and recognized Zeinab's claim to territory.

'So,' she said now, 'what's all this about Mahmoud getting married?'

'It's true,' said Owen. 'And it's going to happen very soon.'

He told Rosa about the mother. Rosa frowned.

'I hope he's not going to take over responsibility for that family too,' she said. 'I always get the feeling about Mahmoud that responsibility with him is a defence. Thinking about others means that he doesn't have to think about himself.'

'Perhaps his wife will sort him out,' said Owen.

'Very probably,' said Rosa, who thought that was what women were put into the world for.

Georgiades came up with the Levantine auctioneer in tow.

'I've been asking him about baby-chairs,' he said.

'Baby-chairs?' said Rosa. 'What the hell do we need a baby-chair for? The bloody child's not born yet. Cradle is what we want.'

'Our other showroom –' began the Levantine.

Rosa turned the full power of her smile on him.

'You don't think you could keep your eye open, and if one comes into the warehouse, let us know?'

The Levantine thought he could.

The space in front of the platform at the far end of the tented enclosure was filling up now. The Levantine gave it a moment or two longer and then climbed up on to the platform and declared the bidding open.

Because there had not been an auction for some time, there was an unusually high number of lots to get through. At last they came to the cotton. Owen stationed himself so that he could see the bidders. He had no great hopes of anything emerging from this. It would be far too risky to leave it to the auction. Safer by far to take the guns somehow straight from the warehouse. All the same, he had to make sure.

'What am I bid?' asked the Levantine.

'What am I bid?' he asked, as no one spoke. 'Who will

start the bidding? Some fine bales of cotton, straight from Sennar. Slightly soiled, but who would notice it? What am I bid? A real bargain this, diverted from a load on its way to the cotton market. What am I bid?'

He looked now directly at Georgiades.

Georgiades smiled sweetly.

'A unique opportunity.'

Still no bid. From anyone.

'I am going to have to withdraw this lot,' warned the Levantine.

His eyes scanned the buyers. Owen watched carefully too in case he missed a sign.

'No bid?'

He looked again at Georgiades.

The Greek smiled.

'For the last time!' said the Levantine.

As he stepped out into the white glare of the Citadel walls afterwards, he felt a certain relief that it had come to nothing. He wondered why. Then he realized. It sent him back to the Nahhasin. In his bones he felt that the answers lay there. That was where the guns had been found, that was where Morelli had died. But it was more than that. In his brief visits there he had sensed the existence of a community not so much closed as integrated, one of the many such small communities that you came across in Cairo once you stepped off the busy main streets. In these communities things did not happen in isolation, they were nearly always connected with something else. If that was so here, then the answers to the questions about Morelli and the guns would be found not so much in the warehouse and his business but in the narrow streets outside, in the community of which he seemed to have been such an accepted part.

# 5

Owen took an arabeah up to the British Consulate, where Paul had invited him to meet some people. It was even hotter in the arabeah than it was outside. Heat clung to the worn leather upholstery and fed back from the sweating flanks of the horse in front, along with the smell of sun-baked harness. It was like travelling in an oven.

Even when they began to thread through the treed alley-ways of the Kasr-el-Aini Gardens there was no relief, and after a while Owen stopped the driver and got out. He took a path over towards the river in search of a breeze. If there was one, he couldn't detect it.

He began walking up along the river towards the Consulate. He could feel his trousers sticking to his legs behind the knees. Looking down, he saw that his white suit was discoloured with great damp patches of sweat. He began to regret not having gone home first and changed. Everyone else would have done.

When he got close to the Sharia ed Dakhaliyeh, he dropped down on to a bench for a moment to cool off.

A water cart was coming along the Sharia ed Dakhaliyeh, presumably with drinking water for the Consulate. It was one of the modern ones which had recently been intro-duced, with a tanker-like top. You could hear the water swilling around inside in time with the gentle movement of the cart.

The driver stopped beneath the trees and wiped his face with a fold of his galabeah. He sat there for a moment looking round him. Then he climbed up on top of the tank and unscrewed the heavy cap. He bent down and splashed water up over his head and arms. Then he stood up, lifted his galabeah, and peed into the tank.

Soon after, Owen saw the water cart turn into the Consulate gardens.

The guests were already out on the lawn when Owen arrived. Scarlet-cummerbunded waiters moved among them with silver trays.

'We're having to go easy on the ice, I'm afraid,' said a cheerful young man, one of Kitchener's ADCs. 'There's been a run on it.'

Owen chose a whisky, which didn't mind the shortage of ice, and wandered across the lawn. Kitchener was there himself, a tall man, tall even by Owen's standards, and with an immense bushy moustache, turned down in a forbidding inverted V. Owen hadn't had much to do with him yet, but according to Paul he caused everyone twice as much work as his predecessor.

A little group was gathered round him. Among them, talking very vigorously, was a woman Owen didn't know. She puzzled him slightly because, since she was new to him, he assumed she had just come out from England; and yet she was very brown. India, perhaps? The group was talking about railways. Owen wasn't interested in railways and moved on.

He fetched up beside the Sirdar, the Commander-in-Chief of the Egyptian Army, who was talking to a man in an elegant white suit; one without any damp dark patches.

'Hello, Owen. Do you know –? No? Cavendish from our embassy at Constantinople. Owen's in charge of security here. From an internal point of view, that is.'

'Ah, internal,' said Cavendish.

Owen couldn't understand the inflection. Nor could he understand what he was doing here, why Paul should have invited him. Nor what the other people were doing here, for that matter. He knew most of them, the Consulate people, the Army people. No one from the Civil Administration, though, surprisingly. There were several people he didn't know, however. He decided it must be to do with them.

'Who's the lady?' he asked.

The Sirdar turned to Cavendish.

'She's a Miss Bell,' said Cavendish. 'We've had quite a lot to do with her. She travels.'

A bit like Trudi, Owen gathered. She seemed to go in for long camel rides like her, and in much the same territory: Mesopotamia and Syria.

'And does a bit of archaeology,' supplemented Cavendish.

There were two other archaeologists there, an older man named Woolley and a short, fair man named Lawrence, who Paul seemed to know.

'Jesus,' he explained.

For a moment Owen didn't understand. Religion? This was unlike Paul.

'The college. Oxford.'

'Oh!'

The archaeologist laughed, contemptuously, Owen thought.

'Are you in Egypt long?' he asked.

'Not any longer than I can help.'

'He wants to get back to his dig,' said Paul.

It was at Carchemish, in Syria, and they had had some trouble there, apparently, with Germans building a railway line.

'They didn't know how to treat Arabs,' he said.

'And you do?' said Owen, slightly irritated.

'Yes,' said Lawrence seriously.

He went on to talk about his workmen at the site. They were of the best sort, he said. Not like the ones he had recently encountered at Petrie's site in Egypt, who had been truculent and difficult.

'Egyptians are all right,' said Kitchener, joining them suddenly. 'So long as they're not spoiled.'

'But that's exactly it, sir,' said Lawrence. 'The Arabs of the Peninsula, the ones I've met, at any rate, are still unspoiled. They're still proud and independent. Whereas the Arabs of the town –'

'There I agree with you,' said Kitchener. 'The Egyptian fellah is the salt of the earth, but once he moves to the city –'

'The army is recruited almost entirely from the fellahin,' said the Sirdar.

'But can you keep them away from the influence of the town?' asked Cavendish. 'Are they still reliable?'

'At the moment, yes.'

The image of the water cart driver up on top of the tank suddenly came into Owen's mind.

'Up to a point,' he said.

Kitchener's slightly bulbous eyes turned towards him and rested. Owen had the feeling that he was being weighed.

'It's all right!' Paul said to him soothingly afterwards. 'It's just the way he looks at people. Actually, he takes to people for aesthetic reasons, as well as because they're efficient.'

Which left Owen rather baffled. At the time, however, he merely held his ground, looking upwards into the eyes, which was an unusual experience for him and which, in fact, he didn't much like.

Kitchener moved away and the group broke up. A little later, Cavendish came up to Owen and took him aside.

'We'll be needing to work together,' he said.

Owen supposed it was over the gun-running.

But the archaeologists, Woolley, Lawrence, Miss Bell, what had they got to do with gun-running?

'Internal, external,' said Cavendish, 'you can't really divide it up like that. Of course, if things come to a head, they'll set up some sort of bureau to cover the whole Near East. Meanwhile, though, you and I had better keep in touch.'

'Fine,' said Owen.

He was still not completely clear what they were talking about. Some kind of general intelligence operation, he supposed. Perhaps it was something that had grown out of the Italian-Turkish war.

'What exactly do you want from me?' he asked.

'At the moment, not much. Perhaps just that you keep an eye on people. Especially people who come and go. We're doing that at our end already, of course.' He smiled. 'I gather that you've come across a certain young lady.'

'Well, yes.'

'We've been keeping an eye on her for some time. I suggest you do the same.'

'Oh, I will, I will.'

'She's in Cairo, I gather?'

'Yes.'

'Well, stick close to her.'

'Don't worry,' said Owen. 'I'm sticking very close.'

Later, he found himself standing beside Miss Bell.

'Could I have a drink, do you think?' she said. 'It's very hot.'

Owen beckoned to a waiter.

'No, thank you,' she said, 'not one of those. I think I've had enough already. Could you bring me a glass of water, please?' she said to the waiter.

'As a matter of fact,' said Owen hurriedly, 'I'm not sure that, just at the moment, that would be a good idea.'

At the end he was left still wondering what it was all about. Some kind of intelligence operation, almost certainly, and one which stretched outside Egypt's borders. Owen was not entirely happy about that. He had always seen his work as internal to Egypt and that had made it easier to reconcile the British Administration's interests with those of the Khedive. They were both trying to run the country, after all. But once you started looking beyond Egypt, their interests might well diverge.

This sounded to him like Britain's foreign policy, not like running Egypt. Cavendish was clearly a prime mover in it.

But had the initiative come from the British Embassy at Constantinople or was it Kitchener's brainchild? Constantinople was the senior embassy around the Mediterranean littoral, but the fact that they were holding the gathering here and not in Constantinople suggested that either the inspiration had come from Kitchener or that he was playing a big part.

Owen felt slightly uneasy about this. Kitchener's predecessor, Gorst, and the Consul-General before him, Cromer, had been content to restrict their role to being Consul-General. It was rumoured that Kitchener's ambitions extended higher. He would have liked, it was said, to have become Viceroy of India. Maybe, now that he had been disappointed in this, he had his eye on building up the Consul-Generalship until he was able to make himself Viceroy of Egypt.

But that would mean changing Egypt's status, making it part of the British Empire, instead of what it was at present, a quasi-independent part of the Ottoman Empire.

Perhaps, from the way Kitchener was behaving towards the Khedive, that was exactly what he had in mind.

If it was, Owen wasn't happy about that either. He really had believed that one day the British would get out and leave the Khedive to run the country on his own. It was that in the end that made the British presence all right. He genuinely had seen himself as serving two masters, the Consul-General and the Khedive, both Britain and Egypt, an odd arrangement, certainly, but which on the whole seemed to work. All right, it was often difficult balancing between them, but that was in the nature of the job.

Now it seemed to him that Kitchener might have in mind altering that balance. If he had, Owen didn't like it.

Cavendish, he thought, as he made his way that evening to the hotel where Trudi was waiting for him, would have approved of him. He found her in the foyer, talking, to his surprise, to Nuri.

She waved a hand.

'I was waiting for you,' she called, 'but then I got waylaid. You will tell them, won't you?' she said to Nuri.

'I certainly will,' said Nuri.

'Right, then. I'll be off to fetch my shawl. I won't be a minute,' she said to Owen.

'Charming girl!' said Nuri fondly, as he watched her posterior climb up the stairs.

'You know each other?' asked Owen.

'First time we've met. Purely business,' said Nuri regretfully. 'However,' he said, cheering up, 'I'll make sure there's a need for another meeting.'

Owen had been slightly discomfited at Zeinab's father learning that he was calling for Trudi, fearing that word might get back to Zeinab. He saw, however, that Nuri's mind was moving along other tracks.

They stood chatting for a little while and then Nuri wandered off into the inner corridors of the hotel.

Business? What sort of business could Nuri Pasha have with someone like Trudi? What sort of business could Nuri have with anyone, as a matter of fact? Nuri's chaotic finances were a byword through the city.

Trudi came down the stairs.

'We've got a moment,' said Owen, glancing at his watch. 'I called the arabeah for half past. Would you like a drink first?'

He led the way into the bar. It was long and dark and split up into recesses. In one of them a small group of men was sitting. One of whom was Nuri. Owen recognized two of the others: the Minister of Finance, and a senior official from the Khedive's office. Owen was surprised. He hadn't realized that Nuri had retained such friends. He must be moving back into favour again. It was something that Nuri was always hoping for, always angling for, but he had been hoping and angling for some years now.

Nuri gave them an acknowledging smile. So did one of the others, one of the two men that Owen did not know. Owen had the feeling, though, that the smile was directed to Trudi.

The others looked away. Almost deliberately, uncomfortably, Owen felt. As if they didn't want him to see them or, at any rate, didn't want him to enter into conversation with them.

It was yet another example, he thought, of the awkwardness that had arisen between the Egyptian servants of the Khedive and the British ones since the start of the war. Or was it since Kitchener had arrived as Consul-General and British Agent? Certainly, he and the Khedive did not get on. His predecessor, Gorst, had been much more popular. With the Egyptians, that was. Not with the British.

He excused himself and moved along the counter to where the barman was standing polishing glasses, and asked for another shot of soda. As the barman bent towards him, he said:

'Who are the men with Nuri Pasha? Not Sidki Bey and not Ibrahim Meck. I know them.'

'One is a Turk and the other a German,' said the barman. 'I do not know their names.'

'Are they staying here?'

'Yes.'

Owen went back to Trudi.

'You must tell me more about your fascinating journeys,' he said, smiling.

The house was a traditional one with a high, windowless wall reaching up from the street to a heavy box window jutting out at the level of the first storey. When he got upstairs he found that the room continued right through the width of the house to another box window on the other side, which looked down into a courtyard.

Mahmoud's future father-in-law came forward and embraced him.

'It is an honour! It is an honour!' he said.

'The honour is mine,' said Owen, returning the embrace.

Ibrahim Buktari led him across the room to where some men were sitting on low divans.

'You know some of my friends, I'm sure,' he said. 'But know them again under my roof.'

Owen did indeed recognize some of the faces. There, for instance, was Fahmy, one of Sidi Morelli's domino-playing friends, and there his young soldier nephew, who raised his glass to Owen.

'Glass!' said Ibrahim Buktari, and rushed off.

There, too, of course, was Mahmoud, looking sheepish. For he was the cause, or at least the excuse, of the occasion. This was the equivalent of what would have been in England a bridegroom's stag night; only here the guests were not so much the groom's friends and fellows as family friends and fellows, unduly tending towards the senior in age and status, their presence summoned by the bride's father.

Ibrahim Buktari returned with a glass of whisky. Most of the other men were drinking coffee or orange juice.

'Medicine!' he said, beaming. 'That's what Bimbashi Macrae

used to say. Hey, Kamal, isn't that right? I see you're having some of the same!'

The young man joined them.

'Quite right,' he said. 'I picked the habit up in the Sudan. That's what the army does for you. Gives you all the wrong habits.'

'Wrong habits!' cried Ibrahim Buktari. 'Fahmy, hear what awful things your nephew is saying!'

'Shocking!' said Fahmy. 'I don't know what the next generation is coming to. And I've done my best to bring him up as a respectable, God-fearing man like myself!'

A roar of mock-outrage rose from the divans.

'Steer clear of him, Kamal!' some advised.

'I try to. But he keeps leading me into vice!'

Mahmoud rose from the divan and came towards them.

'It is good of you to come,' he said to Owen affectionately. 'He is my brother,' he said to Kamal.

'Yes. Yes.' Kamal hesitated. 'But a surprising brother, is he not?'

'When you work together, you grow together,' said Owen.

'Yes. Yes. That is true. I have found that myself. As individuals, I find my British colleagues, *sympathique, très sympathique*. But – but we are not just individuals, we are also Egyptian and British. And that is where the difficulty lies. For the Egyptians and the British have different interests and they pull us apart.'

'That is true,' said Owen. 'And so it is important that as individuals we try to bridge the differences between us.'

'Yes. But, you see, that can conceal or blur – because in the end it is illogical. And that is what I find so surprising about you, Mahmoud, for you are so logical. We were at school together,' he said to Owen, 'and I always looked up to him. I used to say to myself: "Now, come on, Kamal, none of this idling! Model yourself on Mahmoud, who is so able and so hard-working –"'

'Really, Kamal!'

'The future, the future of Egypt, belongs to people like Mahmoud, I said. And now – forgive me, Mahmoud, you are not the same.'

'He has grown up,' said Ibrahim Buktari.

'I am the same and I am not the same,' said Mahmoud, frowning.

'It is the situation that we are all in,' said Owen. 'And about that I find myself saying what the English always accuse the Egyptians of saying: it is fate, the way things have turned out.'

'And I find myself saying,' said Kamal delightedly, 'what the English are always saying: you've got to do something about it, you can't just accept things as they are!'

They both burst out laughing and Kamal threw his arms round Owen in the emotional, over-the-top Arab way.

'But you,' he said, 'I accept. As Mahmoud's brother. Here. For tonight. And I rejoice that you come to Mahmoud's wedding.'

Mahmoud stood there awkwardly, smiling at the two of them.

'If my wedding has brought you together –'

'As individuals,' said Kamal hurriedly. 'As individuals.'

'– then that is a good thing.' He hesitated. 'It is true, though,' he said seriously, 'that there are difficulties.'

'Difficulties!' cried Ibrahim Buktari. 'And he says this even before he is married!'

Mahmoud, Owen learned later, had spent the day going through Morelli's books. It was not, perhaps, the way most people would choose to pass the hours just before their wedding, but as his familiar world began to dissolve about him, Mahmoud turned to his work with even greater ferocity. In the process of examining the accounts, he had come across certain recurring payments which were not matched by invoices or identifiable against goods.

'They are withdrawals for our own use,' the Signora had said.

'No, Signora, they are not,' said Mahmoud. 'Withdrawals for your own use are clearly marked as such.'

'Morelli did not mark all –' began the Signora.

'Ah, but he did. He recorded everything. Damage charged to a porter. An advance to a driver on account of his getting married. Out-of-hand disbursements for extra ice because of the hot weather. But also these recurring payments, made regularly every month, and with a "Sh" marked alongside in brackets.'

'It must be some supplier I do not know,' the Signora had said.

'The last payment recorded,' pursued Mahmoud, 'was made six weeks ago. Why did the payments stop?'

'I do not know,' said the Signora.

Mahmoud had sighed.

'Please, Signora,' he had said, 'why do you not tell me? When I can guess what it is? Everyone knows that such things occur. And I shall find out anyway.'

The Signora had hesitated.

'Please, Signora!'

'All right,' the Signora had said at last. 'We paid. As all business people do.'

She was talking about 'protection' money.

The 'protection' business was highly developed in Cairo. It probably had its roots in payment made for genuine protection, gifts made to some local 'sheik' in return for defence against external marauders, but over the years this had turned into tolls levied by whoever was strongest in the neighbourhood. Increasingly, at least in terms of willingness to use force, this had come to be gangs; and in recent years many of the gangs had come to be the political societies in which Cairo abounded. Most of them were quite legitimate but on the fringe there were quite a few which raised funds through means which were not very different from those employed by the criminal gangs. In any case, the practice of paying 'protection' money was widespread.

'Does the gang have a name?'

'The man who comes has a name.'

'What is it?'

'Shukri.'

'What happened six weeks ago?' asked Mahmoud. 'Did Shukri come and the Signor refuse to pay him?'

'No. Shukri did not come.'

'He did not come at all?'

'That is right. We wondered about it, because he was regular as clockwork. But this time he did not come, and then still did not come. So then we thought it was perhaps an argument within the gang. Or perhaps between that gang and another. These things happen. I know. They happen in Italy too. There is an argument and then things get settled, and then all goes back to as it was. We thought it would be like that this time. And so we put the money by, knowing that in time they would come for it, and waited.'

'It was just like that, was it?'

'It was just like that.'

'The Signor did not refuse? Please, Signora, you must tell me. This is important.'

'He did not refuse. Why should he refuse? It is the way things are. In Italy as here. We may not like it but we accept it. You have to accept it if you wish to do business. And Morelli wished to do business.'

'Nevertheless, Signora, there might come a time when if he wished to continue to do business, he would not be able to afford to say yes.'

The Signora shrugged.

'That time has not come.'

'Each time, the records show, the payments were higher.'

The Signora shrugged again.

'Each time they ask for more, and we give them more. But only a little more.'

'But perhaps this time they were asking for a lot more.'

'They weren't.'

'So the Signor did not refuse?'

'No. And they did not kill him because he refused, if that is what you are thinking. Why should they kill the goose that lays the golden egg?'

All this Mahmoud reported to Owen. Owen nodded. It did not surprise him. The 'protection' business was part of Cairo's way of life. And on the whole he thought that the Signora was probably right. Morelli had not refused: why refuse something that was part of one's ordinary way of life? He, like many other businessmen, probably looked on 'protection' as merely another kind of tax. You might not like it but you paid it.

So he thought it unlikely that Morelli had refused to pay; and he thought it even more unlikely that the gang had killed him because of it. There were other processes that would be gone through before it came to killing: wrecking the premises, for instance, and then a beating-up to show that the gang meant business.

Mahmoud agreed.

'But even so,' he pointed out, 'there is something to be explained. Why did they stop? And, especially, is there any significance in the fact that they stopped just before he was killed? Had they been warned off?'

He thought it might be worth talking to Shukri.

Owen thought it might be worth doing too. For there was another consideration which, just at the moment, he did not feel like putting to Mahmoud. The gangs of Cairo divided roughly into two. There were the ordinary criminal gangs, just in protection for the money; and there were the 'political' gangs, usually offshoots of the entirely legitimate political 'clubs', or societies, their fund-collecting arms, so to speak. These latter were often heavily nationalistic. And what would be more likely, at a time like this, than that one of them, for some reason or another, might take a foreign businessman as their target? Particularly, just at the moment, if he happened to be Italian.

# 6

Heat bounced back from the warehouse doors flung open on to the street and rose up from the dust on which the first group of camels were lying as the porters unloaded them. Other camels were just coming into view at the end of the street, nodding along through the mass of people, their great loads almost brushing the houses on either side. Inside the warehouse the foreman was instructing the porters where to put the packages and the Signora stood, arms folded, among the piles.

'One moment, signor, one moment!' she said, seeing Owen. The foreman was perfectly capable of disposing the loads by himself but she evidently felt that without her attention to stiffen him things might slide.

Shouts from the street announced the arrival of the next group of camels and the foreman bustled out to deal with them. That left the porters to stack their loads undirected, which, again, they were perfectly capable of doing. The Signora, nevertheless, kept her eye firmly on them.

'One moment, signor!'

The arrival of the caravan was a key point in the life of the warehouse and Owen understood that for the moment even Mamur Zapts had to take second place.

He walked out into the street to inspect the new arrivals. The camels' flanks were heaving and they breathed noisily through their noses as their drivers made them lie down. Because of the camels already there, they had to lie further out in the street, and with their heavy loads almost spanning the gap between the warehouse doors and the houses on the other side, the road was closed yet again to further traffic. Custom, however, did not preclude protest.

'Ya, Abdul! Ya, Abdul!' came indignant shouts from behind.

'One moment! One moment, O people!' cried the harassed foreman. All the camels in the first group would have to be unloaded before he would be able to get a single one of them to move and so free space for the others. They had a strong sense of solidarity and refused to act except in a group.

'Move your ass, Mohammed!' came a shrill cry, rising above the hubbub.

One of the drivers, a haughty desert man, looked round indignantly.

'You shut up, you little bitch!' he said.

It was the ice man's assistant, and there was the ice man himself, waiting despairingly with his newly loaded donkey, so loaded that it could not possibly squeeze past.

'Ya, Abdul –'

'One moment, Mustapha. One moment, that is all!'

'The ice will melt, Abdul –'

'Let me hold your hand, Amina, while you are waiting,' pleaded one of the porters.

'I know you, Suleiman,' retorted the girl. 'First it is my hand that you wish to hold; but then it will be something else!'

'Your waist, Amina!'

'Her tits, more likely,' said one of the other porters.

Suleiman turned furiously upon him.

'You shut your mouth –'

'She hasn't got any,' said the offended desert man, inspecting Amina closely.

'If I had, they'd be too good for you!' said Amina indignantly, and jabbed the rear of the desert man's camel with something that looked suspiciously like a knife. The camel lurched protestingly to its feet, the driver swore and tried to force it back into position, the camel swung round and in the uproar the ice man's donkey, prodded by the girl, managed to squeeze past.

The driver cut at Amina angrily with his whip but missed as the girl ducked behind the donkey. The whip fell harmlessly on the packs of ice. The girl raised her head and stuck her tongue out mockingly at the driver, who brought up his arm for another blow. It was caught by Suleiman.

'You do that,' said Suleiman savagely, 'and I'll break it!'

The desert man snatched out a dagger from his belt. Another porter grabbed him and wrestled. In a moment all was uproar.

Owen stepped forward.

Fortunately, the foreman got there first. With surprising strength he pulled the men apart and pushed Suleiman into the warehouse.

'Suleiman, I shall speak to you! And as for you, Mohammed, you, a grown man, to let yourself be put out by a slip of a girl!'

The other desert men gathered round the driver and pulled him back. But then they stood there in a little group facing towards the warehouse.

Owen saw suddenly that the porters had formed a phalanx between the gates.

'Get back inside!' cried the foreman angrily.

'I'll kill him!' shouted Suleiman, struggling against the hands that were holding him.

'Get inside!'

The porters hesitated.

And then there came a voice from inside the warehouse.

'Got any cotton this time?' asked a crumpled-looking Greek standing among the bales.

Cairo was always like that, thought Owen. One moment everything was going along peacefully; the next, they were at each other's throats. It was what made policing tricky. There were so many quarrels waiting to happen: quarrels between those of different religion, different race, different nationality, even. It was the most cosmopolitan of cities. Italians, Greeks, Albanians, Montenegrins – they were all here alongside the native Egyptians, who were themselves a mixture: Copts, Nubians, Bedouin, Sudanese . . .

And yet for the most part they got on together. Trouble was always threatening and yet so often a quarrel would be resolved just as it was reaching the danger point. And without any need for the police to intervene. As in this case, in the end.

Everything simmered down. The porters went back into the warehouse, the drivers shrugged their shoulders and turned to their camels, the ordinary populace got on with its business, and bloody Amina and the ice man moved on. In a moment the street had returned to normal.

'We haven't unpacked the bales yet!' the Signora was saying, in exasperated tones.

'I thought you might have a list,' the Greek said mildly.

'Well, I *have* got a list, but just at the moment –'

'I'll wait,' said the Greek, beaming, and wandered off to look at the loads still on the camels. A little later Owen saw him chatting happily to the drivers.

'I have told you before, Suleiman,' the foreman was saying, 'that I cannot have this. You love Amina, yes, I know, but you are not her husband yet and the trouble she gets into is no business of yours!'

Suleiman nodded sulkily.

'So no more fights, Suleiman. Understand? No more fights!'

Suleiman nodded again and the foreman released him.

The porters had finished unloading the first group of camels now and the foreman wanted them moved so that the second group could come in. The drivers were urging them to their feet, no easy task, as always. With much snorting and grumbling and considerable reluctance now that they had been lying down peacefully for a while, the camels were eventually all upright and their drivers led them off. A similar process then began with the second group of camels.

The Signora looked at Owen guiltily.

'Signor, I have kept you waiting too long –'

'Not at all.'

'I beg you to excuse me. But this is the first time I have seen to the caravan on my own and I thought that if I was not standing over them, they might slacken. They might think that since it was a woman –'

'And in the heat,' murmured Owen.

'Exactly. But I think I can leave them now. And Abdul will be glad of my not being here.'

She led him through into the house and then out into the courtyard he had noticed earlier. They sat down in the shade on a stone bench and a servant brought a jug of lemonade.

'You wish to see me.'

'Yes.'

'I have told you I know nothing about the guns. And I am sure that my husband knew nothing either.'

'That is quite possible, since they were hidden inside the cotton. However, other things are possible too. Only possible, Signora, I do not say they were so. But I have to ask about them as well.'

She nodded acquiescence.

'Signora, your husband was a businessman, as others are: and, as others in the city have been asked, so, your husband was asked.'

'For what?'

'Money. By the gangs.'

'You have been speaking to the Egyptian?'

'Yes.'

'I tell you, as I told him, that is nothing to do with Morelli's dying.'

'Yes, I know. You said that it could not be, because the Signor had not refused to pay.'

'That is so.'

'And I agree with you: they would not have killed the goose that lays the golden eggs. However, there is another thing that I must ask you. Was it that they did not ask him for money but for something else?'

'Like what?'

'Could it be that they asked him to take the guns?'

'Why would they want him to do that?'

'Because they wanted the guns brought from outside and he had caravans bringing things from outside.'

'He was not asked,' she said flatly.

'Are you sure?'

'He is dead,' she burst out. 'Why do you ask these things?'

'Because I want to know why he died.'

'No,' she said bitterly, 'no, you do not. You only want to know about the guns.'

'In seeking the answer to one, I hope to find the answer to the other.'

'He was not asked for money. Nor for anything else.'

Back in the warehouse the unloading had finished. The camels had departed. Just at the end of the narrow street he could see the last one, its rump wagging above the heads of the passers-by. The porters were lying down in the shade. Used as they were to working in the heat, the heat this time had been a bit much. Great beads of perspiration ran down their faces. The foreman, similarly perspiring, was pushing a last bale into place.

'Hot work,' said the Greek sympathetically. 'And none too easy at times, either. Those desert men!' He shook his head. 'Out with their knives in a flash!'

'It was Amina's fault,' said the foreman. 'She shouldn't have provoked him. And as for Suleiman!'

'Well, of course, he's keen on her,' said the Greek. 'One can see that.'

'Follows her around like a dog. Ought to have more sense. But then, he's as thick as a post.'

'Thick or quarrelsome,' said the Greek, 'you've got to handle them haven't you? But I tell you what: I reckon you deserve a coffee after all that.'

Mahmoud came into the warehouse just as Owen was leaving. He put his hand on Owen's arm.

'You will be there tomorrow, won't you?'

'Certainly I will. Don't worry. Everything will be all right.'

'Yes. Of course it will,' said Mahmoud. Doubtfully, however.

'No, I'm afraid I can't, Paul. Sorry! I've got something on.'

'Gareth, this is important. It's a formal follow-on from that previous get-together. Everyone will be there. The Sirdar, Cavendish, the great K. himself – And you've got to be there.'

73

'Paul, I can't.'

'It's to coordinate intelligence for the whole area, internal and external.'

'Can it be some other time?'

'*No*, Gareth. Cavendish is only here for a couple of days and he's a key player.'

'Well, then, I'm sorry, but I really can't come.'

'Gareth, Al-Lurd is chairing this himself. He's making it his top priority. Which means that it's top priority for you, Gareth!'

'I'm sorry, but –'

Really, Paul was getting quite tiresome these days. Ever since Kitchener had arrived, and he had been made Oriental Secretary, he had been taking his work far too seriously.

'K. is really not going to like this, Gareth. And you know what that means!'

He could guess. The ruthlessness with which Kitchener treated his enemies was matched only by the ruthlessness with which he treated his subordinates. All the same . . .

He just could not attend. It would mean letting Mahmoud down. At a time, too, when Mahmoud needed him, or thought he did. He just could not.

'I'm sorry, Paul, it's Mahmoud's wedding and he's particularly asked me to be there.'

There was a moment's stunned silence.

'Mahmoud's *wedding*?'

'Yes, he's getting married tomorrow.'

'Well, I'm damned! Never thought he would. It just didn't seem possible, somehow.'

'You see, Paul, he's particularly asked me to be there. I think he's sort of nervous.'

'Well he might be! Has he seen her yet?'

'I don't know about actually *seeing* her, he's certainly talked to her. Once.'

'I suppose the mothers arranged it all. My God, the things mothers do! I begin to be apprehensive on my own behalf, what with the earth shaking like this. I think I must write to my mother immediately: "Do not, on any account, marry me to some Felicity or other! Not, at least, without telling me."'

'Her father knows Kitchener. Apparently he served with him in the Sudan.'

'Really?' Paul thought for a moment. 'Well, now, that could make a difference. In principle, K. is absolutely unbending on this sort of thing: personal considerations must never take priority over duty. But given that it's an old mate of his . . .'

'You think it will be all right if I don't come?'

'You've got to be there. Otherwise that daft ass Cavendish and his crazy archaeological sidekicks will foist some lunatic policy on us. No, we've got to think of some other way round this . . .'

He brightened.

'I know! I shall simply change the day of the meeting. Yes, that's it. One's got to keep a sense of perspective, after all. Which is the more important? The fate of the British Empire or Mahmoud's wedding? Mahmoud's wedding every time!'

'Sir, Owen has just pointed out to me some major international difficulties with the timing of our meeting tomorrow. I am afraid I shall have to reschedule it.'

'Damned nuisance. It means we'll have to bring Cavendish back from Constantinople.'

'No, no, sir, that won't be necessary. We can arrange it for the following day, while he's still here. It will mean one or two trivial alterations in your own programme, but that will be all.'

'All right, then, go ahead.'

'Actually, sir, there's a happy by-product of the change in timing. It will mean that Owen will be able to attend the wedding of the daughter of an acquaintance of yours.'

'Really?'

'Ibrahim Buktari, sir,' said Owen. 'He served with you in the Sudan.'

'Ibrahim Buktari? Splendid fellow! Give him my regards. His daughter, you say? And congratulations. Yes, and – and – wait a minute. A wedding? I'll see if I can find something. You can take it with you.'

\*    \*    \*

In fact, Owen was not really called on until after dark the following day when Mahmoud went to the mosque to say prayers. As he came out, he was greeted by friends carrying meshals, cressets of blazing wood stuck on tall poles, who formed a procession in front of him to light his way. At their rear some men were carrying a large frame with about fifty lamps on it, arranged in four revolving circles. Then came Mahmoud and his closest friends – including Owen – each of them carrying a candle and facing the frame in a kind of moving circle. And exactly in front of Mahmoud himself were men walking backwards with huge crystal affairs in their hands.

Just behind was a small walking band playing pipes and banging drums, which brought everyone out of their houses to see.

They processed back to Mahmoud's house and the awning-covered street, which was now ablaze with lights. Coloured lamps hung from the balconies and the meshrebiya box windows, bright globes, strung across the street, rotated above the heads of the men chatting below: men, because there were only men there – all the women were indoors. You could hear giggles and laughter from up behind the windows. Servants hired for the occasion hurried around with jugs of lemonade and large trays of sweets and nuts and sugar-covered cakes.

Owen followed Mahmoud and one or two other close friends into the house, where sherbet and coffee was brought to them. No pipes – Mahmoud, strict in his observances, allowed neither smoking nor alcohol.

Upstairs were the mothers and close female relatives, and, in a separate room, the bride.

'Mahmoud,' said Ibrahim Buktari after a while, 'it is time.'

Mahmoud rose reluctantly to his feet. Reluctance was part of the play, but it was clearly not feigned in Mahmoud's case. One of the men went to grasp him.

'We're having none of that,' said Mahmoud hastily.

It was part of the joke to pretend that the bridegroom had to be carried upstairs against his will. Mahmoud, however, climbed the stairs firmly on his own account.

'The price! The price!' whispered Ibrahim Buktari urgently.

Mahmoud felt in his pockets and looked panic-stricken.

His friends pushed money into his hands. Upstairs he would find his bride waiting alone in a room, her head covered with a shawl. He would urge her to remove it, but her maidenly modesty would prevent her from doing so until 'the price of the uncovering of the face' was paid. Then he would see her face for the first time: ever.

This was the key moment of the drama. The men waited below. Upstairs, the women clustered round the door as Mahmoud went inside.

There was complete silence.

And then suddenly the women broke into a joyous paean of celebration and everyone burst into smiles.

A moment or two later Mahmoud came back down the stairs looking sheepish. His friends gathered round him and hugged him and led him back into their room and gave him coffee at once. He seemed to need it.

'Now, Mahmoud,' said Ibrahim Buktari fondly, 'she's not too bad, is she?'

'She's lovely!' said Mahmoud fervently.

Owen wondered if he had ever seen a woman's face before. Seen, perhaps – in his work he would have seen females unveiled, prostitutes, certainly, but also the women of the humble poor, especially in the villages outside Cairo – seen, but not noticed, as that would have been disrespectful.

He pressed Mahmoud's hand.

'You can relax now,' he said.

'Yes,' said Ibrahim Buktari, 'and then you must go outside and receive congratulations.'

'I will come with you,' Owen said, 'and you can introduce me to your friends.'

Out in the courtyard the *fiki* was just finishing his recitation from the Koran. He gave way to the professional singers, who sang some *muweshshas*, or lyric odes to the Prophet. And then the band started up.

Mahmoud waited until the religious singing was over before going forward to greet his friends. To do otherwise would be to treat the verses lightly, which he could not bear to do.

Now, however, though shyly, he would go among his friends. As a married man.

By now it was nearly midnight and the party was just warming up. There was no need for alcohol to assist the warming: on occasions like this, thought Owen, Egyptians were self-fuelling. Some of the men began to dance, either by themselves or with another man. The women remained inside, looking out invisibly through the latticed windows.

At one point the dancers formed a snake. As it wound past him a hand reached out and pulled him on to the end. The hand belonged to Kamal, Mahmoud's, and Ibrahim Buktari's, soldier friend whom Owen had met earlier. Kamal looked back over his shoulder and smiled.

'As an individual,' he said. 'Just as an individual.'

Mahmoud did not join in the dancing but stood quietly to one side, smiling. From time to time people brought him presents. Owen remembered his own.

'And also this,' he said. 'From Lord Kitchener.'

# 7

'Yes,' said Cavendish, 'but are you watching the railways?'

Owen was not watching anything at all at that moment. Indeed, he was barely conscious, because he had got back from Mahmoud's wedding party only an hour before, to find waiting for him a message that the meeting had been rearranged for seven that morning; a time decided on, Paul indignantly claimed, less from malice than from consideration. In this heat the rooms would be insufferable by ten o'clock, the time when meetings normally started. And, besides, Cavendish had to get back to Constantinople.

The French windows, with their shutters, had been left open so that the air, normally still cool at this time in the morning, could freshen the room. Already, though, it was distinctly hot and soon would be hotter. On the other side of the room from the windows, where Owen had been obliged to sit because he had been one of the last to arrive, it was stifling, and, as they seemed to be discussing matters with which he had no concern, such as 'the situation' in the Hejaz, he had lapsed into torpor. From which he now awoke with a start. What was this about railways? The remark seemed to have been directed at him.

What was it Cavendish had said? 'Watch them.'

What the hell for?

'Well, yes, they're the key to it, obviously,' he tried.

This seemed acceptable. There were nods round the table.

'The line to Medina is, of course, now complete,' said the little archaeologist, Lawrence. (And what was he doing here?)

'Which means that they're within striking distance of Mecca,' said Paul.

'It's not Mecca I'm worried about,' said the Sirdar. 'It's Egypt. Now that they've got down to Aba-el-Lissan, they can cut across to Akaba in a few hours. And then they're right on the Canal. On our very doorstep!'

'I don't think you ought to disregard Mecca,' said Lawrence. 'Especially if it becomes a question of mobilizing the desert tribes.'

The Sirdar snorted.

'Mobilizing the desert tribes? About as much use as mobilizing a bunch of camels!'

He stared belligerently at Lawrence. Here, at any rate, was someone else who couldn't see what the archaeologist was doing there.

'The point is,' said Cavendish, 'that with the new railway system they can rush troops down from Turkey in a matter of hours and strike at either Mecca *or* Egypt!'

They? The Turks? But so far as Owen knew, the Turks weren't striking at anyone at the moment, with the exception of the Italians in Tripolitania, when they could get at them.

'So you're quite right,' said Cavendish, addressing Owen. 'The question of the railway system inside Egypt becomes of considerable importance.'

Inside Egypt? What he meant, presumably, was that if there was a railway line going from east to west, instead of from north to south, following the line of the coast as opposed to the line of the Nile, as did most transport systems in Egypt, then it would be much easier for the Turks to get troops across Egypt to Tripolitania.

Certainly true; but so what? There was no such railway line and little prospect of one being built. The government hadn't got enough money, for a start. And the army wouldn't let them if they had. And what, incidentally, was all this stuff about troops on the Canal? It sounded like the usual alarmist phobia that the army engaged in from time to time. Turkish troops on the Suez Canal? That would mean war; not between Turkey and Italy but between Turkey and Britain. And there was surely no chance of that. Daft! He went back to sleep.

The meeting came to an end and everyone went out on

to the Agency lawn for some fresh air. Servants brought lemonade. Owen had been drinking lemonade all night and felt in need of something stronger. He thought he might go down to the Club for a drink before lunch.

'Damned amateurs!' said the Sirdar, standing beside him. He was looking at Lawrence. 'What does a fellow like that know about mobilization?'

'Or me either,' said Miss Bell, suddenly appearing alongside.

'Oh, sorry, Miss Bell!'

'It's a fair point,' she said, 'although Mr Lawrence is, I understand, a military historian as well as an archaeologist.'

The Sirdar snorted again.

'In any case,' said Miss Bell, 'the point is not our military expertise – we leave that to you, Sirdar! – but the fact that we have both just come back from the Sinai and can tell you what's happening there.'

'I'm not saying your information isn't useful, Miss Bell –'

She laughed.

'I hope so. But information has to be professionally appraised, doesn't it, before it's really of much use. Which doesn't stop us, Sirdar, from having opinions of our own.'

'That young man's got too many opinions of his own,' said the Sirdar, looking at Lawrence, who was talking to Paul.

It was an opinion with which Owen was inclined to concur. The archaeologist seemed to set himself up as an expert on so many different things; military tactics, Egyptians, the East. But what did he know about the East? He could only have been out there for a year or so. Intelligent, admittedly. Paul would have had nothing to do with him if that hadn't been so. But with the intelligence was a touch of intellectual arrogance, which always rubbed Owen up the wrong way, especially when he thought that it was at his expense. The memory of that half-contemptuous smile when he had got it wrong about the college at Oxford still rankled with him.

'He's a clever young man,' said Miss Bell. 'I think.' She looked up at Owen. 'But cleverness isn't everything, is it?'

He took her to lunch at the Sporting Club.

\*     \*     \*

On the great wooden doors of the warehouse, in large, sprawling, black letters, were the words:

ITALIANS GO HOME!

The words were written in Arabic and badly written at that. No bazaar scribe's lettering this, thought Owen, but daubed by the hand of some illiterate.

'There!' said the Signora fiercely.

She had sent for Owen immediately.

'Not for the Parquet,' she had said bitterly. 'The Parquet is Egyptian.'

It was still early in the morning. The foreman had found it there first thing when he had arrived to open the doors. Shocked, he had run for the Signora. She had summoned Owen and he had gone at once. The porters were only just arriving. They stood in the street, embarrassed, their faces averted.

Abd al Jawad, Morelli's old friend, hurried up. He stopped, appalled.

'Signora –!'

He tried to wipe the writing away with the skirt of his galabeah.

'Perhaps you should leave it,' said the Signora. 'So that it would remind me of what people think.'

'It is *not* what people think,' said Abd al Jawad. 'It hurts me to hear you say that, Signora.'

Along the street came another of the friends, Hamdan. He was carrying a bucket and brushes. Abd al Jawad and he began to scrub vigorously at the graffiti.

'Here,' said the foreman, 'you're not going to let them do all the work!'

Several of the porters moved forward. Abd al Jawad stopped them.

'No,' he said, 'it is better if we do it. For if you do it, they will say that you did it only because you were bidden.'

'I did not hear what Abdul said,' said one of the porters, 'and I am doing it unbidden.'

Others joined in, not just the porters but people from along the street, shocked, silent. Around the corner came the third of the friends, Fahmy, the one who owned the ice house. He was leading a donkey. Across its back were some saddlebags and in the bags were some large cans.

'This will take it off,' he said.

The foreman unlocked the doors and two of the porters brought out ladders. The writing soon began to disappear.

Hamdan looked over his shoulder at the Signora.

'Do not harden your heart against us,' he pleaded.

The Signora went across and touched him gently.

'Why should I harden my heart against my friends?' she said.

Fahmy wept quietly.

'What is the world coming to?' he said. 'That men should do such things?'

When the work was finished, the Signora went into the house and the servant brought out orange juice.

Abd al Jawad sipped it.

'It is from the tree in your garden,' he said.

'Sidi always said they were the best oranges,' said Fahmy, 'and, by God, he was right!'

'The lemons will soon be ripe,' said the Signora. 'When they are, you must try them.'

'He always used to bring the first,' said Hamdan.

'And so will his widow,' said the Signora.

The friends, their faces working, went back to their businesses. The porters, subdued, began to occupy themselves in the warehouse. The Signora led Owen into the inner courtyard.

'They will not frighten me out,' she said.

'Who are you speaking of, Signora?' asked Owen. 'The foolish people who have done this, or the people to whom you have been paying "protection"?'

She did not reply at once. Then she said:

'Shukri has sent me a message. He says he is starting coming again. When he comes,' she said defiantly, 'I will pay. One must live.'

To his great surprise, he came across Trudi von Ramsberg watching the guards being changed outside the Abdin Palace.

'Well, I *am* a tourist,' she said defensively. 'And, anyway, I like their hats.'

Their hats were certainly splendid. There were the crimson tarbooshes of the Sudanese, which, set upon a man always well over six feet tall, and dressed in a uniform of startling blue, looked very fine indeed; and there were the hats of the two men from the Camel Corps, standing sentry at the gate on their camels, their great cocks' plumes nodding in the wind.

On the far side of the square the guard which had just been relieved was disappearing into the Abdin Barracks, leaving behind them a splash or two of camel dung dark against the blinding whiteness of the square.

Squares were not where you stood in heat like this, and Owen proposed a coffee up one of the darker, cooler side streets. He chose a traditional Arab coffee house with its main room half underground and a stone bench running round the wall inside. There were one or two men sitting there and he felt a flicker from them as he and Trudi entered. He was a little surprised. This was on the edge of the sophisticated Ismailiya Quarter and although the café was a traditional one, he would have expected them to be relaxed about the presence of Europeans. Or was it that Trudi was a woman?

Trudi caught the flicker too.

'The people are different in the desert,' she said.

'Unspoiled?'

'That's just romantic nonsense,' she said dismissively.

'I thought you were a romantic?'

'Not that kind. I told you there were two kinds. I'm the other kind, the rebellious kind.' She looked at the other men in the café. 'If I were them I'd feel rebellious.'

'Against Europeans?'

'Not just Europeans.' She waved a hand in the direction of the Palace. 'Them too. The old order.'

'You want to bring in a new order?'

'I want *them* to bring in a new order,' she corrected. 'Bring it in for themselves. As they're doing in Turkey. Do you know Turkey?'

'No.'

'I've just come from there. And what is happening there at the moment is rather exciting. There's a new movement called "the Young Turks" – it's not what they call themselves, it's what others have called them. Anyway, the thing is that compared with the old politicians, they're young; instead of the old order they want a new one. And what is exciting is that they've just been invited into the government, so they'll have a chance to do something about it.'

'Army people, aren't they?' said Owen sceptically.

'Some of them.'

'How radical will they be?'

'It's different in countries like Turkey. Often the army is the only career open to a bright young man.'

'And you really think they're going to change things?'

'They need to,' said Trudi. 'The Ottoman Empire is about the most moribund institution on earth!'

Owen laughed.

'Except for the British Empire, she thinks, but politely doesn't say!'

'The trouble with us Europeans is that we always intervene to prop up the old orders.'

'Whereas what we ought to be doing is bringing in the new?'

'That sort of thing.'

Owen sipped his coffee.

'I don't know that we "ought" to be doing anything,' he said.

'Ah,' said Trudi, 'that's where I'm different from you. I want to do something.' She glanced at her watch. 'But just at the moment, the thing I particularly want to do is get to the bank.'


Owen was on his way to the Abdin Barracks, at the Sirdar's request. As he was going in, he met Kamal coming out and they stopped for a moment to chat about the wedding.

'Who is it you're coming to see?' asked Kamal.

'Bimbashi Grenville.'

'I'll take you to him.'

He led Owen along a corridor and stopped outside a door.

'This is the Officers' Mess,' he said. 'I think you'll find him there.'

Owen held the door open for him.

Kamal smiled.

'There are two Officers' Messes,' he said gently, 'one for the British officers, the other for the Egyptians.'

He made a little gesture of farewell with his hand and turned away.

Grenville was in there. Owen knew him but not well. He was standing at the bar but came across to Owen as soon as he saw him.

'What would you like?'

They settled down with their drinks in one of the alcoves and then Grenville fished a piece of paper out of his pocket.

'The Old Man thought you ought to see this,' he said.

It was another of the threatening letters. And in the same careful bazaar letter-writer's handwriting.

'For some reason they've picked me out.'

'I wouldn't make too much of it. There are plenty of others.'

'There are?'

Grenville seemed slightly dashed.

'I thought, you know, that as no one else in the Mess –'

'It's just that they hadn't got round to targeting the army before.'

'Oh. The Old Man thought, you see, that this might be a new development – targeting officers individually.'

'You're way down the list.'

'Oh. Like another?'

'Let me.'

Owen had honorary membership of all the Messes.

He brought the drinks back and put them on the table.

'This was the first one, was it? You've not had any before?'

'I've been away for two years. Only just got back. Been in the Sudan. Actually,' said Grenville, 'thought that might be something to do with it.'

The Sirdar came into the Mess.

'Hello, Owen. Worrying thing, this, isn't it? Going for my officers.'

'Owen says we're well down the list, sir.'

'Members of the Administration in general have been receiving letters,' said Owen.

'Don't like that!' said the Sirdar. 'Ought to have been the army! Damned insult, targeting civilians first.'

'Have you yourself received any letters, sir?' asked Owen.

'Get them every day,' said the Sirdar dismissively.

By the time Owen left the barracks it was nearly two o'clock and Abdin Square was at its hottest. The dung he had noticed earlier had already dried hard. The air above the square quivered and on the opposite side to him, next to the Palace, it grew a kind of fault line which then dissolved into spiralling fragments. The fragments came together and formed momentarily a picture of a river. That, too, broke up and then the only things left on the whiteness of the square were the dark figures of the ice man and Amina and the donkey, plodding towards the barracks on their errand of mercy, leaving a trail of drips behind them from the melting ice, which disappeared even as Owen watched.

Zeinab, thought Owen, was being difficult this evening. What was more, he was pretty sure that she was being difficult deliberately. It was the custom on the day after a wedding for friends to go and present their congratulations. This was usually an exclusively male occasion since the friends of the bridegroom – and it was a case, naturally, of the bridegroom only – would all be male and he would receive their congratulations alone.

Owen, however, had had the bright idea of taking Zeinab with him – she knew Mahmoud well, after all – and Mahmoud had leapt at the suggestion, believing that it would provide his wife with an easy introduction into the new social world that she would enter. He wanted her, he said, to feel at ease both in the traditional Muslim world of her family and his, and in the Westernized, cosmopolitan world of the successful professional in which he worked; although, in the latter case, preferably not too much at ease.

Zeinab, though, was being a bitch. For one thing she seemed to be deliberately trying to upstage the shy girl who now appeared before them, probably for the first time in public without her veil. This was relatively easy to do for it was probably also the first time that Aisha had met the daughter of a Pasha, and Pashas were still viewed by many in Egypt as beings from another world. Aisha seemed stunned by this dazzling apparition, so fashionably – and immodestly – dressed (and, now Owen came to think of it, wasn't there something deliberate about that, too?), speaking so boldly even before the men, and dropping in references at every turn to Princess this and Princess that.

'Do you know Princess Fawzi, my dear?'

'I've read about her in the newspaper,' Aisha managed bravely.

Who hadn't? The Princess was notorious for her loose and shocking behaviour. Only last week she had ridden a bicycle round the Bab-el-Louk.

'I'll introduce you to her.'

Mahmoud looked very unhappy.

'I don't think –' began Aisha.

'Nonsense, my dear! I'll get her to arrange something. I know! A picnic. She'll like that. On the river. Just the three of us. Oh, and,' said Zeinab with a defiant glance at Owen and a toss of her head, 'Prince Narouz, Prince Rashid and Prince Yasin.'

The Princes Narouz, Rashid and Yasin were, among a host of dissolute younger relatives of the Khedive, certainly the most dissolute.

Mahmoud had gone pale.

'It's very kind of you,' said Aisha hurriedly, 'but –'

'Not at all, my dear,' beamed Zeinab. 'I'll get her to send you an invitation tomorrow.'

'I, really –'

'Even if she does send you an invitation, you don't have to go if you don't want to,' said Owen.

Zeinab glared at him.

'She certainly does! This is a Royal Invitation.'

'I'll have to ask my husband,' said Aisha desperately.

'But why, my dear?' asked Zeinab sweetly. 'No other woman does.'

Mahmoud looked as if he was about to faint.

'Why are you being so awful?' demanded Owen, the moment he could get her out of the house.

Zeinab broke away from him and ran on ahead.

He caught up with her and tried to take her arm. She shook him off.

'An insipid, useless creature!' she raged. 'A mere child, with no mind of her own!'

'You shouldn't have treated her like that.'

'Why do you take her part?' shouted Zeinab, and burst into tears.

Owen was used to Zeinab's tempers but this one promised to break all records.

Everyone in the street was looking at them. Doors began to open, shutters were flung back. He could sense the sudden interest behind the harem windows.

'For God's sake!'

Zeinab tore herself away and ran off up the street.

She came to a stop just outside a heavily populated café and stood there sobbing loudly.

Heads in the café turned, chairs were eased back, people began to stand up.

Owen caught up with her and tried to take her in his arms.

She half pushed him off, then fell against him.

'Leave me alone!' she shouted.

And now the chairs were definitely being pushed back, and there were concerned cries, and a few angry ones.

An Egyptian woman and an English man! Jesus!

'Come on, now, come on!' he whispered urgently.

'Brute!' shouted Zeinab.

Everyone in the café was getting up.

He looked around desperately.

And then, by the grace of God, an arabeah came into view.

'Here! Here!'

He bundled Zeinab inside and then jumped in himself.

'Just get moving!' he said to the arabeah driver.

The driver shrugged, assuming that this was just another of those Cairo incidents – the woman had probably discovered she was having a baby, or something – and cracked his whip.

Owen held Zeinab close. After a moment or two the violent crying stopped, giving way to the occasional choked sob.

'What *is* all this?'

Zeinab just burrowed her head in his chest.

'Where to?' said the arabeah driver.

'The Ismailiya,' said Owen.

The driver nodded. That was where all these classy bits came from. But they had babies like everyone else.

'Let's not go to the Ismailiya,' said Zeinab.

'Where shall we go to, then?'

'The river,' said Zeinab. 'Let's go to the river. It will be nice there. Nicer than anywhere else when it's hot like this.'

They got out at the embankment and began to walk along beneath the palm trees. Below them the water glugged at the bank.

'Let's get in a boat,' said Zeinab.

'We'd need lights –'

'I wasn't thinking of going anywhere,' said Zeinab.

They found a felucca at the water's edge and climbed into it and lay down. The gentle rocking of the boat was very soothing, and so was the quiet slap of the water against the bank, and the gentle, regular nudging of the felucca against its mooring post. After a while they lay back and looked up at the stars.

'What was all that about, then?' said Owen.

'Nothing,' said Zeinab.

It *had* been about something, though. Surely she wasn't jealous? Not of that kid, surely?

Then a thought came to him. Had Nuri told her about Trudi?

'I met your father,' he said cautiously.

'Oh?'

'Yes, at the Continentale.'

'Oh, yes,' said Zeinab. 'He was seeing somebody about a new railway.'

New railway?

# 8

All sorts of things were tied to the railings of the terrace at the front of the Hotel Continentale: monkeys (for sale as pets, and also the dog-faced baboons which, clad in little red jackets looking suspiciously like military ones, would shortly be performing with the entertainers in the street); dirty postcards of astonishingly abundant ladies; great, extravagant plumes of ostrich feathers; equally extravagant bunches of roses and carnations; little singing birds in cages; hippopotamus-hide whips and fly switches smelling of new leather; men's braces and ladies' suspenders woven ingeniously through the railings; bead necklaces; green eye-shades; slippers with curled-up toes – and, of course, the usual cast-down donkeys of the donkey-boys and the tired horses of the arabeahs waiting patiently for custom.

As well, this time, as two enormous camels, their heads grinning over the railings at the people sitting on the terrace, their jaws dripping a green saliva from the clover they were chewing.

'Do you like them?' said Trudi von Ramsberg enthusiastically, as she came down the steps.

'Up to a point,' said Owen, much less enthusiastically.

'They're racing camels, of course.'

'So I see.'

She looked at him curiously.

'You know about camels?'

'A little.'

When he had first arrived in Egypt he had been posted to the desert patrol and had spent his first few months operating against gun-runners and smugglers; not exactly a good training for policing in Cairo but one which the authorities believed a good training for Egypt.

'I thought you might not.'

'Being merely an ignorant Arabist of the city, you mean?' She laughed.

'That's right.'

'Why do you need racing camels?' he asked, puzzled.

'I don't. I couldn't resist them, that's all. I'll have others with me for the journey, of course.'

He was still puzzled. Racing camels were not something you purchased on impulse. They cost an arm and a leg.

'You must be rich,' he said.

'Oh, I am, I am! And stupid, too. And you,' she said, 'are surprisingly knowledgeable for a mere Arabist of the city.'

They had come in from the south that morning, she said, and she was about to take them over to the Mena Hotel, on the other side of the river, where she was assembling what she needed for her expedition. She invited him over there for dinner the following evening. And then she made one of the camels kneel, perched herself on the huge saddle which was about as big as a ship, took the leading rein from the other camel in her hand, and set off down the street past the surprised parasoled ladies and the impressed tarbooshed men.

After the glare and hustle of the street, the inside of the hotel was soothingly dark and calm. The receptionist was sitting behind his desk, his head bent over the hotel register, a fan whirling on the ceiling above.

'A German? I think that would be Mr Scharnhorst. We have a number of Germans staying with us, of course, but I think Mr Scharnhorst would be the one you want.'

'A businessman, is he?'

'A banker.'

Had Zeinab's father been on the scrounge for money again? It would have to be a foreign bank. All the other banks knew him only too well.

'Do you know the name of the bank?'

'The Dresden, I think.'

'I believe Nuri Pasha was meeting some other people, too.'

'Sidki Bey,' said the receptionist.

From the Khedive's office.

'And Mr Meck.'

The Minister of Finance. Perhaps that was it. It was not Nuri who was doing the asking. The Khedive was equally in need of money. And the same consideration about it having to be a foreign bank would still apply. But what was Nuri doing there? The Khedive would hardly need him as a go-between.

'There was another man, a Turk,' said Owen.

'Ah, yes, Mr Gurnik. From the Turkish State Railways.'

This was more possible. Zeinab's father was on the Board of Egyptian Railways; a post, alas, more honorary than remunerative.

'You have no idea of the subject of the meeting, I suppose?'

The receptionist smiled.

Owen smiled, too.

He picked up the menu card for that evening and appeared to be studying it.

'How long will Mr Scharnhorst be staying?' he asked, without raising his eyes.

'A week, I think. It is a little uncertain.'

'And Mr Gurnik?'

'The same, I believe.'

Owen put the menu card down; only now, inside it, was a hundred-piastre note.

The receptionist tidied the menu card away.

'Something to do with a purchase, I believe,' he said, his eyes dropping back to the register, 'of a railway.'


Owen wormed his way along the bar, not of the hotel now but of the Gezira Sporting Club, where, it being a Friday and the Muslim sabbath, and consequently a day of rest, British officials were gathered in force, and came up alongside Saunders. Saunders was the senior man in Railways and, unusually in the Administration, a soldier. The Egyptian State Railways was still run by the army, which had set the railway system up in the first place, at the time of the Occupation, and had been running it ever since. When he saw Owen, he put his hand in his pocket and pulled out a piece of paper.

'I've had another one,' he said.

'Another –?'

'Threatening letter.'

He gave it to Owen.

'Same writing,' said Owen, glancing at it.

'Not found him yet?'

'Not yet.'

He put the letter away.

'There's something I wanted to ask you,' he said.

'Oh, yes.'

'You're not thinking of selling off anything, are you? Part of the railways?'

'No.'

'Nor buying anything? Some other railways?'

'No,' said Saunders, mystified.

'There aren't any other railways to buy, are there? I mean, not in Egypt?'

'Well, there's the Khedive's private line, I suppose.'

'Private line?'

'Yes. It runs from Alexandria to Mersa Matruh. Along the coast.'

'From east to west?'

'Yes. But, look, that line's not for –'

'He wouldn't do it!' said Paul. 'He couldn't do it! We wouldn't let him.'

'I'm not sure we're in a position either to let or not let him,' said Owen. 'It's his property, after all. And he *is* the ruler of the country, when all's said and done.'

'Yes, but we can't have that! All it would need then would be a link line eastwards and then the Turks could ship people straight to Tripolitania!'

'But it is their country, Paul, and it is his line.'

'We'll have to find some way of stopping it.'

Paul hurried away, leaving Owen staring unhappily at the bubbles in his glass.

\*　　　\*　　　\*

Owen was sitting in his office next morning when he heard shouting in the yard. A moment later, an agitated orderly came running along the corridor.

'Effendi! Effendi! There's a wild man outside!'

In the yard a group of orderlies surrounded, at some distance, a stocky, bare-footed man who stood glaring at them, his hand on a short, curved sword in his belt.

'What *is* all this?' demanded Owen.

The ring of orderlies broke apart and let him in.

'You wanted to see the boss,' said the senior orderly. 'Now here he is!'

The man looked at Owen suspiciously.

'He's not the boss!'

'Foolish fellow!' said the senior orderly angrily. 'Do you not know the Mamur Zapt?'

'Mamur Zapt!' said the man, alarmed. He began to back away. The ring retreated with him.

'What is it you want?' asked Owen.

'You're not the one.'

'Who is it, then? Whom are you seeking?'

The man continued to back away. The ring behind him opened and he found himself up against the wall. He looked desperately towards the gate.

'Come, friend,' said Owen. 'Whom is it you seek?'

'The fat one,' said the man reluctantly.

'Ah! Go and see if Georgiades is in,' Owen said to one of the orderlies, 'and if he is, tell him to come down.'

'He promised me beer,' said the man. 'And money.'

'Oh, yes?'

'I said I was not to be bought. "Who is talking of buying?" he said. "But should a man who sees a piece of gold walk past it with his face averted?" I thrust him away. But this morning I thought that perhaps there was merit in what he said. And, besides, the beer was all finished.'

'These are powerful reasons. And he will be here shortly. All right, you can go back inside,' he said to the orderlies.

They withdrew reluctantly.

The man prised himself off the wall and came forward.

'Are you truly the Mamur Zapt?' he said curiously.

'The same. And who are you?'

'Ali. I am a driver with one of the caravans.'

'I see.'

That explained it. The man was plainly of the desert and not of the city. His skirts were short and tucked up under him, his legs were bare and blackened by the sun, but darker, anyway, than those of the northern Arabs. He had tribal scars cut in his cheeks and wore a white turban. His eyes were slightly bloodshot.

Owen led him into the shade and they both crouched down against a wall.

'Well, Ali, you are far from home.'

'I am; and, to tell the truth, I do not like it much here. But my cousin was getting married, and I said to myself: is it right that she should be alone among strangers when there is a man of her family in town? So I went to the wedding, and there were men there that I could drink beer with. And it was there that the fat man found me.'

Georgiades was coming into the yard now.

'You have discovered, I see,' he said to Ali, 'the man who is the source of much of the beer in Cairo.'

'He is?'

Ali looked at Owen with new respect.

'And some, I daresay, will flow in your direction once we have talked a little.'

'It is thirsty work, talking,' said the driver.

'It is. But for the talk to be clear, it is best if the beer comes after and not during the talking. Ali is one of the drivers with the caravans that come to the Morellis',' he said to Owen, 'and he was with the caravan that brought the guns. Tell him what you told me,' he said to Ali.

'We did not know about the guns,' said Ali. 'If we had known, we would have asked for baksheesh. But we did not know. Although some of the men, I think, suspected it, for they said: "There is a smell of baksheesh in the air." But then they always say that. And Mohammed Guri said: "It is only the smell of your own backsides." But then he always says that too, and it is only if a bale falls off and gets broken, and you see what is inside, that the question of baksheesh arises, for then it is a case of keeping your mouth shut, and money is the best shutter of mouths.'

'Did a bale fall off this time?'

'No, though there was talk of that also. But Mohammed Guri said there was no need for a bale to fall off, for he would pay us extra baksheesh when we got to the Signor's anyway. So we agreed to that, saying: if there are things we do not know, then they are things we cannot tell, and sometimes that is best, especially if we are getting the baksheesh anyway.'

'Mohammed Guri is the leader of the caravan?'

'He is.'

'And he knew about the guns?'

'The leader always knows. And it is right that he should, for he is the one that takes it on his shoulders to see that the goods are delivered safely, and it would not be just if they were other than he supposed.'

'Well, that is true. So, then, someone must have told him before the caravan left. And that would have been at Assuan?'

'That is where the caravan forms, yes.'

'You did not see the man who spoke to him?'

'Effendi, many speak to the leader of the caravan. One comes and says thus: "This is a present for my sister, who lives at such-and-such a place." Or: "My brother has sent me this tusk from Darfur, take it to such-and-such a man in the city." There are many such, Effendi.'

'Of course. And it is easy to miss a few words, quietly spoken. But what of the guns themselves? They would have had to be put in the bales. And surely they would be easily seen?'

'It would have been done at night, Effendi.'

'Are there not guards?'

'But few. And it is easy to say to a man alone: "This is a good time, friend, to go and drink tea with Abdul, for I have many with me and we would not wish to be disturbed." Or they will say, Effendi: "Here is beer for you, go and drink it elsewhere; and let no man know whence it came."'

Owen nodded.

'Where is Mohammed Guri now?' he asked.

'Back at Assuan.'

Owen nodded again and sent Georgiades into the office to fetch some money.

'Take this,' he said to the driver, 'and drink deep. We give it for the information and not for the man.'

Ali walked off with a confident swagger.

'I know what you're going to say,' said Georgiades.

'You can take the train,' said Owen generously.

Afterwards, he couldn't understand how it had happened.

Perhaps it was the heat. It had been stifling in Kitchener's office. The big fan whirling overhead, the smaller one on Kitchener's desk, another one parked on a table behind him, none had seemed to make any difference. The shutters had been closed, of course, with just one of them left open in a fruitless attempt to coax freshness into the room. The gap had let in just enough sunlight to allow him to see Kitchener clearly: the slightly bulbous eyes, the heavy moustaches descending sharply at the corners of the mouth, a mouth normally rather full and sensuous but on this occasion clamped shut.

The rest of the room had been dark, but with a strange greenish half-light, the product of the green paint on the walls and the sunshine filtering through the green slats of the shutters. It had felt like being in a goldfish bowl; an impression enhanced by those bulbous, fish-like eyes fixed unblinkingly on him.

'We can't have it,' Kitchener said.

'In a way it doesn't matter,' said Owen. 'Nothing has changed. There has always been a line going west from Alexandria; and there is no line going east to link up with the Turkish railways system.'

'But something *has* changed,' said Kitchener: 'the ownership of the line. It will now be owned by a Turkish-led, German-financed consortium; that is to say, a *foreign* consortium.'

'Quite a lot of things in Egypt are owned by foreign consortia,' said Owen.

Kitchener stared at him.

'That is just a lawyer's quibble,' he said sharply. 'The fact is that the ownership of this line is of strategic significance.'

'But the strategic significance is limited,' said Owen, 'while there continues to be no link-line eastwards. All I am saying is that this needn't bother us too much because we can always stop the link-line from being built.'

'It's the *principle* of the thing,' said Kitchener. 'It raises the issue of power. He knows that this is objectionable to us and yet he is going ahead all the same. He is cocking a snook at us. He'll have to be taught a lesson.'

'I don't think we can afford to let him get away with this,' said Paul.

'No. If we do, he'll immediately try something else. We've got to stop him in his tracks.'

'How exactly are we going to do that, sir?' Owen had asked.

Maybe it was the 'exactly' that had jarred, for a frown appeared on Kitchener's face.

'Just tell him he can't do it,' he said harshly. 'He's got to back down.'

'It's his own property and he's selling it to a foreign body,' objected Owen.

The frown came back and hung heavily over Kitchener's face.

'Owen is right, sir, to point out that there may be international repercussions,' said Paul hurriedly.

'I *want* there to be international repercussions,' said Kitchener sharply. 'I want Germany and Turkey to understand that they can't meddle with me!'

'It's not the international repercussions I'm worried about,' said Owen, 'as much as the internal national ones.'

Kitchener turned the frown on him full blast.

'Surely they are containable?' he said.

'Of course. But is it wise to provoke them?'

'Are you having cold feet?' said Kitchener unpleasantly.

'No, sir. I am just telling you that if you make the Khedive back down too publicly, it will not be well received.'

'I don't give a damn,' said Kitchener.

'I think you should, sir,' Owen went on doggedly. 'We are here, sir, by legal consent.'

'That is a legal fiction.'

'It is an important one. It is important for Egypt's self-respect. And if you force the Khedive to back down publicly you will damage that self-respect.'

'The average Egyptian detests the Khedive,' said Kitchener.

'That is true. But if you do this you will make him popular as never before.'

'Owen,' said Kitchener slowly, 'how long have you been in Egypt?'

'Five years, sir.'

'Five years. I came here first in eighteen eighty-two and have been here, on and off, ever since. Twenty years, Owen, thirty years. And are you now telling me how to run Egypt?'

'Of course not, sir. I am merely telling you how ordinary Egyptians will react.'

'Ordinary Egyptians? Do you know who the ordinary Egyptians are, Owen? They are the fellahin, the ordinary peasants. Over eighty-five per cent of the population live off the land. They are the ordinary Egyptians, Owen; and do you know what they want? They want security. They want relief from oppression. They want the landowner and the tax-gatherer off their backs. And that is what I am giving them.'

'Yes, sir, and I am with you all the way.'

'Oh, good,' said Kitchener. 'I was beginning to doubt that.'

'Nevertheless –'

Kitchener's eyebrows shot up.

'Nevertheless?'

'We cannot disregard popular feeling entirely, sir.'

'The fellahin don't give a damn for the Khedive.'

'Perhaps not, sir. But in the towns –'

'Ah!' said Kitchener. 'The towns!'

'It is in Cairo, sir, that the running is made.'

'Then I think you should see,' said Kitchener, bending the full weight of his glare upon him, 'that your friends run more slowly.'

\*    \*    \*

100

At least, thought Owen, as he stood outside the Agency waiting for an arabeah, he would be able to marry Zeinab.

In fact, he stopped the arabeah when it got to the river bank and took a boat to the other side, thinking it might cool him down. It didn't. Neither physically nor mentally. The heat hung over the river in a thick layer. It was as if the boat was prising it apart. The woodwork burned the fingers to touch, the water, when he splashed it over his face, seemed hot enough to shave in.

He still felt slightly shaken, not so much from apprehension as from the edge on the arguments. Was Kitchener always like that, he wondered? How could Paul stand it? Paul was a reasonable fellow and liked to proceed by reasoned arguments, and that was the way it had always been in the Administration, at least under Gorst, Kitchener's predecessor. There was none of this bearing down upon you.

It was a question of style, he supposed. Kitchener had always had the reputation of being a bit of a bully. Well, he could put up with that. But he didn't like it.

He suddenly realized that there were a lot of things that he was beginning not to like. Things were changing. It wasn't just Kitchener, it was other things too. They were crowding in on you. It wasn't like it had been in the old, more relaxed days. There had been bombs then, of course, and death threats and killings. But somehow you had had more space, more time.

Or maybe it was just that he needed a holiday.

Maybe he was going to be given one, whether he wanted it or not.

The Mena Hotel stood well back from the river but after the Inundation there was always a great lake left behind which came right up to the doors of the hotel. It had dwindled by now but there was still enough water for ducks to swim and herons to paddle. He and Trudi went for a stroll round it before dinner.

'It's nice here,' she said, 'on this side of the river. It's almost like being in the country. I could never stay long in Cairo.'

'That's a pity,' he said.

She laughed, and then went on: 'I need stillness too much.' She looked at him. 'You're still, aren't you? I think that's what attracts me to you.'

'Still,' said Owen, 'or inert.'

'Sometimes I don't understand myself,' she said. 'I say I need stillness, and yet I'm always on the move. As soon as I've stayed anywhere for a week or two, I get restless and feel the need to move. And yet lately, and increasingly, I've felt I was missing something. Maybe,' she said, 'it's that I need a still point to return to.'

'You'd always be moving away again.'

'Maybe; but I'd always be coming back, too.'

The sky was losing its rosiness and shadows were beginning to creep round the lake. Normally, at this time, so close to the river, there would be an evening breeze and it would be cool. Tonight, though, the water was like glass, without even the hint of a ruffle. It seemed to Owen that it was still as hot as it usually was at three. A long curl hung down the side of Trudi's face, clinging wetly to her cheek; still damp from the pillow.

'Anyway,' she said, 'all this is to tell you that I'm moving on.'

'You're leaving?'

'Tomorrow.'

'Are you coming back?'

'I don't know.'

'I hope so.'

She pulled at a tall bulrush stem growing at the side of the water.

'You wouldn't like to come with me, I suppose?' she said suddenly.

'Mightn't that be awkward?'

She gave him a long, appraising look.

'Yes,' she said, 'it might.'

# 9

'Why, there's that great prick again!' cried Amina.

'Light of my eyes,' said Selim resignedly, 'and pain in my ass: can't you get a husband to keep you in order?'

'He'd have a job!' said a passer-by.

Amina gave him an indignant look.

'One's on the way,' she said.

'I hope it's not that dumb porter,' said Selim. 'He wouldn't stand a chance.'

'I have set my sights higher,' said Amina loftily.

'Well, that's very sensible of you,' said Selim. 'How about a well-favoured soon-to-be sergeant, with the ear of the Mamur Zapt?'

'British swine!' spat out Amina.

'Here, you can't say things like –'

'And you're just an imperialist hireling,' said Amina contemptuously.

'Me?' said Selim, astonished.

'Amina, shall we move on?' said the ice man hurriedly, giving the donkey a whack.

The exchange had begun to attract attention and Owen was irritated because he had particularly instructed Selim to keep out of sight. They had taken up position in a deep doorway; but then the ice man and the donkey had come out of the ice house and the girl, who seemed to have eyes everywhere, had spotted them at once.

'Do you mind if I pat your helper on the rump, Mustapha?' asked Selim.

He stretched out his hand towards Amina.

'Just you dare!' she shouted, skipping out of the way.

Selim affected surprise, then continued with his hand and patted the donkey solemnly on the backside.

'Big shit!' said Amina indignantly, and hurried after the donkey as it disappeared into the crowd.

Shortly afterwards, a man came out of the ice house and went on up the street to where a cart was being loaded with sacks of flour. Men were appearing through a door with the sacks on their shoulders. Their heads and arms were powdered with white and through the door one could see a sort of snow storm. The man went in at the door. When he came out again, he, too, was powdered with white.

He continued along the street to where some steps led down to a cellar. The sweet, sickly smell of crushed sesame seeds came up from below and there was the rumble of a wheel turning. The rumble stopped when the man went down but then resumed as he came back up the steps.

Owen touched Selim on the shoulder and the big policeman moved across the street with surprising speed and folded the man in his arms.

'Shukri?' said Owen, stepping forward.

Back at the Bab-el-Khalk, Selim reached his hand into the folds of Shukri's galabeah and drew out the money he had collected. He laid it on the table in front of Owen.

'It was given to me!' protested Shukri, with a show of bravery.

'I wish someone would give *me* money,' said Selim.

'Ah, but Shukri doesn't get to keep the money he collects,' said Owen. 'He has to give it to somebody else, doesn't he, Shukri?'

'I don't know anything about it,' said Shukri.

'Their names, Shukri!'

'I don't know their names.'

'You know one name at least: that of the man you give the money to.'

'Not even that,' said Shukri.

A few months in jail were nothing. It was dry and they gave you bread. And then you came out and could carry on as before. But if you gave names away, when you came out the gang would beat the hell out of you and, who knows, one of the blows could go amiss, and that could be the end of you.

Owen smiled, knowing exactly what Shukri was thinking.

'Well, perhaps the names don't really matter.'

'Not matter?' said Shukri, astonished.

'Not this time. This time we want something else. Shukri, no one knows that you have been brought here.'

Shukri looked alarmed.

'Here, you can't –'

'So no one will know what you say to us. And what we would like from you, Shukri, just this time, is some information. That's all. And then you can go. This time.'

'What information?' said Shukri cautiously.

'Shukri, you do your rounds in the Nahhasin. And every time you go to the same places. But lately you have not been going to the Morellis'. Why is that?'

Shukri was silent, trying to figure out all the angles.

'It's just information, Shukri. That's all we want. And afterwards you can go.'

'Somebody asked us not to,' said Shukri cautiously.

'Who?'

Shukri hesitated.

'Another gang?'

'Yes.'

'That surprises me, Shukri, and I'm not sure that I believe you. Would you let another gang in on your territory? I find that hard to believe.'

'No, no, it wasn't like that! We weren't letting them in. All they were asking for was a favour. They wanted us to hold off for a bit. Just with him. That's all. They'd got something on and they didn't want anyone else queering the pitch. Well, that's reasonable, isn't it? You don't want trouble if you can help it. They were just taking precautions. And we didn't mind because we knew it wouldn't go beyond that. They are in a different line, see –'

'What line is that, Shukri?'

'I don't know –'

'No?'

'No.'

'Was it political?'

'Well –'

'One of the clubs?'

'Yes, Effendi. But –'

'But what?'

'I don't think they were asking on their own behalf.'

'I don't understand.'

'Look, Effendi, the way it works is this. You're a little man somewhere and you want to put in a request. But it's no good you asking yourself, because why should they pay any attention to you? What can you offer them? So what you've got to do is go to someone they'll listen to.'

'Another gang? Or political club?'

'That's right. One you've got a bit of influence with.'

'OK, so what you're saying is that your gang was asked by another gang, or club, to keep off the Morellis; but that what they were doing was asking on behalf of somebody else?'

'Yes, Effendi.'

'An individual?'

'Effendi, I don't –'

'Someone small, anyway. Perhaps one or two people.'

Shukri nodded.

'That is what I have heard, Effendi.'

'Have you heard anything else about this individual? Or individuals?'

'Effendi, I am but a street man for my gang –'

'Nevertheless, you may have heard something.'

Shukri shook his head.

'Effendi, I have heard nothing. It doesn't affect others in the gang, you see. Only me. And it is not very important. Except that –'

'Yes?'

'The request must be carried out. That is what they have told me. And the way they said it makes me think, Effendi, that those who asked them are not people to be trifled with.'

'This other gang, you mean?'

Shukri hesitated.

'Effendi, it is not really a gang.'

'Club, then.'

'Effendi, it is not a club, either.'

'What is it, then?'

'Effendi, I do not know. I am but a nobody. They do not tell me things. Only what I had to do.'

'You know, however, that it was not a gang and not a club.'

Shukri began to sweat. Owen could get nothing more out of him, however. All he would say was that the organization, whoever it was, that had approached his gang on behalf, probably, of one of its members, was big and powerful. The gang had had little alternative but to go along with its request. It wasn't an organization you would turn down.

'You just wouldn't,' said Shukri earnestly.


Mahmoud listened intently.

'There are other kinds of organization,' he said. 'Business associations, for example.'

'Morelli was an auctioneer,' said Owen. 'That's small business. And any association of auctioneers would be small too. Shukri spoke of the organization as being big.'

'And powerful,' said Mahmoud. 'An association of auctioneers would hardly be powerful.' He thought. 'Maybe a business association that he was dealing with?'

'Do auctioneers deal with big associations of any kind? I wouldn't have thought so.'

They sipped their coffee.

'Maybe it was an association of a different kind. Political? A political party?'

'A political party would hardly put in a request like that,' said Mahmoud.

'And if it did,' said Owen, 'it would do it through one of its clubs.'

Mahmoud grimaced. It was true, but he didn't like to think that.

There was a little silence.

'Religious,' they both said together, and then both laughed. It was hardly likely to be religious, either.

They finished their coffees and stood up.

'How's Aisha?' asked Owen as they walked away.

'Oh, she's fine,' Mahmoud answered him. 'And she is getting on well with my mother.'

'Oh, good.'

'That is important,' said Mahmoud.

Well, yes, it would be, since it was going to be a permanent arrangement. It was where, he had the impression, Egyptian marriages often went wrong.

'As a matter of fact,' said Mahmoud diffidently, 'there was something I wanted to ask you.'

'Oh, yes?'

'Zeinab has invited us to coffee.'

'She has?'

'Yes. Of course, it is very kind of her –'

Hum. Owen hoped so.

'But –'

Mahmoud hesitated.

'You don't happen to know who else will be there, do you?'

'Will it be Princess Fawzi, you mean? Or those dreadful Princes?'

'Well, yes.'

'I wouldn't have thought so. Actually, she can't stand them. Look, I don't know why she was so difficult the other evening, but –'

'She wrote a nice note to Aisha afterwards.'

'She did?'

'Yes. Saying she was sorry. And inviting her to coffee.'

'Oh, good.'

'Aisha would like to go. Of course, she couldn't go by herself.'

'No, indeed.'

'I would have to take her.'

'Well, yes, perhaps.'

'Unless, of course, no men were to be present.'

'You want me to ask her?'

Mahmoud looked relieved.

'Please.'

\*     \*     \*

'Of course not!' said Zeinab.

'No men?'

'Certainly not!'

'What about Princess Fawzi?'

'Not her, either. Actually,' said Zeinab, 'the only other person I have invited is Rosa.'

'Rosa?'

She knew Georgiades, of course, although only as one of Owen's men, and she had met Rosa once or twice. They had got along quite reasonably; that is, as reasonably as Zeinab ever got along with women younger than herself. All the same, Rosa was not someone he would have expected to find in Zeinab's social circle: which was not, in fact, as exalted as she had pretended to Mahmoud and Aisha, but drawn from the artistic fringes of Cairo society, where independent women were more acceptable.

'Georgiades is away,' she said.

'Yes, I know.'

'I thought it would be nice if they got to know each other.'

'It might well be.' He hesitated. 'You will –?'

'Behave?' said Zeinab.


As soon as he got to the warehouse he knew that something had happened. The porters were standing around in deep misery. The foreman was sitting bowed on a packing case, his head in his hands. Beside him, like a judge, stood Mahmoud.

'How can I look her in the face?' the foreman was saying. 'What will she think of me? What will the Nahhasin think of me? Is she not a lone woman? Am not I her protector?'

'You are her servant,' said Mahmoud, 'and she knows that you are a good one.'

'I am a bad one!' said the foreman vehemently. 'That I should let this happen!'

'How were you to know?'

'But I should have known!' cried the foreman. 'I should know everything that happens in the warehouse! Dirt has been poured on my head. How can I look people in the face?'

One of the porters gave a sympathetic sob.

'Abdul, the fault is not yours alone,' said another porter, an older man, evidently of some seniority. 'We share in your shame!'

'No, no,' said the foreman brokenly. 'I have let down the Signora.'

Used as he was to the ready emotionalism of Egyptian street life, Owen could see that this was serious.

'What is it?' he said.

Mahmoud led him up a ladder to a kind of loft where some large cans were stacked in a corner. Mahmoud prised the lid off one of the cans.

'Paint,' he said.

'I don't see –?'

'It was what was used to paint the words on the door.'

'Someone here –?'

'Supplied the paint. They didn't do the actual painting. But they supplied the paint. That is shame enough.'

'Do you know who it was?'

'No, not yet. But in a group like this, it's bound to come out.'

They went back down the ladder.

'We shall leave you,' said Mahmoud severely, 'to listen to your own hearts.'

'How do you know none of them did the actual painting?' Owen asked, as they walked away.

'Because none of them can write,' said Mahmoud.

That was, exactly, what had led Mahmoud to the paint: the fact that it had been writing on the warehouse door; that, and Aisha.

Not everyone in the Nahhasin – it was a source of shame to Mahmoud – could write, so the number of people who could have done the painting was to some extent restricted. And not just the number, but the type of people, since literacy was largely confined to the educated and well-to-do.

Mahmoud had been discussing this with his wife (Owen had the feeling that there was not a wide range of conversational subject matter in the Mahmoud household) and Aisha had come up with the suggestion that possibly a school child had written it. School children were the ones who could actually write, she pointed out. Not only that; they were the ones, in the upper forms at least, who were taking an interest in politics. The Sanieh, she said, was a hotbed of political discussion, and much the same went for the boys' school. And this was especially true, she said, at the moment, when feeling was running so high over the war.

Mahmoud, slightly astonished but always logical in argument, had to concede the theoretical possibility of this. He pointed out, though, that the writing on the warehouse door had been something of an illiterate scrawl, not at all the handwriting you would expect from a properly taught schoolboy or schoolgirl.

Aisha said that could be accounted for by the difficulty of writing on the equivalent of a wall. She had once tried it herself and had found it surprisingly hard, especially if, as was usual in such cases, you wanted to write big. If you were small, you found it hard to reach at the top.

Mahmoud asked when it was that she had tried it.

The previous year, said Aisha, when the war had just started. She had been so angry that one night she had gone back to school and daubed slogans all over the playground wall.

Mahmoud, who was finding marriage delightful but rather more disturbing than he had expected, was obliged again to concede the theoretical justice of her remarks. That was as far as he was prepared to go, however, and he was confining them to the realm of theory when she offered to make inquiries among her former school friends. Mahmoud had not been able to think of an objection in time and so she had gone out and done it.

The next day she had returned triumphant with the news that the culprit had indeed been a school child, a pupil at the boys' school, Fatima's brother. The schools were full of it.

Mahmoud, somewhat taken aback, had deliberated whether

it was proper to make use of information acquired in such a way. He decided that responsibility required him at least to have a word with the boy and so he had visited him in the evening at his home.

The boy had confessed everything readily; indeed, with a certain pride. For weeks, he said, the senior boys had talked of little other than the war and of how they themselves might contribute to the fight against imperialist aggression. They had greeted the news of Morelli's death with satisfaction; but then they had heard that his widow proposed to carry on the business as if nothing had happened. It was at this point that they had decided to take action. They had wanted, he said, to send her a message that Italians were no longer welcome in Egypt, and had chosen him to write something to that effect on the doors of her warehouse.

It was then that he had encountered the problem of finding paint, not to mention a brush. The brush he was able to obtain from a friend; paint was more difficult. But then he had had – according to himself – the brilliant idea of using paint from the Signora's own warehouse to do the daubing. He knew that they kept some paint always in stock and he was a friend of one of the porters –

Which one? asked Mahmoud. The boy had pulled himself up short at this point. He was not prepared to say. Schoolboys' honour; although he did not put it like that. 'We people' engaged in the battle against imperialism, he said, know how to keep secrets. Mahmoud, doubting that the secret was likely to remain a secret for long, did not press him.

What he did do, however, was say to the boy that Signor Morelli had lived in the Nahhasin for a long time and that many there looked upon him as a friend, not as an enemy.

'He was Italian,' said the boy implacably.

'He had become one of us,' said Mahmoud quietly.

The boy had screwed up his face scornfully.

'And even if he hadn't,' said Mahmoud, stung, 'there are many in the Nahhasin who would think it cruel to insult his widow.'

'She is Italian, too,' said the boy, unconvinced: a little shaken, however.

Mahmoud had left him, too, to listen to his own heart.

He had, though, been a little shaken himself by the encounter.

'He seemed so – so unreachable,' he said to Owen, when he was telling him how he had come to find out about the paint.

'I was at that school, too, a long time ago, and when I was there we were always talking about politics. And I daresay we were just as passionate about the occupation of our country by foreigners. But I don't remember us being so – so hard.'

Mahmoud belonged to if not the first generation of Egyptian Nationalists, at least the one that followed soon after. He had been active in student politics at the Law School and, when the Nationalist Party had been formed, soon after he graduated, had been one of the first of its members. He had continued to support it after he had joined the Parquet and remained totally committed to the Nationalist cause. He saw himself, indeed, as did most young lawyers, as at its leading edge.

And now suddenly he became aware of another wave to come, as dedicated as his own but somehow less compromising.

Perhaps he was reading too much into a single encounter, he told himself. In another year the boy might have forgotten about politics altogether. And how representative was he, anyway?

He was still sufficiently in touch with the young of the Nahhasin, however, to know that there were many others who felt as the boy did. And for the first time he sensed the possibility of another generation coming along which did not think quite as he did, would be more extreme, harder; yes, harder.

Owen, too, was left thoughtful by Mahmoud's account. If even girls like Aisha were daubing walls a year ago, what were they doing now? Schoolgirls, like women, were a kind of invisible presence in Egypt. Behind those long, black, shapeless gowns and dark veils and headdresses you never saw them. And because you never saw their faces, you thought that nothing was going in inside their heads. But that, from what Aisha said, was far from the truth. From what she said, the schools, both girls' schools and boys' schools, were in ferment. In a way it was no surprise, at least to him. But it might well be to Kitchener.

By mutual tacit consent they turned into the coffee house at the corner of Mahmoud's street. The usual people, many of whom he had already learned to recognize, were sitting there. Several of them rose to embrace Mahmoud and then, by natural extension, embraced Owen. Sidi Morelli's domino-playing friends were sitting at their usual table. They rose courteously and made space for Mahmoud and Owen. Was it Owen's fancy, having just come from the warehouse, that everyone here, too, seemed woebegone?

'Mahmoud, is this true? About the paint?'

Word had evidently spread with the speed of a bazaar whisper.

Mahmoud nodded.

'This is terrible,' said Abd al Jawad. 'It touches all of us.'

'I shall go and speak to Abdul,' said Hamdan.

'He needs no chiding,' said Mahmoud.

Hamdan looked at him in surprise.

'I go not to chide but to give sympathy.'

Mahmoud made a gesture of apology.

'Her own people!' said Abd al Jawad, distressed. 'What is the world coming to?'

'It is probably only one man among them,' said Mahmoud. 'Let us not call the whole world black when it contains many colours.'

There were general nods at this. The three friends seemed to find it comforting. And Owen, unused to finding himself on the inside of a community where old sayings, and the wisdom they contained, gave important reassurance, felt oddly comforted too.

'The Signora will take this as a sign of hate,' said Fahmy, 'when it is but a sign of foolishness.'

'Certainly the painting was an act of foolishness,' said Hamdan.

'But the giving of the paint! Her own man!' said Abd al Jawad, still unable to get over it.

'Could he have known,' asked Fahmy, he too almost disbelieving, 'that it was to be used for that?'

'If he did,' said Hamdan, 'then shame upon him!'

The other two nodded their heads, and at the neighbouring tables other heads nodded in agreement.

'It touches us all,' said Abd al Jawad again.

Again the heads nodded; and suddenly Owen realized that he was seeing the psychological and social dynamics of the Nahhasin in action. Cairo was still, underneath, not far removed from a tribal society, one in which the honour code had played a crucial part. And where honour was important, so, too, was shame, in some ways the ultimate social sanction of such a society.

It was this pressure that Mahmoud had been content to leave working among the porters, confident that in the end it would tell. He had done the same with the boy; but could he be as confident that it would work there too?

Another small pile of missives from the Box was waiting on his desk when he got back to his office. He glanced through it. They were much the same as usual: a complaint that a certain baker was using disgusting substances to make his bread; another that an oil seller was adulterating his cooking oil. There was the usual letter from a poor old lady claiming that her daughter-in-law was trying to poison her (Owen had checked on this previously; she wasn't, but she thought it was a good idea). And here was something new: a woman enlisting his aid in an attempt to get her son into a certain school. The letter was in a bazaar letter-writer's hand (not the same one) so the woman herself was obviously unable to write. She would have had to have paid for the letter but clearly thought it worth it. Education was moving up the ordinary Egyptian's agenda.

And here was yet another of the threatening letters. He picked it up. The same handwriting as before, and much the same sentiments. No originality here.

He was about to put the letter down when a thought struck him. The same letter-writer wrote all the letters, not just to him but to all the other recipients. That must

115

cost quite a packet; quite a packet, anyway, to someone so (presumably) poor and ignorant as not to be able to write themselves. Apart from the actual writing of the letters, there were the stamps to be paid for. Not everyone had a Box that messages could conveniently be dropped in.

And then another thought came to him. He summoned Nikos.

'Those letters,' he said, showing Nikos the one he'd just received, 'how are they delivered to the other people who get them? Are they simply posted?'

'They are addressed,' said Nikos. 'But they are addressed to people at their places of work. They could simply be handed in at the mail offices.'

Each Ministerial block had its office where the mail was sorted. Messages between Ministries were carried by bearers, as was mail generally throughout the city. Letters were constantly coming and going. It would be easy to slip one into the common pile.

'I will check,' said Nikos, chagrined that he had not done so before. 'At least I should be able to find out whether they are sent by stamped mail.'

Owen continued reading through the other messages the Box had contained. He had half hoped there might be some reference to the guns, but there wasn't.


Zeinab's *appartement* was still smelling of coffee when he went in. Zeinab herself was curled up on a divan, her legs tucked under her.

'How did it go?'

'All right. She didn't say much, but she passed the cakes nicely.'

'She's very young. It must be difficult for her.'

'Yes,' said Zeinab, 'it is very difficult being a woman.'

'How was Rosa?'

'Rosa is pregnant.'

'Yes.'

'You know?'

'Well –'

Zeinab got up from the divan and picked up the empty coffee pot.

'I expect you want to know if I behaved myself?'

'Well –'

'Well, as a matter of fact, I did.'

Then she hurled the coffee pot against the wall. It broke into pieces.

'But I'm damned if I'm behaving now!' she said.

# 10

As Owen was crossing the Bab-el-Luk he saw Trudi von Ramsberg. At first he thought he must be mistaken, for surely she had left Cairo? But the tall, blonde figure was hard to mistake and something about the way she walked –

On an impulse he turned up the Cheikh Sibai after her. Yes, it was her. There was no doubt about it now. He hurried after her and caught up with her when she paused to cross the Sharia-es-Saha.

'Hello!' he said. 'You still here?'

For a moment she seemed disconcerted. Then she kissed him.

'Just making a few last purchases,' she said. 'But you're right, we should have been on our way a couple of days ago. At the last moment, though, something had still not come through. All sorted out now, and I'll be off at dawn tomorrow.'

'Feel like a coffee?'

She glanced at her watch.

'I would,' she said, 'but I've got to get to the bank. These extra days have run my cash down.'

She looked at her watch again.

'But what about later? How about lunch? We could try that place you told me about. It's not far from here, is it?'

'The Mirabelle. You'd need to take an arabeah. But yes, why not?'

They agreed to meet at the restaurant at one o'clock and then Trudi continued on her way.

Owen stood for a moment, wondering slightly. He was a little surprised that she was still here. She seemed so efficient.

118

Perhaps it was not her fault but that of the thing that hadn't come through. And what was all this about cash? She had looked at her watch, as if she had an appointment; but you didn't need an appointment to get cash. Still, it was none of his business.

The Cheikh Sibai continued on the other side of the Sharia-es-Saha, and at the top were the offices of the Dresden Bank. She had almost got there when an arabeah drew up alongside her and a man jumped out. She stopped for him and they went into the bank together. He knew the man. It was Beckmann, the German at the Consulate about whom there'd been that to-do over the librarianship. Perhaps it was his business, after all.

Owen was dropping some things in at the Palace. As he was walking along one of the corridors, a door opened and a group of men came out. Slatin Pasha was one of them. From the way they were shaking hands, Owen guessed that they were saying goodbye to him.

One of the men was Ibrahim Meck, from the Khedive's office. He was talking to Nuri. Owen was pleased to see this further sign of Nuri's acceptability. Perhaps he was on his way back into office. It would make no difference to Owen, but Nuri had been out of favour for a long time and it would cheer him up. He seemed pretty cheerful this morning, giving Owen a warm wave. The recent coolness between him and Owen had evidently been forgotten and Owen was pleased about that too.

Slatin detached himself from the group and came along the corridor to Owen. He seized Owen's hand between the two of his.

'So glad to see you, dear boy, and to be able to say goodbye!'

'You're off, then?'

'Yes, this afternoon. Back to the Sudan.'

They embraced each other in the Arab fashion. Slatin was half Arab by now. Owen rather liked the old boy. In the world of careerists and bureaucrats he was an original.

'Don't let Wingate work you too hard,' he said.

'I won't,' Slatin promised. He embraced Owen again. 'And you yourself take care,' he said. 'These are slippery times.'

Slatin's English was always inclined to the idiosyncratic; but 'slippery', thought Owen, was about right.

'I think Nuri may be going to come back in,' he said to Nikos, as he went through the outer office, back at the Bab-el-Khalk.

'I don't think so,' said Nikos.

He came through with Owen and put some papers on his desk.

'You may need these,' he said.

Owen had a meeting at the Consulate with Paul later that morning. It was a routine one but he thought it likely that this time it might include some questions about the gun-running, so he had asked Nikos to find him the latest reports. He began to go through them now to remind himself.

Something was niggling away, though, at the back of his mind. It was to do with his meeting with Trudi. Beckmann he had figured out now. He wasn't so much the Paul of the German Consulate as its Cavendish. That was what the business of the Librarian had been about. Kitchener had wanted to stop him being planted in a post where he could continue to do his work independent of the existence of a German Consulate. Owen couldn't see why the Germans would want to do that nor why the British should want to stop them. Things hadn't reached such a point, had they? He put it down to a fondness for silly games.

But Cavendish could have been right about Trudi. He and Paul were both convinced that she was here because she was somehow acting as an agent; and now here she was having a meeting with Beckmann. If she *was* having a meeting, and it had not just been an accident. If she was, then what had the meeting been about? And why had it been held in the bank? Something to do with money? But if it was, it certainly wasn't Trudi's need for petty cash.

He realized what it was that had been niggling away

at the back of his mind. It was that the bank was the Dresden. That was the bank that that German – what was his name? Scharnhorst – had worked for. The one who had been involved in the discussions with Nuri about the Khedive's private railway. The Dresden had obviously been lined up to provide the finance.

He wondered where that had got to. On the spur of the moment he picked up his phone.

'Hello,' he said, 'is that the Continentale? I wonder if you could tell me whether one of your guests is still with you? A Mr Scharnhorst. No? He left yesterday? Thank you. And someone else, a colleague of his: a Mr Gurnik? Left, too? I see.'

He put the phone down and sat thinking. The image came into his mind of Nuri, a newly cheerful Nuri, at the Palace talking to Ibrahim Meck.

He got up from his desk and went into Nikos's office.

'I have a feeling,' he said, 'that a meeting might have taken place very recently, either yesterday or the day before. It would have been between two people staying at the Continentale Hotel, a Mr Scharnhorst and a Mr Gurnik, and two of the Khedive's senior staff, Ibrahim Meck and, probably, Sidki Bey. Oh, and Nuri Pasha might have been there too. Could you find out? And if you could let me know before my meeting with Paul –'

At the meeting, as he had suspected, the gun-running issue did come up and he was glad that Nikos had got the reports for him. It gave him something to talk about.

'As you can see,' he said, 'there have been very few interceptions in the past fortnight. It looks as if the steps we have taken are having an effect. The coastal traffic seems to have practically dried up.'

'That's good!' said Paul. 'As long as it has not just moved elsewhere.' He looked pleased. 'I'll tell His Lordship. It might do you a bit of good,' he added.

'Thanks.' Owen hesitated. 'Actually, I've been thinking of writing him a memo.'

'You have?'

'Yes. I don't seem to be able to get through to him talking, so I thought I'd put it down on paper.'

'Exactly what were you thinking of putting down on paper?'

'Well, you know. Look, Paul, I'm really not happy about what we're doing. Stopping the Khedive from selling his railway, if that's what you've still in mind. I thought I'd send him a memo outlining more precisely my objections –'

'Please don't.'

'I feel it's important.'

'Yes, I know. And you've made your point. Only now I think it would be best to leave it.'

'Yes, but –'

'It will only annoy him.'

'Well, I could put up with that if it would only make him think again.'

'It's no good, Gareth. Once he's made up his mind –'

'He's inaccessible to reason, is that it?'

Paul sighed.

'You know, he's really quite reasonable.'

'That wasn't how he struck me.'

'That was because you contradicted him.'

'I didn't contradict him. I merely expressed doubt.'

'Yes, well, he doesn't like doubt.'

'Well, he *ought* to like doubt. About this, at any rate. I tell you, Paul, if he goes ahead on this and forces the Khedive to back down, he'll have the whole country up in arms!'

'Aren't you exaggerating on this, Gareth? Just the teeniest bit?'

'No, I'm bloody not. He's out of touch. Things have changed since he was here before. The whole country has become much more – well – aware.'

'In the towns, perhaps.'

'In the countryside, too. Everywhere. Look, Paul, it's even boiling over in the schools.'

'All we are going to do is point out to the Khedive that he doesn't actually own the thing he is selling. He was given a personal concession to construct a small railway to his private estates in the west. So that he doesn't have to get there on a camel. The land on which it was built remained the property of the state.'

'It's a quibble, Paul. That's how they'll see it.'

'You think they'll come out on to the streets? For this?'

'They'll see it as his, Paul. He's the ruler of the country, after all, and what they'll see is Egypt forced to back down. Not just him, but Egypt.'

Paul shook his head.

'It's no good,' he said. 'It's too late now, anyway. He's made up his mind.'

There was a little silence. Then Owen got up from the table.

'Well, if he has,' he said, 'you'd better tell him to get a move on. Because there was a meeting yesterday at which, I strongly suspect, the railway was sold.'

By one o'clock, the time he had arranged to meet Trudi at the Mirabelle, the unusual heat had made the open street unbearable. The Mouski was deserted. The shops, small, dark, open-fronted and native Egyptian at this end, were apparently empty. In fact, their owners were lying down in the shadows behind their counters, taking their siesta. They would have jumped up at once if anyone had come in, but that was unlikely. Ordinary Egyptians were at their lunch or else sleeping afterwards. The tourists would not come again till later when it was cooler.

Owen went straight into the restaurant when he arrived but Trudi wasn't yet there. The restaurant was only half full, but there was someone he recognized: Grenville, the officer he had met at the barracks, sitting at a table with three elderly ladies, whose complexions suggested they had only just come out from England. He gave Grenville a nod and chose a table which he thought neatly combined cooler darkness with the possibility of a draught from the door.

Shortly afterwards Trudi came in.

'I'm going to make the most of this,' she informed him. 'After this it's durra and beans for three weeks!'

He saw Grenville looking at her. Well, that was not surprising. Trudi was the sort of woman that men looked at;

all the more so in a place like Cairo where women normally went unseen and there were few tall blondes for famished soldiers to feast their eyes on.

This was even more true of the desert, of course, and he wondered how Trudi would fare.

Trudi shrugged.

'I have curiosity value,' she said.

Bearing in mind what Paul had said when he had first heard of her destination, he tried to get from her some idea of her route; not just to satisfy Paul, but also in case she might at some point need help. He couldn't get much from her, however.

'Well, there aren't places mostly,' she said. 'Just rocks and things. You find out the name of them as you go along.'

Owen decided again that the explorer's life was not for him.

He asked her if the thing she had been waiting for had come through.

'Yes,' she said, 'we're all right now.'

Again, without being obvious about it, he couldn't get anything more out of her. After a while he decided he'd done his duty and concentrated on enjoying her company.

They had nearly reached the end of the meal when he saw Grenville looking again: only this time he seemed to be looking at him, not at Trudi. He half rose from the table and jerked his head.

Owen followed him to the cloakroom.

'That girl you're with,' he said, 'she's friendly with one of my officers. An *Egyptian* officer,' he said significantly.

'Oh, really?'

'Yes. Thought you'd like to know.'

'Well, yes, thank you.'

'Saw them talking in the square. Nothing wrong with that, of course. But I thought that if you were taking the girl out, you might like to know.'

'Thank you, yes.'

'Says something about the girl, doesn't it? Of course, maybe it didn't amount to anything, in which case, well, I wouldn't want to make too much of it. But it doesn't look good. You need to stick to your own sort. You know, some of these girls, they come out from home, where they can get away with being free and easy, and think they can be just the same here, with anyone they please. But it's not like that here. You've got to stick to your own sort. I've nothing against a bit of enjoyment, especially if you're a man, but you need to stick to your own sort.

'That's what I tell chaps when they're new out from England. It's not like England, I say, where if you get a girl into trouble you can go ahead and marry her. It's different here with the local ladies. You can't go ahead and marry them; at least, not if you're an officer. It would make for all kinds of trouble. So best not to let the situation arise. Stick to your own sort, I say, and don't get in too deep with the local ladies. A bit of enjoyment is all right, but don't get in too deep! That's what I tell them.'

'Very wise, I'm sure.'

'Not, of course, that I need to tell you that.'

'Well, no.'

Or, alternatively, thought Owen, Zeinab coming to mind, yes.

'And, of course, this lady may not realize that she is cheapening herself. She just may not know the form here. She is English, I suppose?'

'German.'

'German!'

'Of course, it may not apply to German women,' said Owen, straight-faced.

By the time they came out of the Mirabelle the city was beginning to stir once more. The water-sellers and ice men were starting up their rounds again and one or two shopkeepers were standing yawning at the front of their shops. There were still no arabeahs about in the Mouski, however, so they walked down towards the Khan-al-Khalil, where Owen knew there was a rank of them. There was a solitary donkey coming towards them. As it drew nearer, Owen saw that it belonged to Mustapha, the ice man for the Bab-el-Khalk; and there behind him, as ever, was his assistant, Amina. They

125

exchanged greetings; but then, after the donkey had passed them, Amina turned her head and spat, with considered deliberation, at Trudi's feet.

Office work at the Bab-el-Khalk, as at almost all the government offices, finished for the day, because of the heat, at two. Owen, however, frequently went back at the end of the afternoon to see if anything had come in.

Today some things had. There was a letter from the Italian Consul complaining that the recent measures with respect to the guns traffic appeared to have had no effect at all. There was also a letter from the Sublime Porte complaining that the measures were interfering with legitimate traffic from Turkey to Tripolitania. Then there was another letter from the Italian Consul deploring the lack of progress in the investigation into Morelli's death and asking what was being done to protect Italian citizens; together with a memo from the Khedive's office protesting about the constant harassment of native-born Egyptian citizens in the so-called interests of security. Finally, there was a memo from the British Financial Adviser pointing out the cost of the recent measures and reminding Owen of the need to hold expenditure back, while at the same time, of course, maintaining the level of his operations.

Owen considered that none of these required any action on his part. He asked Nikos – Nikos never went home; Owen thought it possible that he lived in a filing cabinet – if anything had come in from Georgiades at Luxor. Nikos said it hadn't.

Owen felt slightly guilty at sending Georgiades to Luxor at this time, just when Rosa was pregnant. The thought suddenly came to him that it might be a bad time for another reason, too: she was a Greek, and therefore a foreigner, like Morelli.

Somehow he had never thought of her as a foreigner. Her family had lived in Egypt since, well, at least, he guessed, since her grandmother's time. The old lady tended, at home, to speak Greek, whereas the rest of the family, like many Cairenes, switched about constantly from French to English to Arabic to anything else that happened to be handy.

The Greek community had been here so long that it thought itself Egyptian. But then, so did the Italian community. And Morelli had lived here for a long time. 'One of us.' That was what people had said about him and that was what he had thought. But it had not saved him.

The war was opening cracks in what had seemed firmly cemented. If Morelli, why not Rosa? If the Italians, then why not the Greeks? Why not anybody? Egypt was one of the most cosmopolitan countries of the world, hospitable, in the past, to almost every nationality. That was one of the things that Owen liked about it, that was one of the reasons why he felt at home. Egypt was getting to be his home as much as it was theirs.

And now this!

It would end only when the war ended. If then. He had a vision of it all breaking apart and falling in pieces. What Trudi had said about Turkey came into his mind: an old order falling and a new order coming into being. She saw the new order. What he saw was the falling apart.

Well, all you could do was try and contain it. And it didn't help, it didn't help at all, if, while you were trying to keep the gun powder in the barrel, someone like Kitchener came along and threw a match in it.

He decided to visit Rosa.

He guessed that while Georgiades was away she would be staying with her parents. They owned a small shop in the Khan-al-Khalil, selling antiques to the tourists: armour from the crusades, old Persian embroideries and enamels, brass boxes and bowls inlaid with silver, ancient illuminated Korans, amulets and jewellery of all sorts, turquoises – the beautiful pale-blue turquoises that you seldom see in London – by themselves. The shop was not exactly thriving – Rosa's father being more interested in the goods than in the business – but was doing well enough. It was held together by her grandmother, a formidable old lady who dominated her son and daughter-in-law but had met her match in her granddaughter.

Rosa was there and came out to see Owen, pleased.

'With Georgiades away, I thought I'd come and see if you were all right.'

'All right?' said Rosa. 'Why shouldn't I be all right?'

'Well, you know, with the war on and there being a bit of feeling against foreigners. There was an Italian killed in the Nahhasin.'

'An Italian!' said the grandmother dismissively. 'Well, they're the ones who started the war, so what did they expect?'

'You haven't seen any sign that it might be affecting you?' said Owen, turning to Rosa's father.

'No.' He hesitated. 'A little, perhaps.'

'If they come,' said Rosa's grandmother, 'we shall know what to do.'

'Abou is here,' said Rosa, 'and Thutmose.'

'Much use they would be!' snorted Rosa's grandmother, who tended to feel that way about men in general.

'If there are any signs,' said Owen, apparently to Rosa's father but actually to her mother, who, although never daring to open her mouth at home, could be counted on to act independently, 'let me know.'

Rosa announced that she had been on the point of leaving to go back to her own home and Owen offered to walk with her. She and Georgiades had a flat up near the Greek Orthodox church. To get to it you went along the Nahhasin and then through the maze of streets to the Khalig-el-Masri.

It was evening now and the city had come to life. All along the Nahhasin men were sitting out at tables. The coffee houses were full. Lights were on in the shops and their owners out on the street to greet their acquaintances. There was a steady throng of people going in both directions, not particularly purposefully but just taking the air, bringing the fodder camels and arabeahs almost to a halt.

As they passed the tables, Owen, almost by habit, listened in on the conversation. For the most part people were talking about their own affairs; no one was talking about the Khedive or his railway. At some of the tables, though, especially those where groups of young men were sitting, the discussion was political. It often was in Cairo.

There was one table, for instance, at which almost a dozen men were sitting, all young office effendis by the look of them, where discussion was particularly passionate and Nationalist newspapers much in evidence, and words like 'capitalism', 'imperialism' and 'Capitulations' (the system of commercial and legal privileges that foreigners in Egypt enjoyed) came spilling out into the street, where, beyond the circle of light, children played and Amina sat listening, rapt.

She turned her head as they approached and Owen wondered if she would spit at Rosa, in which case he would speak to her; but she didn't. It wasn't, perhaps, quite the same. Trudi was obviously foreign, clearly, with her blondeness, incongruent. Rosa was darker and, although not in the birka, in a long dark dress and something which came over her head and half covered her face; if not Arab, then, arguably, decently Egyptian.

They passed the coffee house where Morelli had died. The usual people were sitting at the usual tables. Mahmoud was among them. As they walked past he happened to look up and saw them. He jumped to his feet and rushed across. He embraced Owen and greeted Rosa respectfully but with real pleasure.

'You must come in!' he insisted. 'Both of you. Aisha would be so pleased.'

Owen saw that, now that he was married, Mahmoud's life was changing.

Inside the house, too, things were changing. Aisha came confidently forward, clearly with the intention of joining them. Even more surprisingly, Mahmoud's mother came in too, sitting, however, somewhat shyly on a divan at the outskirts.

The two younger women sat together and began an increasingly animated conversation. Owen and Mahmoud chatted about general matters, by common consent avoiding anything to do with work; but then the conversation drifted towards the subject of the current state of things, the 'feel', as it were, of the city. Owen spoke of his sudden worry about Rosa, and others like her; and mentioned, as an illustration of what he thought was a different attitude coming into being, Amina's gratuitous spitting at Trudi.

'That was wrong of her!' said Mahmoud, shocked.

'You ought to speak to that girl, Mahmoud,' said his mother, who had been quietly following the conversation. 'She's running wild.'

'I will,' said Mahmoud. 'But perhaps it would be better if Fahmy did.'

Fahmy, he explained, had taken the girl in when her grandmother had died (her parents had died some time before) and given her lodging at the ice house. Owen realized suddenly that they were talking about the domino-playing friend of Morelli.

'He would take anybody in,' said Mahmoud's mother. 'He's much too soft-hearted, that man.'

'It was good that he took Amina in,' said Mahmoud.

'Yes; but see how she repays him! She never does anything about the house. She's always out!'

'She goes with Mustapha and the donkey,' objected Mahmoud.

'Yes, but when Mustapha and the donkey come home, she stays out. Late at night, hanging around the Nahhasin.'

'Yes,' said Owen, 'I saw her, on the way here.'

'Always hanging around the men,' said Mahmoud's mother tartly.

'I don't think she's that kind of girl,' demurred Mahmoud.

'She was just listening,' Owen felt obliged to say in her defence.

'Yes, but it's the people she listens to – Ishmail and Ali and Abbas and that idiot Habashi, who would be better off doing his work at the Ministry than always sitting around a table talking!'

'It is true that they are not the wisest of men,' said Mahmoud.

'What sort of nonsense does the girl pick up? And, anyway, it's not true that's she's not hanging around the men. Look at the way she's carrying on with Kamal!'

'Kamal doesn't even know that she's there!' declared Mahmoud.

'That makes her behaviour even worse. He's quite out of her reach. And if she makes such a fool of herself over him in public, who else will want to marry her?'

'Suleiman wants to marry her.'

'Suleiman!' Mahmoud's mother was silent for a moment. Then she said: 'I'm not sure she wouldn't do better to stick to making sheep's eyes at Kamal!'

Owen was sitting in his office at the Bab-el-Khalk when an orderly came and said that 'one' wanted to see him. An effendi, asked Owen? No, said the orderly, with the lordly gesture of disdain of someone secure in the hierarchy, a man of no account.

Owen rose from his desk. If it had been an effendi he would have received him in his office; but for other people he went down to the courtyard. He had found that ordinary Egyptians were often intimidated by the huge building, with its tall pillars, its multiplicity of doors, the uniformed orderlies sometimes waiting to greet them, by the anonymity and impersonality of it all, and simply froze. By the time they got to his office they were incapable of saying anything.

In the courtyard, often squatting together in the dust, they felt on equal terms and were better able to communicate what it was that they had come to say.

He wondered who it was; possibly the driver, returning in the hope of more beer. Or maybe someone not to do with the case at all.

In fact, it was the Morellis' foreman. He stood diffidently in the shadow, his fingers plucking worriedly at the embroidered edge of his galabeah. Owen led him away to a quiet, shady corner, away from the stream of orderlies going in and out of the gates, and they crouched down together.

'Effendi, I don't know what to do.'

'Be easy,' said Owen, supposing he was talking about the discovery at the warehouse. 'It was not your fault.'

'It is not that, Effendi. Except that one thing leads to another.'

'What is it, then?'

The foreman hesitated.

'Effendi, I have always been a true servant.'

'And for that the world commends you.'

The foreman sighed.

'That is not what it is doing at the moment,' he said.

'It is not? How can that be?'

'Effendi, there is a word going through the streets and around the coffee houses: it is that the Signor himself bespoke the guns that came to his house.'

'That is most unlikely. Why should he do that?'

'Effendi, that is what I said. The Signor was a just man, I said. He would not want to have anything to do with that. No, no, they said, he was an Italian, wasn't he? And I said, what of that? And they said, well, then, he was buying arms to send to the Italians in Tripolitania.'

'That is utter nonsense!' said Owen. 'Have not the Italians enough arms of their own? It is the Turks in Tripolitania that need arms, not the Italians.'

'That is what I said, Effendi. But they would not have it so. "Blood is thicker than water," they said. The Signor was an Italian and it was only to be expected that he should seek to aid those of his blood.'

'It is complete nonsense.'

'That is what I said, Effendi; but such is the word.'

'But what grounds are there for speaking such a word? There must be grounds; otherwise the word is but wind, and bad wind at that.'

The foreman hesitated.

'Effendi, once the Signor spoke of arms.'

'Well –'

'At night. In his warehouse.'

'Who to?'

'That is not known, Effendi.'

'At night? In the warehouse? With the doors barred? How then was he heard?'

'I do not know, Effendi. I know only that such is the word.'

'Who was it who heard him?'

'That I do not know either, Effendi.'

'And nor does any man. At night? With the doors barred? How could a man be there to hear? This is foolish talk.'

132

The foreman shrugged.

'Nevertheless, it bears heavily upon me, Effendi,' he said quietly, and looked down into the sand.

'Why should it bear upon you, Abdul?' said Owen, after a moment.

The foreman raised his head.

'Because they say I work for those who serve the enemy. Effendi, I have always tried to serve the Signor and Signora truly; and when the Signor died, I thought: it is now that the Signora needs me most. But now, Effendi, I do not know. What if the word were true? I am like everyone else, I am on the side of those who hold true to the Prophet. But, Effendi, even if the word were not true, what am I to do? For I have a family, and children who go to the local *kuttub*, and this place and these people are all I know.'

'You have been true and should remain true.'

'That is what I would wish. But, Effendi, I have to be able to hold up my head among men, and at the moment I cannot. First, that other thing, and now this. I am torn, Effendi. The Signor and Signora have always been good to me; and shall I return evil for good? But –'

His voice died away and he stood looking down into the sand.

'What is it you want from me?' said Owen.

'I do not know,' confessed the foreman, 'except that I come for help.'

Afterwards, Owen sat in his office, thinking. Another victim of the war. He passed the foreman's story, for what it was worth, on to Mahmoud.

# 11

The next morning a bearer brought Owen a note from Mahmoud asking him to come and see him in his office that afternoon. It was the office bit that was unusual. Normally they met at coffee houses or in some other neutral place. Mahmoud never visited Owen at the Bab-el-Khalk; nor did he invite Owen to his office at the Ministry of Justice. This was because he refused in principle to accept the legality or propriety of any such post as Mamur Zapt or Head of the Secret Police; much less that it should be occupied by an Englishman. There must be some powerful reason for this departure from custom.

When Owen entered Mahmoud's office he was taken aback to find it full of children. After a moment he took in that they were all boys and that they were all dressed in the same school uniform of the rather good boys' school in the Quartier Rosetti, the more well-to-do and Europeanized quarter that adjoined the Nahhasin.

Mahmoud was looking severe.

'This is the Mamur Zapt,' he said. 'Tell him what you have told me.'

There was a moment's awed silence. Then one of the boys said in a whisper:

'I don't recognize the Mamur Zapt.'

'You don't recognize the Mamur Zapt?'

'I think it wrong that the Khedive should make use of Englishmen,' said the boy defiantly.

Mahmoud sighed; his own positions rising up against him again.

'Very well, then: repeat what you have told me.'

The boys looked at each other.

'You have already told me; now tell me again.'

They hesitated. Then one of them said in a rush:

'It wasn't Abou's fault.'

'Nevertheless it was Abou that did it,' Mahmoud observed.

'We had all agreed. It just happened that Abou was the one to carry it out.'

'I thought of it,' said the one who had spoken first, with pride. Owen had worked it out now. This was the boy who had daubed the words on the door of the Morellis' warehouse.

'It was a foolish and cruel thought,' said Mahmoud.

The boy tightened his lips stubbornly.

'So it is not just that Abou alone should be punished,' said one.

'No,' agreed Mahmoud: 'nor that Abou alone should be the one to apologize.'

'Apologize!'

'Never!'

'To a foreigner?'

'One should always apologize for cruelty,' said Mahmoud quietly, 'never mind to whom it is done. But especially if the person is a defenceless widow.'

Several of the boys looked troubled at this. The first boy, Abou, however, remained firm.

'She is our enemy!'

'Talk to the elders in the Nahhasin. Talk to Fahmy and Abd al Jawad and Hamdan; and then call her our enemy.'

The boy was silent.

'Nevertheless,' said another boy, 'it is not right that Abou alone should be punished.'

'He was not brought here to be punished,' said Mahmoud.

'No?' said the boy, surprised.

'He was brought here to answer a question.'

'What question?' said Abou.

'Who was the man who gave you the paint?'

'I – I cannot tell you,' said Abou in a low voice.

'Why cannot you tell me?'

'I really cannot.'

135

'What if I already know the answer?'

'Even then,' said the boy, almost inaudibly, 'I cannot.'

The other boys looked at each other.

'Sir, he really cannot.'

'Why not?'

The boys looked at each other again but said nothing.

'Is it because he is family?'

Abou went pale.

'Yes,' said a voice from among the boys.

'That is what I guessed,' said Mahmoud.

'It would be wrong for him to say, sir.'

'You do not need to say, Abou,' said Mahmoud, 'now that I know who he is.'

Abou looked miserable.

'You have found out through me,' he said, 'and I am ashamed.'

'Your whole family will be ashamed,' said Mahmoud. 'But that is something they will have to bear.' He looked at the other boys. 'And so will you,' he said.

The boys filed out in silence.

'I asked that you should come,' Mahmoud said to Owen, 'so that you should be able to tell the Signora that justice has been done.'

Owen nodded. In the Nahhasin shame was punishment enough.

'How did you know the man?' he asked.

'It was when he said he couldn't tell me. At first I thought it was, well, schoolboys' honour? Is that what you say? But then, when he still refused to tell me, I began to think. And then when the other boys confirmed that he couldn't tell me, I guessed that it was family. I know the family, of course. Everyone in the Nahhasin knows all the families. And as soon as I thought, I could see who it must be.'

The warehouse was simmering in the heat. Little beads of tar bubbled in cracks in the wood of the doors and the silver grains of sand in the street outside winked so brightly in the sun that you had to look away.

The porters were gathered in the darkness inside. It was

136

the rest hour and they were lying down or else eating their midday meal. Some of them had brought food tied in a handkerchief: flat pancakes of bread, with an onion and some pickles.

'I seek Suleiman,' said Mahmoud.

He was sitting apart from the others and had just fetched a bowl of water from the fountain house which he was drinking in impatient sips. Suddenly he threw the rest of the water over his head.

'Suleiman,' said Mahmoud, 'I have words for you.'

'Speak them then.'

'Why did you give the paint?'

The other porters went still.

'What paint?' said Suleiman.

'The paint that was used to write the words on the door.'

'I know of no paint. I know no words either,' he said, and laughed uneasily.

'I know you know no words and therefore did not write them. But you gave paint to the one who did.'

Suleiman was silent for a moment. Then he said:

'Has he spoken?'

'He has not spoken of you.'

'Well, then.'

'But he has confessed.'

'But he has not spoken of me?'

'He wouldn't, would he? Not of his own family. But I know.'

The silence was broken by the foreman.

'Suleiman, is this true?'

Suleiman raised his head and looked at him.

'Yes,' he said defiantly.

'Then you may go.'

Suleiman lumbered to his feet.

'Not so fast,' said Mahmoud. 'I came to ask you a question and you have not answered it.'

Suleiman looked puzzled.

'The question?'

'Why? Why did you give the paint?'

'I give paint to whom I choose,' said the porter truculently.

'You gave because one of your family asked. That I can understand. But you gave it knowing that it would be used against your mistress. And that I do not understand.'

'What is she to me?'

'I know you to be a foolish man, Suleiman, and therefore I am not surprised that you gave the paint to a foolish child. But I had always taken you to be a man of honour.'

'And so I am,' said Suleiman angrily.

'Why did you do this, then?'

'Because she is here. And because she is a foreigner. They eat the country like locusts. And then they make war on us.'

'She brings you bread. And it is not this country that they are making war on but another. And it is her countrymen who are making the war, not she.'

'Suleiman, you know nothing about these things,' said the foreman.

'If it is not she who is making the war, then why was her man sending guns to the Italians?'

'Do you know he was sending guns to the Italians?'

'Everyone knows it.'

'It is but a tale,' said Mahmoud. 'A tale made from the wind of the bazaars.'

Suleiman shrugged.

'Where did you get this tale?'

'Here,' said Suleiman. 'I got it here.'

'That is true, Mahmoud,' said one of the porters diffidently. 'We were talking about it. You remember, Ibrahim,' he said, turning to his neighbour, 'it was the day the Signor came down and asked about the Box.'

'Box?'

'Yes. The Mamur Zapt's Box.'

'What did he want to know about that for?'

'I do not know. He had never asked about it before. That is why I remember it. That and the fact that it was the Signor. We had to shut up, you see, because we were talking about the quarrel. That is why I remember that it was that day.'

'What was this quarrel?'

'It was between the Signor and someone else. They were talking about the guns. That is how we know.'

'One of you overheard them?'

The men looked at each other.

'Well, no. Not one of us, exactly.'

'Who was it, then?'

They looked at each other again.

'Someone else.'

'Yes?' said Mahmoud patiently.

There was a little silence.

'We do not know, exactly. It was just that word was brought to us. We do not know by whom.'

'Perhaps it was Amina,' said one of the other men. 'She's always coming and going and she's the one who usually brings us the news.'

'Perhaps. Anyway, we were talking about it, and Abdul said it was but wind, but Ibrahim, here, said that there was no smoke without fire –'

'And then the Signor came so we shut up.'

'He said nothing about the quarrel?'

'Oh no. He merely asked about the Box.'

'And this was how you came to hear the tale, was it, Suleiman?' said Mahmoud, turning back to the porter.

'Yes.'

'And so you decided to give the paint to your nephew?'

'Yes.'

He looked at Mahmoud.

'What are you going to do? Take me?'

'Not at this moment. But there may come a time when I shall come for you.'

'You won't find him here,' said the foreman. 'Suleiman, I have had enough from you. Be gone, and do not come back.'

They found Amina at the Ministerie de la Guerre; or, rather, she found them. Learning from Fahmy at the ice house what route Mustapha, the ice man, was following that day, they had set a course to intercept him at the Ministry. Owen knew an aide-de-camp who worked there and they parked themselves in his office, asking the post man to let them know when the ice man arrived. Instead, Amina arrived herself.

'You wanted to see me,' she said.

'That is so, Amina,' said Mahmoud courteously. 'Would you please sit down?'

She did; on the floor, from where her sharp eyes looked up at them.

'Amina, there is a story going round the Nahhasin that the Signor knew of the guns in his warehouse.'

'I have heard the story,' said Amina cautiously.

'And perhaps passed it on?'

'Certainly not!' said Amina. 'What do you think I am? A gossip?'

Mahmoud smiled.

'Not a gossip, no. But perhaps one who carries the news of the world with them as they go on their rounds. Or so the porters think.'

Amina didn't know quite what to make of this.

'Well,' she said. And then again: 'Well.'

'They thought it might have been you who carried the story to them.'

'No, I don't think so.'

'On the day that the Signor came and asked about the Box.'

'I heard him ask about the Box, certainly.'

'And, perhaps, just before, had passed on the story?'

'I don't think so.'

'Where did you hear the story, Amina?'

'The story was in the air and it fell into my ear.'

'But the story must have come from somewhere?'

'Who knows where these things begin?'

Mahmoud, used to such fencing, considered his next step.

'I think you are a good newsteller, Amina,' he said, 'and tell only what is fresh and what interests. I think you told the porters that day, and that therefore the news was new. I think too, then, that you might remember where you heard it.'

There was a little silence. Then Amina said: 'No, I don't think I do.'

'No?'

Mahmoud smiled, and waited.

'Perhaps it was the fakir,' said Amina after a while, reluctantly.

'Fakir?'

'The boss-eyed one.'

'I do not know the fakir.'

'You might not,' said Amina. 'He comes and goes.'

'Tell me more about this fakir.'

'When he is in the Nahhasin, he sleeps at the door of the warehouse. The wood is warm to his back and he sleeps well. He was sleeping there one night and he heard voices inside the warehouse. There were two and they were arguing. One said: "You shouldn't have done it!" And then the other said: "But I had asked you!" And the first came back: "But you didn't tell me it would be guns!" And the other said: "Some things it is best not to know." The first speaker then became angry and said: "It was a trick that you played on me." But then they moved away and the fakir heard no more.'

'But what is the Signor to do with this?'

'The first voice was his.'

'And the second?'

'The fakir did not know.'

They walked down with Amina to the courtyard, where Mustapha was waiting with his donkey, having delivered his ice.

'Effendi,' he said to Owen, 'if she has done aught amiss, let me be the one to beat her.'

'Stay your blows. She has done nothing amiss. Except –' said Mahmoud, remembering, 'Amina, I want to have a word with you.' He led her aside. 'Amina, I will not have you spitting at foreigners. It is discourteous.'

'I do not –' began Amina furiously.

'The woman I was with,' said Owen. 'The tall, fair one.'

'I was not spitting because she was a foreigner. I was spitting because –'

She stopped.

'Anyway,' she said to Owen, 'I did not spit at you.'

*     *     *

141

He had been uncomfortably aware that he had been receiving hospitality but not returning it. Even Zeinab had done better. She had at least entertained Aisha at her *appartement*. But the thought of entertaining anyone in his *appartement* quite unnerved Owen. He reckoned to take all his meals out. The coffee houses and restaurants were as much his home as his *appartement* was; indeed, far more, since that was where he met his friends and did his reading.

He decided, therefore, to invite Mahmoud and Aisha out for a meal; and then it was only a question of checking that Zeinab was willing, and calling in at the restaurant.

The restaurant he had chosen was a Lebanese one in the Ismailiya, dark, cool and quiet, the sort of place, with its low tables, its near-Arab food, and its seclusion in which he hoped Aisha would feel at ease. This would be the first time that she had ever dined out in public.

When he and Zeinab arrived, Mahmoud and Aisha were already there, Mahmoud in his serious dark suit, Aisha in a dark, European-style dress and a dark, but European, veil. Zeinab was veiled, too, but *à la Parisienne*, with a touch of flamboyance and rather more than a touch of provocation; seemly, however, by the standards of the Cairo rich. With Owen's dark, Welsh colouring, they could easily have passed for a rich Lebanese foursome out for the evening: rich, because this was the sort of thing that only the confident, emancipated rich would do.

Aisha was liking it, he could see. She began to blossom, leaning forward to join unself-consciously in the conversation, her dark, rather pretty eyes absorbing everything.

Mahmoud, too, began to expand. He talked about his youthful university days, something which seemed to interest Zeinab particularly, and which rather surprised Owen, for he had never supposed that Mahmoud had had a youth. It was a new Mahmoud that he was seeing.

And suddenly he realized what it was. It was the marriage. They were both very happy. Owen couldn't work it out. An arranged marriage, arranged between two people who didn't know each other, arranged by someone else – and yet it appeared to be successful!

Whereas he and Zeinab; Zeinab sitting there so unusually silently –

He just couldn't work it out.

The next day Kitchener forced the Khedive to withdraw his offer to sell the railway; whereupon the Khedive departed in high dudgeon for one of his estates on the Mediterranean coast. Not before making clear his fury at the Consul-General's action, however. On the following day the newspapers were full of the 'dreadful insult' to Egypt's ruler; an insult which was also, as *Al-Liwa*, the most popular, as well as the most Nationalist, of the Arabic newspapers, pointed out, one to the Egyptian people.

The Egyptian people were not, however, despite Owen's prediction, up in arms. This was because the Sirdar had got there first. He had filled the streets with British soldiers, and for the next few days they were much in evidence. The crowning piece of his show of force was a massive parade in Abdin Square, just in front of the Palace.

His original intention had been to announce that it was in honour of the Khedive's birthday, which was, admittedly, some way off, but would do as well as anything. When the Khedive, apoplectic with rage, declined to attend, he had at first altered it to the Queen's birthday, trusting that not too many people would realize that Victoria had died some years before. Persuaded by Paul that, even so, this was not a good occasion on which to celebrate England's royalty, he had then, in desperation, claimed that it was the anniversary of the Aldershot Review, an announcement which left everyone, both British and Egyptian, mystified. The Egyptians, however, saw from the name that it was something to do with shooting, so took, on the whole, the right message.

And so there they were, drawn up in the square, in full dress: the Dragoons in their scarlet, the Borderers in their tartan, the Horse Artillery in their gold-laced jackets. And there beside them, although in prudently smaller numbers, representing the Egyptian Army, were the Camel Corps with their cocks' plumes and the Sudan Infantry with their crimson tarbooshes. Trudi, thought Owen, would have loved it.

Around the square, restraining the over-enthusiastic onlookers, or, depending on your point of view, stopping them from throwing stones, was a thin line of policemen. There was, in fact, a crowd there to restrain, come partly because of the Cairene inassuageable thirst for entertainment, partly because, like the ice man and his donkey, they had been stopped during passage of the square in the ordinary pursuit of their business. Owen saw Mustapha sitting resignedly on the ground on the shady side of his donkey.

Amina at first he could not see, but then he caught sight of her on the very edge of the crowd, wormed through to the front and peering, rapt, at the soldiers opposite.

Normally on such occasions there would be dignitaries present, sitting in armchairs arranged in front of the Palace railings. Today, of course, with the Khedive's boycott of the event, there were no Egyptians and it hadn't seemed worth setting aside special chairs for the few Europeans. Instead, seating had been subsumed into the general arrangements for the military wives and families, consisting of a separate roped-off enclosure to one side.

The occasion was, however, to be graced by the attendance of the Consul-General himself, and soon Kitchener appeared, the tall figure towering above those of his attendants. He stood for a moment reviewing the formations in general and then began to walk along the lines, stopping for a word or two here and there, not always with British soldiers but sometimes with Sudanese or Egyptians whom he recognized from his time in the Sudan.

This was a moment when Owen always felt tense, because, with Kitchener standing still, he presented a better target to anyone who wanted to take a potshot at him. Of course, the crowd was kept back sufficiently far as to make such an attempt unlikely to succeed. All the same, he scanned the mass of people anxiously.

Soon, however, Kitchener was done. He exchanged salutes, took one last look around, and climbed into his carriage. His mounted escort closed round him and in a moment he was gone.

The parade came to an end. The various detachments began to move off. The Camel Corps, always popular, made a long wheel-round close to the crowd. Behind them the Egyptian Artillery, also a favourite, was harnessing up its guns and getting ready to follow them.

The onlookers redisposed themselves to get a better view. Children pushed forward right under the linked arms of the policemen. At the point where the soldiers would come closest, the crowd was at its most dense. Amina, having wriggled forward on hands and knees, suddenly appeared at the feet of one of the policemen.

Selim looked down.

'Since you're so close to the ground already, my love,' he said, 'why don't you just turn over and lie on your back?'

'You shut up, you big bastard!' hissed Amina, keeping her eyes fixed intently on the approaching Artillery.

Selim followed the direction of her gaze.

'Out of your reach, I would have thought,' he said critically.

Owen could see now the object of her attention. It was Mahmoud's friend, Kamal.

Amina's eyes drank him in. He passed by, however, without noticing her.

# 12

Over the next week there was a sharp increase in the number of attacks on foreign persons and property. Stones were thrown, windows broken, walls daubed. It was all, however, satisfactorily minor.

'Unfortunate times,' he murmured to Nuri Pasha, when he chanced to meet him one day, wishing to play down his satisfaction.

'Unfortunate times indeed,' said Zeinab's father, 'and doubly unfortunate for me.'

'But why? Surely it is at times like this that the Khedive will especially value the advice of an old friend?'

'He has been hurt,' said Nuri, 'deeply hurt. And he has kicked out all his advisers.'

'Dear, dear!'

'But that's not the worst part about it,' said Nuri. 'The fact is, I had hopes of personal benefit from this latest scheme of his – the railway, you know. I was hoping to be able to sell some land.'

'But the land the railway is on all belongs to the State. It's not even the Khedive's.'

'Well, that's doubtful, isn't it?' said Nuri. 'It's the Khedive, after all, and the Khedive, surely, is the State. But, actually, my land isn't there, it's on the other side of Alexandria.'

'But there isn't a railway there at all!'

'Not yet,' said Nuri. 'But there will be. At least, there would have been if this had gone through. It's logical, isn't it? Connect up the systems. Turkey to Tripolitania. Visionary! That's what I call it: visionary. And now,' said Nuri sadly, 'the vision is not to be realized. And my estate is exactly in the line that an extension would take! It's a small estate, complete desert, of course, not a chance of anything growing. But strategically placed. Its value, one might say, is all in the vision. And now all chance of realizing the vision has been dashed. I call Lord Kitchener's action high-handed!' said Nuri reproachfully. 'High-handed!'

He shook his head mournfully.

'And – and short-sighted! Well, isn't that the truth of it? It is no longer to the West that one must look for vision; not to the bankers of London or' – with a tinge of regret – 'the boulevards of Paris. No, all that belongs to the past. The future lies east. In Constantinople. Those new fellows. Men of vision.'

It was a view that was coming to be widely shared in Egypt; although, perhaps, not quite in the form it took for Nuri.


Nikos came in and laid the latest batch of threatening letters on Owen's desk. Most recipients had got into the habit now of sending the letters to Owen directly they arrived. Not, as someone tartly pointed out, that that seemed to do much good.

The latest letters were more or less the same as the earlier ones: all handwritten by a bazaar letter-writer, and usually the same letter-writer. Owen was sure now that the sender of the letters must be illiterate.

No personality came through the letters. There was something slightly mechanical about them, almost as if they had been composed to a formula. There was never any suggestion that the recipient of the letter was personally known to the sender, even that he was seen as an individual. Each letter could have been sent to anyone on the list.

Nor did the letters ever seem modified by events. There was no change in this respect between the earlier letters and the more recent ones. Owen found this odd. The latest ones had been written after Kitchener's brush with the Khedive. No reference was made to it. Owen had had the impression that this was something on which the whole country had a view just at the moment; but nothing of that emerged in the letters. It was as if the sender was somehow cut off from events. A recluse? Or just someone very ignorant.

He summoned Nikos and asked him if he had found out anything about how the letters were being delivered. As before, said Nikos; by hand. Someone was going round and dropping them in regularly at the government offices. Although he had asked the clerks in the post rooms to keep an eye open for anyone handing them in, no one had so far reported anything. This was not really surprising, for most mail, including all that between offices, was sent by hand. The post rooms were busy places and there were people coming and going all the time.

Was it just people in government offices who were getting them, asked Owen? Or was it foreigners in other institutions, banks, say, as well? It was confined to the British Administration, Nikos replied. Just the government offices. Oh, and the army as well.

This raised the question again of how the names of the officials, and their government addresses, had been obtained. They would all be in the *Ministry Handbook*, which was, of course, available in all the offices; but to get access to it you really had to be in the offices yourself. Now how did that square with the ignorant illiterate that he had been positing?

An orderly? But how was it that he was able to get around to government offices during working hours? Unless, of course, he was a bearer himself.

Owen at last managed to catch up with Zeinab. She had been busy, she said, raising money to send ambulances to Tripolitania. Owen assured her that even Miss Nightingale had had to raise money. Zeinab, however, did not even smile.

Lately there had seemed something distant about her. Used as he was to her swings of mood, he found this troubling. It was not, now, as if emotion was violently swinging but as if it had been somehow drained away. He challenged her about this.

'What's the use?' she said.

'Use?'

'The use of going on like this. You and I.'

'Now, look –'

She interrupted him.

'The fact is,' she said, 'you're British and I'm Egyptian, and nothing's going to alter that.'

'Yes, and you're a woman and I'm a man, and I hope nothing's going to alter that, either!'

She regarded him expressionlessly.

'It's no good,' she said.

'No good? Look, just because Kitchener and the Khedive get across each other, it doesn't mean that you and I –'

'It's not just that,' she said. 'Of course, it's not making it any easier. But if it wasn't that, it would be something else. There's always going to be something pulling us apart, and I don't know that I can go on. Time is no longer on my side and I'm not sure I can wait any more for things to get sorted out.'

'Look, we don't need to wait for things to get sorted out. We could marry tomorrow!'

She looked at him again with that dead, expressionless look.

'Could we?' she said.


Mindful of the increasing number of attacks on foreigners, Owen went to see how Rosa was getting on. His route took him along the Nahhasin. As he was walking past a coffee house he saw Mahmoud sitting at a table with some of the men who had been at his wedding. They were talking fiercely; but then, as they saw him coming up to them, there was a sudden silence.

'You are not welcome!' said Kamal angrily.

Mahmoud put up his hand. Kamal turned on him.

'I know he is your friend, Mahmoud, but he is not welcome!'

'I come at the wrong moment,' said Owen. 'I am sorry.'

'No moment is the wrong moment for a friend to come,' said Mahmoud courteously.

'Nevertheless –'

149

He prepared to leave.

'No, no!' Kamal jumped up. 'It is I who will leave.'

'Kamal –' began Mahmoud.

Another man jumped up.

'Habashi –'

Kamal brushed aside Mahmoud's protests and stalked off. Several of the men left with him.

'Hothead!' said Ibrahim Buktari, looking after him affectionately.

Owen hadn't noticed at once that Mahmoud's father-in-law was one of the group. They exchanged embraces. One or two of the other men, who knew Owen from the wedding, also did so, awkwardly.

Ibrahim pulled him down into a seat.

'At least join us in a coffee,' he said.

'Ibrahim, I am sorry, but I have to go,' said another man, getting up. 'It is not meant discourteously,' he said apologetically to Owen. 'I really do have to go. People await me. I am late already. I am sorry I cannot stay to help you resolve your dispute,' he said to Mahmoud, 'but I must, I must go!'

He rushed off.

'I consider the opposition to have abandoned the field,' announced Ibrahim Buktari.

Mahmoud smiled.

'I would not have wished to offend my father-in-law, anyway,' he said.

'What was the dispute?' asked Owen.

Ibrahim turned to him.

'Well, in a way it concerns you, too,' he said, 'for you brought the gift.'

'Gift?'

'The one from Kitchener,' said Mahmoud.

'They argue it should be sent back,' said Ibrahim. 'But I say no. It was a gift between friends; and what has that to do with Khedives or railways or the British government? It was not the British government that gave the gift, it was an old friend; and shall I now send it back saying that friendship is nothing?'

'The trouble is, Mahmoud,' said one of the other men good-humouredly, 'that now you've acquired a father-in-law, you've also got yourself landed with some awkward friends.'

'Ah, but he had some awkward friends before he got married!' said Owen with a smile.

Ibrahim Buktari beamed: the others laughed, and the incident passed off smoothly. Owen suspected, however, that similar problems were occurring all over Egypt as a new strain was placed on relationships.

The story that Morelli had known about the guns in his warehouse bothered Owen. He didn't believe it for one moment, but there was no doubt that it was all over the Nahhasin. Where had the story come from? Amina had spoken of a fakir but Mahmoud, who seemed to know everyone in the Nahhasin, couldn't place him. Did that mean he had come in from outside? Was there an extra agent in all this? It would be helpful to have a word with this fakir, if he existed. Owen put his men to work.

Meanwhile, his thoughts returned to the porters and to the warehouse. That was where the conversation was supposed to have taken place and where Suleiman claimed that he had first heard the story. Suleiman was not necessarily to be believed, but the other porters had supported his story, in that they agreed that they had been talking about it – they had even been able to identify the day because of Morelli's strange inquiry about the Box – so it was possible that on this occasion he had been speaking the truth.

But how had they heard the story? From the fakir? From Amina, carrying it on her travels? Or had it been, as she had suggested, hanging in the general air of the Nahhasin, ready to fall into any open ear?

There was another thing, though, that made him pause. He had been assuming that the story was false; but suppose it were true? Suppose there really had been a conversation in the warehouse. Then the person most likely to overhear it would be one of the porters. All right, the conversation had taken place at night, when they would all have gone home.

But it was far more likely that one of them had been hanging about than that anyone else had. The warehouse was secured at night. And all this stuff about someone sleeping against the door outside – well, it was not impossible, but surely less likely than that a porter, perhaps the last to leave, might have overheard something.

He took his sun helmet off the peg – these days he had taken to wearing a helmet rather than a tarboosh when he walked about the city during the daytime because it gave greater protection against the sun – and set off for the warehouse.

He found the Signora and the foreman standing alone in an almost empty warehouse.

'We're having an auction today,' said the Signora. 'Everyone's up there.'

'And that's where I must be,' said the foreman. 'Pretty quick, too.'

He touched his breast and made a little bow to the Signora.

'Before you go,' said Owen, 'there's just one thing I'd like to ask you.'

'Effendi?'

'That night, the night of the conversation – or quarrel – in the warehouse: who was the last to leave when the warehouse was locked up?'

'I was.'

'You yourself did the locking up?'

'I did. I always do.'

'Was anyone with you?'

'They do not linger,' said the foreman caustically, 'when the hour comes for them to go.'

'Abdul is always the last to leave,' said the Signora, 'and sometimes he works late.'

'I understand. Was it possible, though, that on that occasion someone was working with him?'

'Would that that were so!' said the foreman.

'Why do you ask?' said the Signora.

'Because I wondered if by chance someone – one of the porters – had been in the building that night.'

152

'They don't work in the day,' said the foreman. 'Never mind the night.'

'Why do you ask?' said the Signora again.

'Because I was wondering who might have been in a position that night to overhear a conversation in the warehouse.'

'Not me,' said the foreman. 'I locked up and went home.'

'There was no such conversation,' said the Signora.

She led him through into the little inner courtyard. It was filled with trees: orange trees, lemon, grapefruit. The heavy, half-ripe fruit was bowing down the branches. There were no flowers. It was one of those Southern gardens designed to give shade, not colour.

There was a table beneath one of the trees. She indicated that he should sit down. Then she stood there for a moment.

'There was no conversation,' she repeated.

'Probably not,' Owen agreed.

She nodded her head as if satisfied and then went off into the house. He heard her calling for the house-boy.

And yet he was beginning to think now that there could have been a conversation after all; at least of some kind. Not, perhaps, as the foreman had reported it. He had thought then and he thought now that it was inherently improbable that the Signor himself had 'bespoken' the guns. But perhaps as Amina had reported it. There was a certain circumstantiality about the reports: a conversation, at night, in the warehouse, the Signor as one of the speakers. He thought it possible that a conversation of some kind had indeed taken place.

But the two accounts were very different. Amina's was far more particular. All right, as an accomplished news-teller, Amina had perhaps imparted an extra vividness – the direct, as if verbatim, report of the speech, for instance. But in what was still a predominantly oral culture people *did* remember speech verbatim and it was not at all unlikely that if someone had heard the words, then he would have been able to reproduce them fairly accurately.

And the purport of the words, as Amina had reported

them, was very different from that of the conversation as the foreman had reported it. It was only in the foreman's account that the Signor was alleged to have 'bespoken' the guns. Amina's account was quite different.

Owen thought it likely that the foreman's account was further from its source. It smacked to him of popular simplification and distortion, a Nahhasin embroidering. Amina's account, he thought, could be much nearer the truth.

Did that mean that Amina herself had heard it? She was always about the place and certainly might have done. Or was she merely reporting pretty exactly what she had heard from the fakir? He would like, he thought again, to have a word with this fakir.

The Signora returned with a tray on which were two glasses and a jug of lemonade.

Owen took a sip.

'Your lemons?'

'Last year's.'

'I now know why the Signor's friends praised them.'

He put the glass down.

'Signora, do you know what the Signor is supposed to have said in this conversation?'

'I know only that he is said to have bespoken the guns. And that is nonsense.'

'Yes, that is nonsense,' Owen agreed. 'However, that is not what the words, as they are reported, actually say.'

'There were no words.'

'Oh, but I think it possible that there were. But that their meaning was not quite as the popular report has it. Signora, did a conversation of any kind take place that night? Between your husband and another?'

'How should I know what conversations he had?'

'Well, I think you might remember this one: if it was held at night.'

'At night,' said the Signora; 'I am in my bed; and so was Morelli.'

A thought struck Owen.

'Could it have been earlier? The evening, perhaps? Yet when it had become dark?'

The Signora shrugged.

'Conversations?' she said. 'What conversations? He had many conversations.'

Owen persisted.

'Did someone come here that evening?'

The Signora gave another dismissive shrug.

'Perhaps it *was* early. Before the warehouse closed. You said that Abdul sometimes worked late.'

'What if the warehouse was still open? What if someone did come?'

'Then there could have been a conversation. In the warehouse, in the dark. And someone could have heard it.'

'There was nothing to hear.'

'An argument? A quarrel?'

'There was no argument. Or quarrel.'

'I think there might have been. For something left the Signor disturbed. So disturbed that the next day he did something unusual. He came to the porters and asked about the Mamur Zapt's Box.'

'Why would he do that?'

'I can only think,' said Owen, 'that he was considering sending a message to me.'

After a long while the Signora spoke.

'What were the guns to him?' she said, as much to herself as to Owen. 'A load to be carried, that's all. He would have done it without question if asked. But he wasn't asked, and so he was angry. But the guns – the guns themselves were nothing to him. He was a busy man and in this country a busy man turns a blind eye to a lot of things. Protection, for instance. What is protection money? It is insurance, that is all. What are guns? A load, that is all. But he wasn't asked, and so he was angry.

'Angry, but – well, what shall I say? – not too angry. Words, words – that was all it amounted to.

'But the next morning, when he woke up, there were the guns still. So it wasn't only words. What should he do with them?

'Where did he stand? That was what it came to. Guns are

not, after all, just a load, they are things that can be used. And used wrongly. Was that what he wished? He wished that he had told him to take the guns, take them away, forget about it, let everyone forget about it. But they were still there, the next morning.

'They could be used to do wrong. Was that what he wished? They could be used against the government, against the British. But what were the British to him? What was the government, for that matter? He lived his life, let them live theirs. He was of the Nahhasin, that was all he wanted to be. Let the British fight their own wars. What the guns might be used for, what they might do, was nothing to him.

'But there they were. In his warehouse. And the British were people, too, were they not? Even the British. And it might not be the British, it might be Egyptians on the wrong end of them, who knew? They might even be used against the Nahhasin. How could he let that be? He was of the Nahhasin. The British, the government, they were in the end nothing to him. But the Nahhasin was.

'He wished he had asked him what they were to be used for, who against. Perhaps made him promise. But could his promises be trusted? He had deceived once; might he not deceive again?

'And so he thought the best thing to do would be simply to get rid of them. But how? Leave them lying some-where? But then might they not fall into the hands of others who might do wrong? Take them to the police? But they would ask questions. To the Mamur Zapt? He would ask more.

'And then he remembered the Box. He would tell the Mamur Zapt anonymously and let the Mamur Zapt find the guns and say it was nothing to do with him. Better; he could take the guns from his warehouse and put them somewhere else and tell the Mamur Zapt and who would know who to put questions to? That is what he thought.

'And, who knows, that is what he might have done, had he not – not been killed.'

She came to an end and folded her arms.

'Signora,' said Owen gently after a moment. 'You have told us much, but you have not told me all.'

'All?'

'You have not told me the name of the man he argued with.'

'If Morelli would not have told you who the man was, why should I?'

'Because, Signora, you have a double reason to tell. The guns, perhaps, mean nothing to you. But surely Morelli does.'

'I do not understand.'

'Why shield the man who killed him?'

She stared at him.

'Killed him?'

'Perhaps in order to make sure that he stayed silent.'

'Oh, no. No.' She laughed. 'It was not like that. He would not have killed him. He would never have killed him,' she said confidently. 'It was an argument, no more. Words, just words.'

'Signora, please tell me his name.'

'How can I? Am not I of the Nahhasin, too?'


Mahmoud listened attentively.

'I do not understand, either,' he admitted. 'But it is clear that the Signor knew the man and that he came from the Nahhasin. In which case, I shall find him. Especially if, as you suggest, it all took place earlier in the evening. There will have been people about and someone will have seen him. Leave it to me. But why could she not give his name?'

'I think,' said Owen, 'because he was of the Nahhasin and she, too, thought of herself as of the Nahhasin; and that she thought it was a question of guns only, and what are guns to the Nahhasin?'

'Well, yes,' said Mahmoud, 'and, clearly, the Signor knew the man well. But why should she shield him? He could not have been family.'

'I think,' said Owen, 'that perhaps to the Morellis, the Nahhasin *was* family.'

\* \* \*

He had arranged to take Zeinab to the opera that evening. When he called for her, however, he sensed that something was amiss.

'What's the matter?' he said.

'Nothing.'

'Look, if you'd rather not go –'

'No, no. I would like to.'

He settled her into the arabeah and climbed in beside her. She turned her face away from him.

'Something *is* the matter. What is it?'

Zeinab shrugged.

'The Khedive is going to Constantinople.'

'Well?'

'My father has decided to go with him.'

'So?'

'He wants to take me.'

'I see. What do *you* want?'

'I think I might go.'

'Well, why not?' he said. 'You've never been there, and it might be interesting.'

'The thing is,' she said, facing him, 'I might not come back.'

He had half guessed it but now that she had said it, he couldn't quite take it in.

'I see. Why is that?'

She made a little gesture of helplessness.

'What about us?' he said.

'It's no good,' she said. 'It's not going to happen. Things are too difficult.'

'Nonsense!'

'I'm not blaming you,' she said. 'It's me as much as anything. I'm just not seeing it any more. The two of us. It's too difficult.'

'No, no, no, no. It's just that it's a bit difficult at the moment.'

'It's no good,' she said.

He was sitting in his office the next morning when Nikos stuck his head tentatively in at the door.

'There's a message from Lord Kitchener.'

'It can wait.'

Nikos swallowed.

'And one from the Khedive –'

'That can wait, too.'

'Yes. Right.'

Nikos still hesitated in the doorway.

'Oh, and something's come in from Georgiades . . .'

# 13

Assuan, over five hundred miles to the south, was like a furnace. When Owen stepped out of the train, he was hit by a blast of hot air. From the engine, he thought. It wasn't.

Georgiades, waiting in the shade, detached himself from the wall and slouched forward.

'Is it always like this?'

'So they say. In summer.'

Just standing there seemed to drain him.

'OK,' he said, 'so what is it?'

The Camp of the Bisharin was on the eastern side of the railway station, the desert side. Spread across the sand were dozens of low brown tents. Among the tents, everywhere, were camels: and among the camels were the Bisharin themselves, short, swarthy men with great mops of wiry hair. They crouched together in little groups among the camels, seemingly oblivious of the sun, or swaggered past with the truculent strut of the desert man, their short skirts hitched up to their knees, camel sticks and whips in their hands.

For they were camel men through and through, the drivers who brought the caravans in from the south, from Sennar and Kassala and Khartoum, and from the east, from the ports on the coast. Sometimes they went on further, to Kharga and the great oases of the west, even to Timbuktu and Tripoli. Mostly, however, the caravans ended at Assuan and the Bisharin would return to their home in the Red Sea Hills.

Some of them, though, stayed at Assuan and drove for the smaller, more specialized caravans going north; caravans such as that of the Morellis, for whom Mohammed Guri worked as leader.

'Guns?' said Mohammed Guri uneasily. 'I wouldn't have anything to do with them!'

Georgiades sighed. He had been through all this with him before.

'Normally,' he said.

'Normally,' Mohammed Guri accepted.

'But on this occasion –?'

'Well, I had to, didn't I? He being my sister-in-law's cousin's herdsman's son.'

'He?' murmured Owen.

Mohammed Guri ignored this.

'Besides,' he said, 'I owed him a favour. Well, I didn't exactly owe it myself, but my brother did, and that's about the same thing, isn't it?'

'So you had to do it?' prompted Georgiades patiently.

'Exactly!' agreed the leader, relieved, and seeming to conclude that the conversation stopped there.

Georgiades let him have a couple of minutes and then said:

'Of course, you didn't approach him, he approached you.'

'That's it! That's it exactly! I mean, I would never have approached him. Not about guns. I never have anything to do with them. I mean, they take up too much room. You've got to think of the load. Camels are all right, they'll carry a mountain, but guns are really heavy, you know –'

He stopped, sensing that, once again, he might have said too much.

'Yes, I know,' said Owen.

'That's why I never have anything to do with them,' said the caravan leader unhappily.

Georgiades let him stew for a moment or two and then said:

'What exactly was it that he asked you to do?'

'Well, nothing. I mean, that was the beauty of it. "All you've got to do is what you would ordinarily do," he said. And for that he was going to pay me extra! Well, I mean . . .'

161

'Come on, you must have had to do something!'

'No. Not a thing. Sometimes, you know, when you deliver something for somebody you have to go out of your way. But I didn't even have to do that. "No, no," he said, "it just goes to the Morellis' warehouse as usual."'

'What about putting the guns in the bales?'

'That would all be seen to, he said. "The less you know about it, the better," he said. "You just assume they're there, that's all." Well, I didn't argue, and after that I didn't ask any questions either, except about the money.'

'I can see, Mohammed,' said Georgiades, 'that in all this you were but the unknowing servant of evil men. That will reassure my friend, for he has heard bad words about you. But now he can see that you are a man of good standing; and, to prove it, all you have to do now is tell us the name of the man who approached you.'

The caravan leader swallowed.

'I'm not sure I know his name,' he said faintly.

'That is odd,' said Georgiades, 'for I have spoken with those who saw you talking to him and they remember it well.'

'Hilmi,' said the caravan leader.

The river bank was lined with feluccas loading and discharging, and on the shore there were huge piles of sugar cane and also, for some odd reason, bright-orange pottery. But where was the great Camp of the Traders of which he had heard so much?

Georgiades pointed, and there, almost lost among the hills of grain beside the Grain Bazaar, he saw camels coming down to the river to drink, and an area, much smaller than he had imagined, where goods of a rather different kind, skins and carpets and ostrich feathers and spices, were lying scattered around in little heaps, and a caravan was being loaded.

'It's much smaller than it used to be,' said Georgiades. 'The drivers used to stay here but they don't any more. They don't like it. They say the town is taking over. They prefer to stay up at the camp at the top, where, they say, they can smell the air. They come down only to load up.'

So the bales, thought Owen, would have been left standing

in the open, possibly for several nights, and it would have been easy to put the guns in.

'There are watchmen, of course,' said Georgiades. 'But then, there are ways with watchmen.'

And a man who knew the ways with watchmen, and, indeed, the ways of the whole dockside, and of the traders and of the traders' camp, was Hilmi; a man who, it was said around the docks, could arrange anything.

But where was Hilmi this morning? Sick, said the man in the little coffee house where Georgiades had arranged to meet him. Gone to visit his mother, said someone else. It was his mother that was sick, volunteered a third.

Georgiades was unperturbed by all this and led Owen along the dock front to a space where they could sit down and study the feluccas as they came into the shore and savour the rich aromas of spices and coffee.

After they had been sitting there for some time, Owen became aware they had been joined.

'He is in the House of Fatima,' said the small boy.

Georgiades nodded.

'Can you take us there?'

The boy led them away from the front and into the maze of side streets that came down to the river. He stopped at a corner.

'It is the third house,' he said. 'I will not come with you, lest he find out and beat me.'

'You have done well,' said Georgiades, and gave him the money he had promised him for watching.

Fatima was a lady of astonishing fatness, much blued with henna.

Georgiades took no notice of her protestations and pushed past her.

There were only two rooms in the house so it was not difficult to find Hilmi. He was lying naked on a rope bed. The heat in the windowless room, and the smell, was so overpowering that Owen almost retched. He stood prudently at the door until Hilmi was ready to come with them.

'Have you recovered?' asked Georgiades solicitously.

'Recovered?' said Fatima suspiciously.

'You are his mother, are you not?' said Georgiades.

Fatima turned on Hilmi wrathfully.

They walked along the river front almost to the Camp of the Traders and sat down among the hills of grain. They did not give much shade but Owen did not mind. Anything was better than the House of Fatima.

'You see, Hilmi,' said Georgiades, 'that we had no trouble in finding you. That is the way it is with my friend. He has eyes that see at a distance. They have been watching you even from the Great City. So do not mess us around.'

Hilmi nodded, much cast down.

'Tell my friend what you told me,' Georgiades commanded.

'One came to me,' began Hilmi obediently, speaking in the sing-song manner in which he might have given evidence in court, 'and said that he wanted guns to go to the Great City. They were to go by such-and-such a caravan, and only that caravan. And I was to arrange it with the leader and also see to it that the guns were put in the bales.'

'Which was done how?'

'It was easy,' said Hilmi. 'The guns were lying nearby. They had been brought in that day by separate camel. All I had to do was see that they were put in the bales. And see that the watchmen went for tea.'

He stopped.

'Well?' said Georgiades.

'That's about it,' said Hilmi.

'Not quite. How did the guns come to be there?'

'I had asked for them,' said Hilmi reluctantly.

'Who did you ask?'

'There are caravans,' said Hilmi, 'which take guns westwards. They do not come into the Camp of the Traders but make a stop out in the desert. They send men in for what they need. While they were in the Camp of the Bisharin I spoke to them. I said I had a friend who would pay them more for their guns than they would get at the end of their journey, and so they agreed to sell some.'

He stopped.

'That is all.'

'No, it is not all. You did not do this unbidden. Their names, Hilmi; my friend wants their names.'

'I do not know his name –'

Owen stirred.

'I do not, Effendi. Truly. All I know is that he is a soldier at the barracks.'

He had shown Georgiades the soldier and in the evening, when the military day was done, they went down to the barracks and met him as he came out of the gates.

'You see, Rashid,' said Georgiades, 'I do as I promised. Remember that, for that is how it will be. Do as I say and you will be rewarded. But if you do not, then things will go hard. And do not seek to flee, for my friend's breath is hot upon your neck. It burns already. But I can come between you and his wrath, as I have promised to do if you deal with me justly. Tell us now how it comes about that you order guns.'

'Effendi,' said the soldier, raising his eyes to Owen almost beseechingly, 'I do not order for myself but for others.'

'Others here?'

'No, Effendi, they are in Cairo. And I do not know their names – truly, Effendi! – for they are friends of friends and –' He hesitated. 'Effendi, it is as a brotherhood. Only it is a large brotherhood, Effendi, in which not every man knows his brother's name. Only this, that –' his voice faltered but then became determined – 'we wish for a better Egypt.'

He kept his eyes fixed on Owen's face.

'Does not every man wish for a better Egypt?'

'The Egypt we wish for, Effendi, is one not ruled by Pashas. Nor by the British.'

'I see. This brotherhood of yours: are you all soldiers?'

'Yes, Effendi.'

'And it is the brotherhood which asked you to obtain the guns?'

The man hesitated.

'Not quite, Effendi.'

'No?'

'Not this time. It was – it was one of the brotherhood.'

'I don't see the difference.'

'He asked for himself, Effendi, not for the brotherhood.'

'I see. So it was just a case of using the brotherhood connection?'

'That is so, Effendi.'

'Various things puzzle me, Rashid. The first is, why does he have to obtain guns in this way? If he is a soldier, surely there are easier ways?'

'It is possible, Effendi, but it is not easy. The armouries are kept locked and guarded. It is easier to obtain guns through trade.'

'I understand. The second thing that puzzles me is this: why, if, as I take it, he is a soldier in the garrison here, why should he want guns sent to Cairo?'

'He is not in the garrison here. He was passing through.'

'On his way to Cairo?'

'Yes, Effendi.'

'When was this?'

'A month ago. Perhaps six weeks.'

'I see. And he knew that guns could be obtained here, but he also knew that he could not carry them with him.'

'That is so, Effendi.'

'Rashid, what you have told me is gold. And perhaps there could be gold in return if you could but tell me one thing.'

'That is?'

'The name of the man.'

The soldier shook his head.

'Not for gold nor for anything will I do that, Effendi. For he is one of the brotherhood, as I. I have told you much, perhaps too much, but this I will not tell you.'

'It doesn't matter,' Owen said to Georgiades as they walked away, 'for now that we know this much, we shall be able to find him. And we know, too, now, what organization it was that Shukri was talking about. Like a society but not a society. Like a club but not a club. Call it a brotherhood. And big and powerful. As big and powerful as the army. That,' said Owen, 'I don't like. In fact, it's worrying.'

'It's not the army that's behind this,' said Georgiades, 'it's just a one-man effort. Shukri said that as well.'

'Let's hope it stays like that,' said Owen.

But he knew that there was little he could do about it. Whether it stayed like that or not depended upon other things; not least upon Kitchener.

There was one other thing he had learned, and this was important; that there were caravans carrying guns from east to west. This surprised him, for he would have thought that the route was too difficult. It would need good camel men. However, it seemed that the traffic along the coast might have been displaced southwards. He told Georgiades to stay for a while and look into it. Meanwhile, he himself caught the train back to Cairo.

The railway from Assuan to Luxor was the older military line and narrow gauge, but at Luxor he transferred into the more comfortable coaches of the ordinary State Railway. From then on he had only to sit and sit and sit and sit.

The line ran along the western bank of the Nile and he was hardly ever out of sight of the river for long. He could follow the graceful lateen sails of the feluccas, the occasional steamer, the more frequent dahabeahs, and this gave some interest to what was often a monotonous journey through featureless desert landscape.

As they drew nearer to Cairo they began to run more and more through cultivated fields, with fellahin stooping among the plants, women going down to the river with pots on their heads, and the continuous creak of the water wheels along the river banks. Water buffalo browsed on the sandbanks in the shallows and, in almost every village, dilapidated pigeon towers nosed up among the palm trees.

This was immemorial Egypt; and suddenly he could see why Kitchener so favoured the fellah. It wasn't just that he had a soft spot for the fellahin, although he clearly did, but rather this very fact of immemoriality. What drew Kitchener was the stability of it all.

But that, he realized abruptly, was where he himself

differed from Kitchener. It was not what drew him. What he missed, what he needed, was movement, the physical movement of Cairo, with its carts and crowds and cafés, all the noise and bustle of the big city, and not just the physical movement but the intellectual movement, the talk in the coffee houses, the passion of the newspapers. That was why in the end he could not go along with Kitchener.

And why, in the end, he would never be able to go along with Trudi's sort of movement, either, those vast, austere rides. In the desert there was nothing.

But Trudi was right in one thing and Kitchener was wrong: there was movement, movement of a different kind, in Egypt, and those who sought to govern her had to move too.

However, it was not Kitchener who occupied his thoughts for most of the journey but Zeinab. In a way, that was Kitchener too for it was he who was driving Nuri to Constantinople, and with him Zeinab. But was it just that, or were things anyway, as she had said, too difficult? Was it in the end impossible for someone like him, a servant in the British Administration, to have a relationship with someone like Zeinab, an Egyptian?

But it wasn't that really. They could have a relationship and no one would mind. It was the next step: marriage. Could someone like him marry someone like her?

But he knew that, deep down, it wasn't even that either. They were both, he and Zeinab, sheltering behind the difficulties. Neither of them was quite sure, quite sure enough, that it was what they wanted. And so they had been content to leave the issue dangling. That, he realized, had been the basis of their relationship: a tacit agreement to leave the issue dangling.

But now Zeinab was beginning to feel that she could not go on like this. He sensed that she was wanting some kind of resolution. Things were closing in on her, time was closing in. She was no longer satisfied to leave things dangling.

And he?

He found Paul, as he had expected, in the bar at the Sporting Club and pulled him aside.

'Paul, how would Kitchener feel if I got married?'

Paul looked doubtful.

'He doesn't like people close to him getting married.'

'I'm not close to him.'

'No.'

Paul examined his glass.

'Zeinab?' he said.

'Yes.'

'Wouldn't that create difficulties?'

'Not any more than at present, surely?'

'I don't know about that. People wouldn't know whose side you were on. At the moment they do: our side, the British. But if you were married to an Egyptian, they might not be sure. And with a job like Mamur Zapt, it's best that they are sure.'

'Paul, I really don't think −'

'And then you've got to consider it from our side. British interests are not quite the same as Egyptian interests and each one of us out here has to balance the two. If you were married to an Egyptian, people might have doubts about your ability to maintain that kind of balance.'

'Too close to the Egyptians?'

'That's right.'

'Why don't they have doubts about that now? Or perhaps they do,' said Owen bitterly.

'I don't think they feel bothered if the woman's just a girlfriend,' said Paul. 'Illogical and unreasonable of them, I know, and reflecting a strangely exalted view of the influence of Administration wives.' He hesitated. 'You don't think you could just leave things as they are?'

'Zeinab's not happy.'

'That's what all this is about, is it?'

'Yes.'

'Well, I can understand that.'

Owen was silent for a moment. Then he said:

'There's nothing in the regulations that actually stops me, is there?'

'From getting married?'

'From getting married to an Egyptian.'

'I think that's beside the point. The point is that a job like Mamur Zapt is sustainable only if you have the confidence of the key players.'

'On both sides, Paul, on both sides. And just at the moment that's a bit difficult.'

'Or on the side that's got the power.'

'And you think I wouldn't have Kitchener's confidence if I went ahead and married?'

'I think that would just about put the lid on it,' said Paul.


'Currant salesman. Aleppo. Fluent Arabic required.'

'Inspector of Police, Burma.'

'Customs Officer, Abu Dhabi. Good arithmetic.'

'Commander of the Royal Guard, Zanzibar.'

Hum. Owen put the newspaper down. Not exactly promising. The Royal Guard, perhaps? It was an Arab country, after all. But would Zeinab agree to go there? Almost before he had finished framing the question, he could hear the answer. Paris, possibly, Zanzibar, never.

Nikos stuck his head in at the door.

'There was that message from Lord Kitchener –' he began cautiously.

'It can wait.'

'Yes. Well. And then the Khedive –'

Owen jumped up.

'He can wait, too.' He searched for his tarboosh. 'I've got more important things to do.'

'More important –?'

Nikos looked after him bewilderedly as he hurried off along the corridor.

At the other end of the corridor, an agitated knot of orderlies.

'Effendi, Effendi! There's a snake in the lavatory!'

'Another time,' said Owen, pushing his way through.

As he passed through the orderly room, the clerk at the desk looked up.

'Effendi, a message from the Minister of Finance –'

'Sod him!'

'Sod –?'

Owen strode on, leaving behind him an impressed Bab-el-Khalk.

The consensus among the orderlies was that this must be serious. Another war, perhaps? Or maybe the same war, only a new development? Yes, that was probably it. And soon the nature of the development was taking on a precise form. The British were coming in! And then, even more precisely, and, unfortunately, even less probably: the British were coming in on our side!

Bearers entering with messages picked up the news and spread it excitedly through the city. The British were coming in on the Egyptian side. The Mamur Zapt had said so.

# 14

It was almost as if Zeinab had been expecting him. When he went in, there she lay, posed on a pile of great leather cushions, eyes looking tragically up at him, as if she was playing a part in one of the operas she loved so passionately, whose stories Owen always found bizarre but which Zeinab took completely seriously, finding in them a perfect vehicle to express her own heights and depths of feeling.

'It's no good,' she said now, sombrely.

She was surrounded by books; in fact, too many books for her to have been reading them, unless she had been dipping into them, as she sometimes did, to reread favourite passages. They were all in French. On the floor, not far away, big head-lines proclaiming the iniquity of the British, was a newspaper, Egyptian but also in French; and, scattered around the room, almost too casually, were other things French: the latest journals from Paris, some French catalogues, pieces of French music. It was as if today it was important to her to assert her distance from anything English.

He had a suspicion that it was also intended to assert her Egyptianness. If so, something had gone wrong, for she was doing so in a language that was not Egyptian and using symbols – if that's what the books were – to make the statements that were not those of her own culture but those of another. Perhaps, though, this *was* Egyptian: doubly dispossessed as a country both of culture – at least so far as its governing class was concerned – and power.

But going to Turkey would not help. She would feel just as dispossessed there. She did not speak Turkish. French might be a foreign language, but it was the language she had been brought up to, the one in which she felt most at home. The Turks, too, were not Arabs. The Cairenes always regarded them as puddings, a bit too solid and stolid; reliable and efficient, no doubt, but, oh, so boring! And she would find the social and religious structures there as oppressive as those she objected to in Egypt, with, perhaps, less opportunity of slipping out from underneath them.

'You're right,' said Owen. 'It's no good.'

She looked surprised.

'No good,' he explained, 'going to Constantinople.'

'At least the British aren't there!' she said bitterly.

'There are a lot of other things that aren't there, either,' said Owen, 'and they're all things that matter to you.'

'I don't know that anything matters to me much,' said Zeinab listlessly, 'just at the moment.'

He was used to her troughs, but this was a deep one.

'Come on,' he said gently, 'come on! This isn't like you.'

'I don't know what is like me any more,' she said despairingly, 'and that's part of the trouble. I don't know who I am any longer or who I want to be. I thought I did, but that's all gone now, closed off. There's nothing left for me here. So,' she shrugged, 'I might as well go to Constantinople.'

'There *is* something left for you here. I'm here.'

She regarded him expressionlessly.

'You're what's closed off,' she said.

'No, no, no –'

'Yes, yes, yes. Can't you see it? They let us play, but the moment it looked like getting serious, they stepped in to end it.'

'No one has stepped in to end it.'

'They've opened up a gap, which has become a great divide. I always knew it was there but I thought I would bridge it. I thought you could bridge it. But we couldn't, could we? I'm not blaming you, I'm just blaming . . . things. Actually,' said Zeinab, with a flash of her old form, 'I blame the British.'

'Let's leave the British out of it. In the end it comes down to you and me, and we're individuals and can do what we like.'

'Oh, no, we can't.'

'We can. And must.'

'We can't. You're British and have got to do what the British tell you. And I'm Egyptian, and –'

'And no one is telling you what to do. Come on, now.'

'Oh, but they are! Can't you see it? I can't have a job of my own, I can't go out on my own in public, I can't live on my own – or, at least, I can, but only because my father is rich enough and powerful enough to bend the rules, I can't even choose the clothes I wear. That's what Egypt is telling me. All the time. And all the time it's telling me there's only one thing you can do if you're a woman, and that is to marry. And even that, now, is cut off from me. Can't you see? I'm trapped!'

'If you're trapped,' said Owen, 'then so am I.'

She shook her head.

'Oh, no,' she said, 'not like I am. You've got a job. You've got a life.'

'Actually,' said Owen, 'the thing I came to tell you is that I am giving up my job.'

She stared at him.

'Really?'

'Really.'

'For me?'

'For you. And me.'

She sat silent for some time, fingering the stitching on one of the cushions.

Then she said suddenly:

'I can't let you do it.'

'The decision's made. I've been thinking about it for quite a while. Up till recently, though, I've always had a vague hope that when it actually came to it, perhaps they'd go along with it. Now I know they won't. Not while Kitchener's here, at any rate. So I've made up my mind.'

'No,' she said.

He leaned across and kissed her.

'Yes,' he said.

'Yes,' said Zeinab, after a moment, dreamily. This was how she had always imagined it. He would come along (ride up?) and lay himself, his wealth, his lands at her feet. And she would –

But hold on a minute. Himself was one thing but wealth and lands, unfortunately, another; and although Zeinab in one vein was passionately romantic, in another she was severely realistic. She pushed him off.

'What would we live on?' she said.

'I'd get a job.'

'What sort of job?'

'Oh, I don't know. There are lots of them in the newspapers.'

'You've said you'd get a job before.'

'Yes, well now I really mean it.'

'You've said that before, too.'

'This time I've actually been looking.'

'And what have you found?'

'Well, Chief of Police, that sort of thing. Commander of the Royal Guard.'

'Commander of the Royal Guard?' said Zeinab incredulously. 'Where?'

'Zanzibar –'

'Zanzibar!'

Zeinab fell about laughing.

At least, he reflected afterwards, it had had the effect of snapping her out of her gloom.

In front of the Post Office, as he went past, was the usual row of letter-writers sitting on their mats. There, too, capitalizing on the illiteracy of the population and on the handiness of the Post Office, were seal-makers – a seal took the place of a signature for those who could not write – and stationers offering cheap paper and envelopes. There, even, hanging on the Post Office wall, were wet rollers for those who had an aversion to licking stamps.

There were individual letter-writers in the bazaars but it was only here that there was a concentration of all the services. You came along, bought your paper and envelope and picked your writer; and afterwards you bought the stamp from the Post Office counter and put the letter in the letter box.

That was, of course, if you wanted to send your letter by

stamped mail. If, for some reason, you didn't; if, for example, you intended to deliver it by hand, but needed someone to write it for you, then you could get it written here and simply take it away with you.

It was a long shot but worth trying. He had one of the anonymous letters in his pocket. He took it out and looked at the handwriting and then began to walk slowly along the line of letter-writers.

Nikos had obtained from the army a list of all the Egyptian soldiers who had passed through Assuan in the last three months, whether on leave or as part of a detachment. There weren't many of them.

He concentrated on the officers. These were still the days when any insurrection was likely to be led by officers. The time of the sergeants was yet to come. This was hardly an insurrection. Nevertheless, as Trudi had pointed out with respect to Turkey, it was among the future leaders of the army that the most lively minds were likely to be found; the men most likely to take action.

He thought that perhaps he ought to have a word with Mahmoud. He glanced at his watch. It was still early in the evening. Mahmoud might well be still at work. He didn't want to call upon him at his office. This was one of those subjects best broached on neutral ground. He had an early meal at one of the restaurants and then walked down to the Nahhasin, confident that these days he would be likely to find Mahmoud at home.

At this hour the Mouski was full of people, out thankfully taking the benign evening air after the extreme heat of the day, or shopping at the stalls which lined the street and which, together with the press of people, made passage difficult for the arabeahs taking tourists to the bazaars. They were obliged to move at a slow walk and had to stop occasionally for camels carrying forage or firewood, their great loads almost spanning the street, or for porters carrying almost equally gigantic loads across their shoulders.

Owen didn't mind the crowd; indeed, he rather liked it.

He liked to see the ordinary women, with their dark veils and nose-pipes, emerging for once into the daylight, and to pick out the Arish women with no veil at all but often little plaits of silver coins dangling from a headband. He liked to see the men in their long galabeahs and their little beaded skull caps, often with a small boy perched round their necks, and also the smart young men about town, with their dark suits and tarbooshes and walking canes.

In a crowd like this, wearing a tarboosh himself, he could usually pass for a Cairene. Nevertheless, when he reached the turn-off to the Nahhasin, where there were fewer people, he saw that someone had spat on his trousers.

There were coffee houses on both sides of the Nahhasin and they were full of men, smoking bubble-pipes, playing dominoes or talking earnestly. The coffee houses seemed to segregate naturally, dividing between those favoured by the older men and those preferred by the young. At a table in one of the latter he saw Mahmoud and made towards him.

When he got near, however, he saw that an argument was in progress. He hesitated, fearing that to arrive at such a moment might be awkward.

The arguing seemed to be directed at Mahmoud.

'But, Mahmoud,' someone was saying, 'how can you do nothing? At a time like this?'

'I express my feelings through the Party,' said Mahmoud.

'But that's not enough! No one will listen.'

'They won't listen,' said someone else, 'until we can show that public support for the government has been withdrawn to such an extent as to leave the country ungovernable.'

'And we can only do that,' said the first speaker, 'if people like you do as Habashi has done.'

'I won't claim to have done any more than set an example,' said someone – Habashi, presumably – modestly.

'But that is enough if others follow.'

They all looked pointedly at Mahmoud. Mahmoud said nothing.

'I really don't understand you, Mahmoud. You, who claim to be in the vanguard of the struggle –'

'I certainly don't!'

'You were one of the first to join the Party, anyway. And we look to you for a lead.'

'You always spoke of the need for action,' said someone bitterly, 'and now that the time for action has arrived, you do nothing!'

'I respect Habashi's decision,' said Mahmoud quietly, 'but I do not think that anything would be gained by following his example.'

'Well, of course, it takes courage to resign –'

'That is true,' said Mahmoud, 'and I respect it. But there is also the question of what purpose is served by resigning. And I do not think that the resignation of an orderly in the post room of the Ministry of Religious Bequests is likely to have a great effect on Lord Kitchener's thinking.'

'But that is where you come in, Mahmoud! I agree with you about Habashi, but surely if a member of the Parquet were to resign –'

'I think you overestimate my significance,' said Mahmoud, 'and probably also that of the Parquet.'

'But –'

Owen could see that a lot of the people seated at the other tables in the coffee house were listening in to the conversation. Not only them. Just beyond the rim of the wick of light cast by the vapour lamps of the coffee house, children were sitting attentively. Among them he fancied he saw Amina.

He backed away. This was not the moment for his conversation with Mahmoud. Mahmoud had enough on his plate.

It had brought home to him, though, how much pressure Kitchener's action had put on ordinary Egyptians working in the government service, forcing them to question exactly where their allegiance lay. For ones like Mahmoud, both scrupulous and committed to the cause of independence, it would be hardest of all.

The other thing he thought, as he walked away, was that this was how the Nahhasin exerted its influence: pressure in the coffee houses, pressure in the streets, the pressure of neighbours, friends, family. No one could escape it. It was all around you, all the time.

*     *     *

178

The next morning, when Owen got in, he found a message waiting for him from Georgiades. It had come in the previous evening.

Owen caught the next train to Assuan.

As before, Georgiades was waiting on the platform, as before, the heat was appalling. He had found the heat in the carriage almost unbearable. Outside, it hit you like a blow.

Georgiades looked at him.

'You don't mind,' he said, 'a bit of a walk?'

Georgiades's shirt was dark with perspiration. The sweat ran down his face, his neck, along his forearms. He had a floppy cotton hat on and even that was soaking wet.

They went down to the barracks, to the gate where, when he had been here before, they had met the soldier.

'He won't be free,' said Owen.

'He will,' said Georgiades. 'I've had a word inside.'

And, sure enough, he was soon coming towards them. He showed his pass to the sentries and padded across the sand to where they were waiting. Georgiades led them round behind a wall where they could stand in the shade.

'OK,' he said to the soldier, 'tell him what you told me.'

The soldier hesitated.

'Why do I speak?' he said.

'Because you know that these things will be found out,' said Georgiades, 'and because you know that there is no chance for you unless you do.'

'I have had a message,' he said. 'The same message.'

'I don't understand,' said Owen.

'To send guns,' said Georgiades, 'as before.'

'As before?'

'Exactly as before,' said the soldier. 'To the same place and by the same means.'

'Were you told more?'

'That is enough,' said the soldier, 'and more than enough.'

'How will payment be made?'

'By the same man as brought the message.'

'He is a driver,' said Georgiades, 'with one of the caravans.'

'Can you find him?'

'He has returned to Cairo.'

'We will find him there.'

'You hear?' Georgiades said to the soldier. 'Even in the big city he will not escape.'

The soldier nodded, subdued.

'What do you want me to do, Effendi?' he asked, after a moment.

Owen stood thinking. Then he touched the man on the shoulder.

'Here is what you will do,' he said. 'You will do exactly as you would have done had you not spoken to me. You will ask for the guns as before.'

'As before?'

'As before.'

'But –'

'You will not, of course, say that you have spoken with me. You will not say that to anyone. Just ask as you did before. Do this and you may escape my wrath. For you are but a small creature, and why should the small be beaten when it is the big who are to blame?'


Hilmi was again in the House of Fatima. This time Owen sent Georgiades in to fetch him out. Hilmi came resignedly, fearing the worst. They walked along the dock front together.

'I shall not come again,' said Owen, 'for it is bad for your business if you are seen walking with me too often.'

'Yes, Effendi,' said Hilmi mechanically. And then: 'Yes, Effendi!' brightening, as he took in what Owen had said.

'That is, if you do as I ask.'

'What do you wish me to do, Effendi?' said Hilmi cautiously.

'I wish you to do nothing that you would not have done had you not spoken with me,' said Owen.

'What?' said Hilmi.

'A man will come to you, as before. He will ask you to buy guns for him. And, as before, I wish you to buy them.'

'You do?' said Hilmi, astonished.

'And, as before, you are to speak with Mohammed Guri,

180

and to the same purpose. And then you will put the guns in the bales.'

'If that is what you want, Effendi.'

'It is what I want. Now, tell me, Hilmi, how long will it be before you can get hold of some guns?'

'Effendi, a caravan is passing even at this moment.'

'Will you be able to get in touch with them?'

'Oh, yes, Effendi,' said Hilmi confidently.

'Then do so.'


In front of the caravan leader's tent a woman was kneading dough. She had built a small fire in a hole in the ground. As Owen and Georgiades approached, she took a metal plate out of the fire and rested it on a stone. Then she smacked dough on it to form a kind of pancake. She left it for a moment and then took it off. Then she plastered the plate again.

Mohammed Guri came out from under the awning.

'You come once more,' he said.

'That is so. But not again, if you do as I ask.'

'That is an encouragement.'

'When is the next caravan to the House of the Morellis?'

'It leaves in three days' time.'

'Good. Now, a man will come to you and he will ask you to take something there for him. It will be guns, as before.'

'I never have anything to do with –'

'You will this time.'

'I will?'

'You will.'

The caravan leader shrugged.

'Very well, I will.' He reflected a moment. 'Will I get paid extra?'

'Very probably.'

'Then I definitely will. Even though it will be difficult, for the camels are already fully laden.'

There was something about him, though, that made Owen doubtful. He thought he had better make sure.

'The bread smells good,' he said.

Mohammed Guri beat himself on the breast.

'And I have not offered you some!'

The woman brought them a pancake and they broke it, sitting beneath the awning, and ate it together.

Owen was more confident now that the caravan leader could be relied on.

Some riders were coming into the camp. They were riding particularly fine camels and the Bisharin stood up to inspect them. He thought he recognized one of the figures even though the face was muffled up inside the tails of a turban.

'Hello!' he said.

The figure unwrapped the tails.

'Why, hello,' said Trudi, looking down at him. 'What are you doing here?'

'I thought you were heading for the Old Salt Road?'

'I am. I've just dropped in here to pick up a few extra things.'

She slipped off the camel without bothering to make it kneel. One of the riders with her leaned across and attached a leading rope and the camels swayed off through the tents in the direction of the river.

'If I had known you were here,' said Trudi, 'we could have arranged something.'

'That would have been nice.'

'I can't stay, though. I have to get back.'

'To your caravan?'

'Yes.'

'Far?'

'Not on camels like these.'

'Where are you?'

'Out west.'

'How far west?'

'Well, I don't know. There aren't exactly signposts.'

'Near the border?'

'Border? I don't know that there are borders, either. Not out there. That's one of the nice things about it.'

'There are always borders.'

'That's not what the Arabs think. There are territories, yes, but no borders. I prefer that way of thinking.'

'Borders make less sense in Africa, I admit.'

'They're completely ridiculous. Just something imposed by other countries, European countries, to stake their claim. Do you know what I'd like to do?' said Trudi. 'I'd like to ride west, and carry on riding west, first to Tibesti, and then on to Timbuktu, and then, oh, I don't know, on, right on, perhaps to the Atlantic. And all the time without ever thinking about borders.'

'They make no sense, I agree. And yet people fight about them.'

'That makes even less sense.'

'But the trouble is that they do. And when they're doing it, it is sometimes best not to make more trouble by not observing them.'

'There are times, you know, when you sound just like a policeman.'

'There are other times, too, I hope.'

'Well, yes,' said Trudi, considering, 'I'll grant you that.'

Some Bisharin at a nearby fire offered them more coffee. It was harsh and bitter but somehow refreshing and they stood for a few moments sipping it thankfully.

'How long are you here for?' asked Owen.

'About a couple of hours. Three would be better, from the point of view of the camel.' She squinted at the sun. 'Perhaps three,' she decided.

She looked at Owen.

'I can give you an hour,' she said.

'Meal?'

'I don't eat when I'm riding.'

'The river?'

The river was a blaze of light, too bright to look at, too exposed to the heat to stand beside it for long.

There were several camels splashing in the water. Three of them were Trudi's. She stood for a while watching them critically.

'Don't let them drink any more,' she said to the men, 'or they'll be useless on the way back.'

The men nodded and led the camels out on to the bank.

'Take your two and leave mine.'

She made her camel kneel.

'We could go out into the desert,' she said. 'That's what the herdswomen do.'

'Jesus!' said Owen. 'It'd be like a cauldron!'

It was.

As soon as Trudi had gone, Owen went back to the barracks with Georgiades. The soldiers were under the command of a British Bimbashi. His name was Lofthouse and he was an experienced man who had served in the Sudan. Among the soldiers was a unit from the Camel Corps.

'They're good,' said Lofthouse enthusiastically.

'Who would they be under?'

'Fuad. He's their lieutenant.'

Fuad was sharp and professional.

'Twenty minutes,' he said. 'That's all we need. And then we'll be ready.'

'There's a caravan out there,' said Owen. 'It's not going to come in to Assuan. It's running guns to Tripolitania. I want it intercepted.'

'That will be no problem,' said Fuad, with a flash of white teeth.

'But, look,' said Owen, 'the timing is important. I don't want them taken, or even alarmed, until a certain transaction has taken place. Georgiades, there, will tell you when it has. But then you'll need to move very fast because they won't hang around.'

'Don't worry,' said Fuad, smiling. 'We move very fast too.'

'Have you got trackers?'

'We can get them.'

'Good.'

Owen hesitated, and stood hesitating for quite a while, so long, indeed, that Fuad began to look puzzled.

'It may help them to find the caravan,' he said at last, 'if you tell them that just over two hours ago three camels left the Camp of the Bisharin heading very probably for the caravan. I'm not sure, but I suspect so. The camels are racing camels.'

'If they're racing camels, we won't catch up with them.'

'Unless you meet them at the caravan,' said Owen.

# 15

Back in Cairo, as Nikos reminded him the next morning, there was still that message from Kitchener. It asked him to call in on the Consul-General at his earliest convenience. Nikos rang to see if the Consul-General happened to have space that morning. Unfortunately, he had. The Appointments Secretary added that there was a degree of urgency about the summons.

When Owen went in he found Kitchener standing impatiently by the window looking out on the residency roses. He probably tended them with his own hands, too, thought Owen.

'At last!'

He wheeled and sat down at his desk. The fish-like eyes regarded Owen coldly.

'I don't like to hear accusations that my officers are insufficiently diligent,' he said. 'Where have you been?'

'Assuan.'

'On work?'

'Yes.'

'Oh!' Kitchener seemed momentarily disconcerted. 'Thought you were exclusively a Cairo man,' he said.

'If you remember, I was given an extra responsibility for regulating arms traffic.'

'That's what I wanted to see you about,' said Kitchener, unbending. 'Ferducci is complaining that the arrangement isn't working, that nothing's being done. That *you're* not doing anything!'

Ferducci was the Italian Consul.

Owen shrugged.

'Assuan?' said Kitchener. 'What were you doing at Assuan? I thought the traffic was along the coast.'

'That's what we all thought,' said Owen.

'And it's not the case?'

'They're running them across the south.'

This did make him pause.

'Well, I'm damned! You're sure about this?'

'Yes.'

'Well,' said Kitchener, after a moment, 'that puts a different complexion on things. Yes,' he said, almost rubbing his hands, 'quite a different complexion.' He looked at his watch. 'I have a meeting very shortly which I was not looking forward to. Now' – he smiled, not altogether pleasantly – 'I am.'

He picked up the small bell on his desk and rang it.

'It's with Ferducci and Ismet Bey,' he said. 'You'd better come too.'

An orderly hurried in.

'Coffee,' instructed Kitchener. 'For two.'

He smiled, almost savagely, and this time he really did rub his hands.

He waved a hand in Owen's direction and Owen sat down. He hadn't realized how much he had been sweating. He almost stuck to the leather.

'How did you find out?' asked Kitchener curiously.

'Oh, intelligence, sir.'

'You're not saying?'

'I'm in the middle of an operation, sir.'

'Well, that's probably right. Yes, it's probably right.'

He gave Owen a smile which was almost friendly.


'Absolutely nothing!' said the Italian Consul indignantly. 'I hate to say this, Lord Kitchener, of one of your men, but –'

'Not my man,' said Kitchener. 'He works for the Khedive.'

'Sometimes,' murmured the Khedive's representative.

'The arms are still getting through! And I'm afraid I am forced to ask, Lord Kitchener, whether this is just incompetence or whether it is something more sinister, a reflection of a position that His Majesty's government is taking up!'

'Incompetence,' said Ismet Bey genially.

'Constructive incompetence,' suggested the Khedive's representative, smiling.

'In either case,' said the Italian Consul hotly, 'I demand a change in the arrangements. And in the personnel!'

'That seems a bit hard,' said Kitchener, 'when Captain Owen has just made such an important discovery.'

'Discovery?'

Kitchener turned to Owen.

'You tell them,' he said.

'We have discovered that the route the arms are following is not, as we had previously thought, along the Mediterranean coast but further south, south of Assuan, in fact, across the desert.'

'Across the desert?' said the Khedive's representative incredulously.

'Ridiculous!' said Ismet Bey, geniality fading.

'What!' cried the Italian Consul, almost starting out of his chair. 'But this is outrageous!'

'It is quite impossible,' said Ismet Bey. 'How are the arms being transported, for a start? No roads, the heat –'

'By caravan from the Red Sea coast,' said Owen.

Ismet Bey sat back.

'I do not believe there have been any such caravans,' he said flatly. 'If there had been, they would have called in at Assuan and word would certainly have –'

'They are not calling in at Assuan,' said Owen.

'But that makes it an incredible journey!' said the Khedive's representative. 'From the coast to Assuan, I could understand. But to go straight across to Tripolitania without calling in anywhere –! It would require some remarkable riders.'

'They are some remarkable riders.'

The Khedive's representative still looked doubtful.

'Have you any evidence?' he said sceptically.

'Oh, yes,' said Owen, and hoped that by now he had.


The Ministry of Waqfs, that is to say, Religious Bequests, was not like the other Cairo Ministries. For a start, its Minister had no British Adviser sitting alongside him. This was because the Ministry's function was essentially religious. Muslims were enjoined in the holy scripture to give generously to charities and over the centuries some of their bequests had built up to quite considerable amounts. Whether or not that had happened, there were thousands and thousands of such bequests and a whole Ministry had been set up to regulate them.

The difference in character between it and the other Ministries was apparent the moment you entered the building. Instead of clerks with their tarbooshes neatly parked on the desk beside them, the workers all wore turbans, and instead of smart, dark suits, long flowing gowns. There were fewer modern appurtenances; fans, for instance, but to make up for that the rooms were high and dark and spacious, which gave some degree of relief from the heat. There was, too, a different smell from that of the other Ministries, the smell of old books, of parchment, a general kind of dustiness.

A young man came forward to greet Owen and, when he announced his errand, led him into a small office where an older man was sitting at a desk. He rose and they shook hands.

'It's not often that we see the Mamur Zapt here,' he said curiously.

'Well, no, and I shall not interrupt you for long. I come on something small. It is really, I must confess, almost just a matter of satisfying my personal curiosity.'

'Our Mr Habashi, I believe?'

'Yes. No longer yours, I gather?'

'That is so. He left last week.'

'Can you tell me something about him?'

'There is little to tell. He hadn't been with us long, he was very junior, and he wasn't particularly good.'

'An orderly, I believe?'

'Well, a little more, perhaps. Though not much. He used to bring the files up from the basement when someone needed them. Of course, you have to be able to read to do that, so he was a little more than a simple orderly.'

'What sort of person was he?'

The man hesitated.

'You know why he left, presumably?'

'Yes.'

'I must tell you, Captain Owen, that I have some sympathy with his gesture.'

'I am not without sympathy myself,' said Owen. 'Still, it is a surprising gesture, is it not? From one so junior?'

'Not when you know him. He was always a big talker. He led, how shall I put this, a larger life in conversation than he did in humdrum reality. He had Nationalist sympathies, as, of course, you know, and felt strongly about this recent action of Lord Kitchener's, and I can quite see him drawing himself into a dramatic gesture such as this.'

He looked at Owen.

'But I don't think you need to make too much of this, Captain Owen. It was just talk. There are many who feel at the moment rather as he does but we don't all act with such precipitancy.'

'He's just a young lad.'

'Well, yes. And more given to talk than action. So I don't think, Captain Owen, if I may say so, that you really need to be very concerned about him.'

'I am not really concerned, not in the way that you think. It was something smaller that was interesting me. I was wondering if, in the course of his work, he had access to the *Government Handbook*? You know, the directory of addresses of government personnel?'

'The *Government Handbook*?'

'Yes.'

'Well, we do have a number of copies, of course. We even have one in our section. I was looking for it myself the other day –'

A message came from the Signora asking him to call. When he arrived, he was shown into the courtyard, where he found, a little to his surprise, not just the Signora but also Morelli's three domino-playing friends, Abd al Jawad, Hamdan and Fahmy. They rose and embraced him courteously.

'It is good to meet old friends,' said Abd al Jawad.

'And good to see them together,' responded Owen, his smile taking in the Signora as well.

Hamdan made a deprecatory gesture.

'We come only to sample the Signora's lemon juice,' he said with a laugh.

'Well, not quite that,' said Abd al Jawad.

'It was I who asked them to come,' said the Signora. 'For when one needs advice, to whom should one turn but one's friends?'

'What are friends for?' said Fahmy, with an apologetic shrug.

'Shukri has stopped coming again,' said the Signora.

'For the money?'

'Twice now he has missed.'

Owen looked at the other three.

'Is it just the Signora that he has left out?'

They nodded.

'Twice, you say?'

'He has come two weeks running,' said Fahmy. 'The first time it was just that he was late because of the Moulid. He did not wish to come when the streets were busy. And then he had others to visit. And then he came again this week for this is his normal time.'

'And on neither occasion did he come to me,' said the Signora.

'Next time he comes, I will ask him,' said Hamdan.

'But meanwhile –' murmured Abd al Jawad.

'The last time he did not come,' said the Signora, 'Morelli died. Who will it be this time?'

Abd al Jawad, very unusually for a man to a woman, placed his hand on hers.

'It may mean nothing,' he said softly.

'Or, it may mean something,' she said. 'And so I went to my friends.'

'And we are glad you did,' said Fahmy, 'for this is not to be borne alone.'

'I think I know what it means,' said Owen, 'and it does not mean death. At least, not, I think, for anyone in the Nahhasin.'

Abd al Jawad turned to him.

'You think so?'

'I do. And I have reason.'

Abd al Jawad turned back to the Signora.

'Well, that is good.'

'It is good, too, that you have told me,' said Owen, 'for there are things I can do.'

'There are things we can do, too,' said Fahmy.

It transpired that the three friends had offered to take it in turn to sleep at the Signora's house each night at the foot of the stairs: 'Until this thing shall pass.' The Signora, touched, said that there was no need.

'But there is,' said Fahmy, gently insistent.

So it was agreed; but then the whole argument was rendered incidental because the foreman, learning of the outcome and shocked beyond measure at what he considered a slight to himself, insisted that it was his duty to guard the Signora. 'Besides,' he whispered to Owen out of the corner of his mouth, 'what use would they be if it came to blows?'

'Let it be, Abdul,' said the Signora, 'but thank you, my friends. It is at times like this that one learns the value of friendship. And it is in the Nahhasin that friendship shows most truly.'

'You are of the Nahhasin, signora,' said Abd al Jawad, pressing his hand to his breast. 'How could it not do?'

Coming away, Owen met Mahmoud. He told him about the conversation.

'I am glad she has found her friends again,' he said. 'Or, rather, her husband's friends. I thought at first, immediately after Morelli's death, that she was, you know, reacting a bit against them. Against the whole of the Nahhasin. But the Nahhasin is a warm place and its warmth is just what she needs.'

He had thought that Mahmoud would be pleased by the compliment to the Nahhasin but, to his surprise, he didn't seem entirely to acquiesce.

'These bonds are good, of course,' he said, frowning, 'the bonds of friendship; but sometimes they work in, well, not so good ways.'

Owen didn't know what he was driving at and they walked

on for a little time in silence, while he was trying to work out what Mahmoud had meant. In the end he couldn't, so he asked him.

'I was thinking about the Signora,' Mahmoud said, 'and about why it was that she wouldn't tell the name of the person her husband had been talking to on the night before he was killed. We know that Morelli knew the man and that he was, very probably, a friend. We know, too, that the Signora also knew the man and, I suspect, also viewed him as a friend. Which is why, I think, she wouldn't tell us his name. She was confident that he had nothing to do with her husband's death and that, for her, was enough. As for the guns, well –'

'Not important in the Nahhasin's eyes, I agree.'

'And she was enough of a Nahhasiner for them not to matter to her. And also,' said Mahmoud, 'enough of a Nahhasiner to hold her tongue about a friend. But that,' he said, 'is just the trouble! It is good to be loyal to one's friends. But sometimes not so good. And in the Nahhasin you have to have both. The Nahhasin,' said Mahmoud, 'is sometimes quite impossible.

'Take that business about the fakir, the one who is supposed to have spread the story about Morelli's visitor. Now, one thing about the Nahhasin is that everybody knows everything. So if there *was* a fakir everyone – or, at least, someone – would know about him. Someone other than Amina. But they don't. No one's ever seen him. So what I deduce from this is that Amina hasn't seen him either. He doesn't exist.

'So why did she say he did? Well, Amina is a great passer-on of news but also a great storyteller. If the news is dull, she improves it, and goodness knows what sometimes goes on in her head. So she could have made it up just to improve the story; or perhaps because in fact she did not know and did not want to say so in case it reflected on her standing as someone who knows everything.

'But there is another possibility. She was doing it to protect someone. That is what I mean about the Nahhasin. You stay loyal to your friends when sometimes you shouldn't. Now, if all this is true, the question is: who did she think she was protecting?'

In the little streets behind the bazaars everything drooped in the heat. The women kept to the shade of their doorsteps and talked across the street to their neighbours on the other side. The men at the tables in the coffee houses – for there were already men at the tables even though it was only mid-morning – had withdrawn into the deeper darkness inside. There was hardly anyone at the fruit and vegetable stalls. These days, with the heat so intense, people did their shopping early. The produce on the stalls wilted and shrivelled almost visibly. The stallholders themselves were abandoning their stalls, stretching out beneath the tables already for their midday sleep or, in some cases, packing up for the day. A listless dog nosed at the spilt vegetables lying in the dust, a reluctant donkey nodded along the street.

Beneath Owen's feet he could feel the sand burning through his shoes. Beside him the sweat dripped from Selim's arms and formed a little pool in the dust which evaporated even as he noticed it.

Selim stirred. Owen pushed him back into the doorway of the shop, then stepped back into it himself. He didn't want to risk being seen a second time.

The shopkeeper raised his eyes, then saw Selim's uniform, and the effendi standing alongside him, and discreetly lowered them again.

Around the corner the ice man's donkey came padding, Mustapha sitting on its back above the blocks of ice, Amina walking alongside, poking the animal from time to time with a short stick. She seemed preoccupied, hardly bothering to look around her. Or perhaps it was just the heat.

The donkey passed, leaving a little trail of drops behind it.

Amina did not see them. The donkey moved on down the street and turned up in the direction of the ice house.

And now someone else was coming along the street, keeping to the shadow. Selim stirred again.

The figure turned into one of the shops. By the time it

came out again Selim had already stationed himself beside the door.

'You again,' said Shukri resignedly.


'It is an act of friendship,' protested Owen, when they had got him back to the Bab-el-Khalk.

'I could do without such friendship,' said Shukri.

'One day you will bless me for it,' promised Owen.

'I bless you every day, Effendi; but especially on those days on which I do not see you. Which are, alas, becoming less and less frequent.'

'Do what I say and you will not see me again.'

'Ah!' said Shukri. 'You want something? But in what, then, does this act of friendship consist?'

'An early warning,' said Owen, 'that it is time for you to look for another job.'

'That does not seem very friendly.'

'Oh, but it is. For if it were not for the friendship I bear you, Shukri, you would join the others of your society in the caracol.'

'It is not for friendship that you do this but because you want something.'

'And in return for what I want I give a reward.'

'All right,' said Shukri resignedly. 'Tell me.'


'I think I have found,' said Mahmoud, 'the man who went to see the Signor the night before he was killed. He went openly and there were those who saw him. But because he went openly, and because they were used to seeing him, they did not remark on it.' He looked at Owen. 'I must say, his identity surprised me. Although perhaps it should not. Nevertheless, because it does, I feel that in fairness I must make one more check. There is one more person who I must ask.'

'The name of that person?'

'Abdul, the foreman at the warehouse. But I shall tell you no more. For the moment.'

Owen laughed.

'You are of the Nahhasin too, Mahmoud,' he said, laying

his hand affectionately on Mahmoud's arm for an instant, 'and you show it even in this.'

The fountain house at the end of the street in which the Morellis' warehouse lay was a beautiful structure with a delicately latticed upper storey. Doves rested in the recesses and you would sometimes see them tumbling out. In this heat, though, they preferred to remain inside, and the only sign of their occupation was a continuous low purring like the engine of one of these superior new motor cars that you were beginning to see in the streets of Cairo. That, and the fact that a pigeon would sometimes drop down to sip the water spilled by the fountains and to eat the grains which Amina had thoughtfully left for them on the stone lip of the basin.

Where the sun had been on it, the stone was warm to the touch, but the water from the fountain was delightfully fresh and cool, and Owen took the small iron cup attached to the basin by a chain and splashed it over his face. Along the street he saw Shukri coming.

He bent over the basin again and a moment later Shukri bent beside him.

'You asked the reason,' he said, 'why they had told me once more not to call at the Signora's. It is as before.'

'They have been asked? By the same people as before?'

'Yes.'

'That was the easy bit,' said Owen. 'Did you find out the rest?'

'It is not easy, Effendi. But I did.'

'Well, then?'

'Effendi, I must not go on asking questions. For they are beginning to look at me strangely. Soon they will have me followed.'

'It is for that reason that we meet like this. And we need not meet again.'

'Very well, then. Effendi, what I have learned is this: it is as before. Those who have asked us, do it on behalf of another. The same one as before. However, Effendi, there is, this time, this difference: that whereas before, those who asked us did not care greatly, this time they do.'

'I do not understand.'

'Effendi, if the words are dark, it is because the business is dark. I report but a feeling, and what is a feeling?'

'But it is a feeling felt by those who have spoken to you, and who are in a position to know?'

'That is so, Effendi. The way it was put to me was thus: last time, those who asked did not care greatly about the outcome. If it succeeded, good; if not, well, little was lost. This time they want it to succeed.'

'Whatever "it" might be.'

'That I do not know, Effendi. Nor did I think it was wise to ask.'

'It does not matter.'

'Effendi, it is little that I have to report,' said Shukri apologetically.

'It is enough,' said Owen.

'What does that mean?' asked Georgiades.

'It means,' said Owen, 'that the big boys are thinking of coming in.'

Another of the fruits, he thought, of Kitchener's ill-judged action.

'Unless, of course, this example discourages them.'

The caravan was late in arriving. It had been held up crossing the river. The iron of the Kasr-al-Nil Bridge had expanded so much in the heat that the bridge had refused to open and the traffic over all the bridges had been affected in consequence. The delay seemed to have been the last straw for the drivers, if not for the camels, for two of the drivers were lying semi-comatose on their camels' backs.

The journey this time had been unusually gruelling. The Bisharin would normally have regarded such a short, easy trip as a mere saunter, but the heat this time had turned even a saunter into a major effort of endurance. Owen suspected that they had been too casual and had omitted to supply themselves with sufficient drinking water, for several of them were looking dehydrated.

They drew up wearily in front of the warehouse. The foreman rushed out.

'Welcome, Mohammed! You have had a good journey?' His eyes took in the condition of the party. 'No, you have not.'

'We have not,' said the caravan leader, touching his camel on the head with his riding stick. The camel knelt.

'Some water, Mohammed?'

'First, the camels,' said Mohammed Guri. His eye travelled back along the caravan and stopped at the two slumped drivers. 'No,' he said, 'first, them. They're young,' he explained apologetically to the foreman. 'It's their first time. Although I must say I don't know what's got into the young these days. A mere step like this!'

'Ah, well, Mohammed, you've got to make allowances.'

'It wouldn't have done in my father's time, I can tell you. If we'd fallen off, he'd just have let us lie there.'

'Ah, well, things were a bit different then.'

'They were. Still, we'd better do something for them, I suppose. Get them into the shade! No, wait a minute, take them to the ice house. They'll do better there.'

Two of the other drivers turned the camels and led them off up the street, the two incapacitated men still slumped forward motionless over the camels' necks.

The caravan leader made a sign and the other drivers got their camels to kneel down.

'We'd better get them unloaded,' he said. 'If we water them first we'd have endless trouble.'

'Right, Mohammed!'

The porters came out of the warehouse and began to carry the loads inside. The drivers stood beside their camels to see they gave no trouble. Camels were always quarrelsome and occasionally they took a bite at a person unloading them, especially if they thought he didn't know much about camels.

When the unloading was finished, the caravan leader remounted and led the camels off to the river. First, the camels; then the men. That was the rule of the desert.

\*    \*    \*

197

Owen had men watching the warehouse. They watched it day and night but no one attempted to break in. On the evening of the third day, after the porters had gone home, Owen borrowed the key from the Signora and went in himself. He and Georgiades combed through every bale and then went through them again; but the guns weren't there.

# 16

With the doors closed, the temperature had risen, even though outside it was dark.

Georgiades wiped his face.

'I saw them put it in!' he protested.

'We've had people watching all the time. No one could have got in!'

Georgiades sat down on a bale.

'Maybe they just didn't get there, then.'

Owen couldn't believe it. He had been so sure. They had even eaten bread together!

'I need to talk to Mohammed Guri,' he said.

'He'll be on his way back to Assuan by now,' said Georgiades.

'I still need to talk to him.'

'I'll talk to him,' said Georgiades bitterly. 'I'll even go back to Assuan to do it.'

Owen sat thinking. He had been so sure of Mohammed Guri. Tricky, the man might be, and honest only within limits, but within those limits you could surely rely on him, if for no other reason than that you *had* to be able to rely on a caravan leader. He had said he would deliver, and surely, surely – But tricky. Could there be some kind of trick here? Suppose, for some reason, he didn't want to go all the way with Owen; suppose, yes, that even he was not immune to the burst of anger that had run through Egypt because of Kitchener's action; suppose . . . ?

He ran through the whole thing in his mind.

Then he stopped. Maybe, in a sense, in his own way, up to a point, the caravan leader *had* delivered.

'Those camels,' he said, 'the ones that were led off to the ice house: did they ever come back again?'

'Yes. They dropped the two men off and then the other drivers brought them back.'

'But they went to the ice house first.'

There was a lamp still on in the ice house. Fahmy himself came to the door. He looked at them in surprise.

'You were lucky to catch me,' he said. 'I've been working late and was just on my way to the coffee house. How can I help you?'

'We are looking for something.'

'Oh, yes?'

'Guns.'

Fahmy seemed stunned for a moment. Then he stepped aside.

'May God be my strength,' he said quietly.

They found the guns in an unused corner of the ice house.

Even though it was late, a small crowd had gathered by the time it came to take Fahmy away. The ice men, who normally slept outside in the street beside their donkeys, stood in shock. Amina was openly weeping.

From all parts of the Nahhasin people came running. The crowd outside the ice house grew every second.

As Fahmy appeared, escorted by two policemen, there were cries of anger.

'Why are you taking an innocent man?' someone called out, and for a moment it looked as if the situation might turn ugly.

It was eased by Fahmy himself.

'Friends, I am not innocent,' he had said, looking straight before him. 'Take me away.'

'What are they going to do with him?' cried Amina, distraught.

'Take him before the Kadi,' said Selim.

'He has done no wrong!' she said angrily.

'That will be for the Kadi to decide.'

Owen appeared at that moment.

'You stupid asshole!' cried Amina.

'Now listen,' said Selim, shocked, 'me you can call an asshole because I'm not a sergeant yet. But you don't call the Mamur Zapt an asshole!'

'I call anyone I like an asshole,' said Amina defiantly.

'That is because you are an ignorant slut,' said Selim. 'If you knew anything about the world, you would know that you don't call Mamur Zapts assholes. Or anyone else that big. Because they're not like me. I would just put you across my knee. But they would cut you in half with a curbash. You don't cheek the great, you silly bitch. Though it's all right to cheek people lower down.'

'I cheek who I like,' muttered Amina.

'She cheeks who she likes,' said Suleiman.

'Shut up,' said Amina.

'Shut up,' said Selim automatically. Then he looked at Suleiman.

'Hello, my little petal,' he said in surprise. 'What are *you* doing here?'

'I work here,' said Suleiman defiantly.

'I thought you worked for the Signora?'

'I did,' said Suleiman.

Selim laughed.

'And she threw you out? Very wise of her!'

'It was that bastard Abdul who threw me out,' said Suleiman.

'It just goes to show where the brains are round here,' observed Selim. He looked at Suleiman critically and then tapped the porter on the head. 'Not in here, that's obvious.'

Suleiman struck his hand away angrily.

'So how come you're here?' asked Selim.

'Fahmy took pity on me.'

'That's more than you deserved,' said Selim.

Surprisingly, Suleiman agreed.

'It *is* more than I deserve,' he said. 'But Fahmy is a good man.'

'Not that good,' said Selim, 'or he wouldn't be where he is now.'

'You stupid bastard!' said Amina angrily.

'Yes, you stupid bastard!' said Suleiman.

'Little flower,' said Selim, tapping Suleiman on the chest, 'if you open your mouth just once again, I'll close it for you for a long time.'

Suleiman squared up angrily. Amina pushed him away, then ran off.

Suleiman's eyes followed her hungrily.

'I wouldn't waste your time,' said Selim. 'She doesn't give a toss for you. What she's keen on is a pair of shiny officer's boots.'

Someone pulled Suleiman away hastily.

The following evening Owen got the message he had been waiting for. It came from Mahmoud and asked him to come to his house as a matter of urgency. When he entered the upstairs room he found several familiar faces: Mahmoud's, of course, and that of his father-in-law, Ibrahim Buktari, but also those of others of Fahmy's friends, including Abd al Jawad and Hamdan.

There was an awkward silence for a moment and then Ibrahim Buktari came across the room and pressed Owen's hand in both of his.

'You do us honour,' he said.

'I bring you pain,' said Owen.

Ibrahim Buktari nodded.

'Yes,' he said, 'you bring us pain. However –'

He led Owen over to a divan, where Hamdan made space for him.

Then, however, there was another silence.

Owen broke it.

'You wish, no doubt, to ask for clemency,' he said. 'But there is no need. I give it without your asking.'

'We ask it for a friend.'

'I know; and know, too, that friendship counts for much in the Nahhasin.' He paused. 'I, too, counted Fahmy as a friend.'

Hamdan looked at him quickly.

'You did?' he said.

'And do. But even though he is a friend, I must do justly.'

Abd al Jawad sighed.

'That,' he said, 'is precisely the point.'

'I know he would not have used the guns himself. But he held them for those who would.'

'He was asked,' said Hamdan quietly, 'by someone he could not refuse.'

'Why couldn't he refuse them?'

Hamdan hesitated. The others nodded encouragement.

'He was bound,' said Hamdan, after a moment. 'They were of his blood.'

'It was someone from his own family?'

They exchanged glances and then nodded; all of them.

'His nephew,' said Ibrahim Buktari. 'That I should be the one to say it!'

'Kamal?'

Ibrahim nodded.

'If it is any consolation,' said Owen, 'you tell me nothing that I do not already know.'

'He shouldn't have asked him!' said Hamdan in anguish.

'It was wrong of him,' said Abd al Jawad, 'for he knew his uncle could not refuse.'

'And doubly wrong,' said Ibrahim Buktari, 'to let his uncle go to prison while he stayed silent.'

'We waited,' said Hamdan.

'But he did not come forward,' said Ibrahim Buktari.

'And so in the end,' said Abd al Jawad, 'we felt we had to speak.'

'The blood-tie bound Fahmy,' Hamdan explained, 'but it does not bind us.'

'Friendship is much,' said Abd al Jawad.

'But justice is more,' said Hamdan.

There was a timid tap on the door and Aisha came into the room, eyes lowered.

'Mahmoud,' she said, 'someone asks to see you.'

'Could you tell them,' said Mahmoud, 'that I have serious business, and ask them to wait?'

'I think they have come,' said Aisha, 'about that serious business.'

Mahmoud rose and left the room.

'Who is it, Aisha?' asked Ibrahim Buktari.

'The Signora,' said Aisha.

Even the Signora found it uncomfortable to come, as a woman, into a room full of men. She held a veil across her face and kept her eyes lowered.

The men rose to their feet.

'Signora –'

'I ask you to forgive me for interrupting you. I would not have done so had there not been great need.'

'There is no need for forgiveness,' said Ibrahim Buktari. 'We know you would not have come if you had not thought it important.'

'If you say there is need,' said Hamdan, 'then there is need.'

The Signora inclined her head in thanks. Abd al Jawad wanted to lead her to a divan but she refused, protesting that it was not meet for a woman to sit in the presence of men. The men insisted, however, and finally she took up a place, alone, on one of the divans.

There were not enough places for the others and Aisha went out of the room and returned with cushions, which she spread on the floor. Then she left the room.

The Signora fixed her eyes on Owen.

'I come,' she said, 'because you have taken Fahmy.'

'You come,' said Owen, 'like the others here, in friendship.'

The Signora nodded.

'I do,' she said. 'But, more than that. I come because I can speak and they cannot; and because I know what they do not. Fahmy is innocent.'

'Not quite,' said Owen, 'for he took the guns, knowing that they were guns.'

The Signora made an impatient gesture.

'What are guns?' she said. 'What do they matter to the Nahhasin?'

'We are talking of innocence,' said Owen, 'and that, in Egypt, is not just a matter for the Nahhasin.'

'They were not for his use.'

'I know that.'

'He did it out of love.'

'I know that too.'

'Signora,' said Abd al Jawad, 'we have told.'

The Signora did not speak for a moment. Then she said:

'It would have been better if it had not come from you. Let it come from me.'

She faced Owen.

'The man you look for is Kamal.'

'How do you know, Signora?'

'You came to me,' the Signora said to Owen, 'and asked me who Morelli was speaking to in the warehouse that night, the night before he was killed. And I would not tell you. Now I will. It was Kamal.'

'Why could you not tell me?'

The Signora shrugged.

'Because it is the Nahhasin's business, not yours.'

'And yet Morelli thought of telling me.'

The Signora looked at him.

'Through the Box, yes. But that would have been about the guns only. Not about the man.'

'Why would neither of you talk about the man?'

'Because he was Kamal. A friend. Because we had known him since he was a child, and loved him and laughed at him, as with a child. We had always known him as hotheaded and somehow we could not believe –'

She stopped and was silent for a moment.

'I still do not believe,' she said, 'do not believe that when it came to it he would have used them. Because although he was hot-headed, he was also warm-hearted. He looked on Morelli as an uncle, as someone he could do wrong to, a little wrong, knowing that the uncle would understand and in the end forgive. The guns were a small wrong.'

She looked at Owen.

'You asked why I could be sure that whoever had argued with Morelli that night had not killed him. I have given you the answer: because he loved him. Guns were a small wrong; and when Morelli upbraided him that evening, it was for a small wrong. He chided him as a father and Kamal took it as a son. It was between them only. And so he would not have told you Kamal's name, and neither did I. Should one betray one's son?'

'And yet now you do.'

The Signora was silent again. Then she lifted her head and looked Owen in the face.

'It was the wrong done to Fahmy. There comes a time when there have been enough of such wrongs. And so,' she said, 'I have come to tell you that the man you want is not Fahmy, but Kamal; that it was Kamal who bespoke the guns; and that it was Kamal who argued with Morelli that night in the warehouse.'

'Not night, but evening,' said Mahmoud.

The Signora looked at him in surprise.

'That is so.'

'After Abdul had shut up for the night.'

'Yes.'

'Kamal was seen. And seen, too, by the foreman as he left. There was no need for you to speak, Signora. I already knew.'

'And there was no need for you to speak, either,' Owen said to the men, 'for I already knew that Kamal had bespoken the guns. He ordered the guns as he was passing through Assuan on his way back from the Sudan. He was able to do so because he is a member of a brotherhood which has other members in Assuan. The brotherhood is one of soldiers and so he was able to bespeak their aid. But there are not many soldiers who pass through Assuan and so once I knew the guns had been ordered there, I was able to find him. It was, in the end, not necessary for any of you to speak; but I am glad that you did.'

A sudden puff of wind came through the open lattice work of the box window and made the oil lamps flicker and the shadows fanned round the room. It made the charcoal in the brazier flicker and a little flame started up. Ibrahim Buktari picked up the coffee pot mechanically.

'So,' he said to Owen, 'Fahmy will be released?'

Owen nodded.

'With a caution to live more virtuously in future: an enjoinder which is perhaps not necessary.'

The Signora laughed: a short bark of a laugh.

'And Kamal?' she said.

'Kamal!' Ibrahim Buktari shook his head and put down the coffee pot. He looked at Owen. 'You will go now to take him, I suppose?'

'Yes.'

Ibrahim Buktari cleared his throat.

'I have been thinking,' he said. He looked round at his friends. 'Perhaps we should come with you. It is right that he know who his accusers are.'

'There is no need,' said Owen.

'Ibrahim is right,' said Hamdan. 'We will come.'

They stood up.

'You do not need to come if you would prefer not to,' Owen said to Mahmoud. 'The guns are my concern not yours; and perhaps it would be better if that were seen to be so.'

Mahmoud had been sitting silent, his face unreadable in the half darkness. Now he, too, stood up.

'I will come with you to see Kamal,' he said. 'But not about the guns.'

There were footsteps on the stairs. Aisha, coming in, caught his words.

'There is no need,' she said. 'Kamal is here.'

Kamal came into the room and walked straight across to the group of elders.

'You did not need to,' he said gently. 'I would have spoken.'

'But why not before, Kamal?' said Hamdan reproachfully. 'Why not before?'

'I was in the barracks and did not hear at once. And then – then there were things to be thought about.'

'Others to be thought of?' suggested Owen.

Kamal looked at him defiantly.

'No,' he said. 'I acted alone. Others would have joined me. Once I had the guns.'

'You should know,' said Owen, 'that I had found you anyway. I had followed the trail of the guns. There was no need for these friends to speak.'

'It was right for them to speak,' said Kamal. 'Since they thought I was not coming forward. I am sorry,' he said, addressing them directly. 'It was wrong for me to stay silent.'

'It was wrong of you to involve your uncle in the first place,' said Ibrahim sternly.

'I did not mean to. But suddenly there was a need and I couldn't think fast enough. I had found a route for the guns and could not suddenly change it. But then I needed a place to store them and the only place I could think of, the only place with storage space, was my uncle's warehouse.'

'It was wrong,' said Abd al Jawad, 'for you were taking advantage of your uncle's love.'

Kamal bowed his head.

'As, before,' said Owen, 'you had taken advantage of the Signor's love for you.'

'That, too, was not intended,' said Kamal. 'I had intended that he should know nothing of it. The guns would be delivered without his knowing and I would collect them without his knowing. Yes, I was taking advantage of him, in that I used his caravan; but not, I told myself, of his love. It was only when he discovered the guns and I went to plead with him that, yes, you could say I took advantage of his love. And for that, signora,' he said to her, 'I am deeply sorry.'

The Signora made a little, almost fond, gesture of acceptance.

Kamal turned to Owen.

'So,' he said, 'you had found out anyway?' He shrugged. 'Well, perhaps that is fitting, since you are, of them all, the one who is closest to us. And perhaps it is best, as they say, if it is a friend who finds out one's faults.' He held out his hands to Owen. 'Come, take me.'

'I do so,' said Owen, 'not as a friend, not as an individual, but as the Mamur Zapt.'

Kamal gave him a quick smile.

'Why, yes,' he said delightedly, 'and the person you arrest

is not Kamal but tomorrow's Egypt. Although I am taken, there will be others.'

He looked at Mahmoud.

'But, Mahmoud,' he said, 'how is it that you are standing alongside the Mamur Zapt in this? When you, as one who looks towards tomorrow's Egypt, ought to be standing alongside me?'

Mahmoud moved forward.

'Because,' he said, 'one thing connects with another, as guns with bullets, and bullets with people. It is not guns alone that is the issue here.'

'No?'

'It is Sidi Morelli.'

'I do not understand.'

'When you came to Sidi Morelli that night, the night after he had discovered the guns, what happened?'

'He upbraided me.'

'That was deserved,' said Ibrahim Buktari.

'Well, yes,' said Kamal, 'it was deserved.'

'Was what followed deserved, though, Kamal?' asked Mahmoud.

Kamal stared at him.

'I do not understand, Mahmoud.'

'Did Sidi deserve to be killed?'

'Killed?'

'You killed him, didn't you?'

'Killed him? Why would I kill him?'

'Not when he upbraided you, but afterwards. When you had had time to think that he might give you away.'

'No, Mahmoud, no!'

'You wondered why I stood beside him. Now you know.'

'No, Mahmoud, no!'

He seized Mahmoud by the lapels of his suit.

'I did not kill him, Mahmoud! I swear it! I deceived him, yes. I arranged for the guns to be hidden in the bales of his caravan without telling him. And then when he found the guns and bade me come and see him, we spoke hot words, yes, but that was as far as it went. Sidi Morelli? Kill him? Sidi Morelli? What kind of a man do you think I am?'

'You would have killed others,' said Owen.

'The British, yes, I would have killed the British. They are my enemies, they are holding my country. But Sidi Morelli! He was a good man, he was my uncle's friend – *my* friend! He had lived among us. He was one of us. Almost.'

# 17

In the incredible way of the Nahhasin word spread like lightning; and by the time they emerged on to the street a small crowd had already gathered. Among them was Amina. She stepped forward and barred their path.

'It was not he who killed the Italian,' she said.

Mahmoud stopped.

'That is for the Kadi to decide, Amina,' he said courteously.

'But I know he didn't do it.'

Mahmoud, who had been speaking with his eyes slightly averted, as he always did when he was addressing women, looked her full in the face.

'How do you know that, Amina?'

Amina took a deep breath.

'Because I did it,' she said.

'Now come, Amina. It may be that you care for Kamal but it is not sensible to say –'

'I killed the Signor,' she said.

'It is not possible, Amina. You are a slight girl and Sidi Morelli was a strong man. And whoever killed him was even stronger.'

'No, no,' she said. 'I – not like that.'

'I killed him,' said a deep voice.

It was that of Suleiman, the porter.

'Shut up!' said Amina.

'No, Amina, I will not. Not this time. I know you love Kamal and I hate him for it. But I do not hate you. Even though you love him. And even though I know now that I am nothing to you. But still I love you, Amina, and I will

211

not let you do this. Come, take me,' he said to Mahmoud, thrusting out his hands.

'Suleiman, go!' said Amina. 'I have done enough to you.'

'I will not go! I waited for the Signor that night and when he left the coffee house I took hold of him and killed him. I did it. Come, take me.'

'He did it at my bidding,' Amina said to Mahmoud.

'No, Amina –'

'I told him to,' she said fiercely. 'I said that if he loved me, he would do this for me.'

'But, Amina,' cried Abd al Jawad, 'why would you wish to kill Sidi?'

'Because I thought *he* wished it,' said Amina, looking at Kamal.

'I?' said Kamal, stunned.

'I heard about them quarrelling. I had followed Kamal that night. I always follow Kamal. And then afterwards I thought: perhaps the Signor will tell someone about the guns and the police will take him away. And then the Signor came and spoke to the men about the Mamur Zapt's Box, so I saw that it was in his mind. It was then that I went to Suleiman and bade him kill the Signor that evening. I did it to save you,' she said to Kamal.

'Oh, Amina!'

'And, besides –'

She stopped.

'Besides, what, Amina?' said Mahmoud gently.

'Besides, I knew Kamal hated foreigners and I thought this would please him. I wanted to please him. I thought it might make you love me,' she said to Kamal. 'At least make you notice me.'

'Amina, Amina!' groaned Kamal.

'The Signor was Italian and I knew you were angry with the Italians. You said so. You said they were bad men and should be driven out. You said it would be well if they were all killed. So I thought –'

'But, Amina, I did not mean –'

'I understand, I think, now. But I did not understand then. I was blind. I thought only of you, of pleasing you. I thought

I had to do something to raise myself in your eyes, and I thought this would be it. I knew the guns were to be used against the British, I knew you were going to strike at them, and I thought that was wonderful, that *you* were wonderful. I thought it would be wonderful to be with you, to strike with you. Only I knew that if I went to you, you wouldn't listen to me. You would laugh at me. So I thought I would do something to show you that I was worthy. It was not the first time I had thought this. I had thought of it before, had actually done —'

'It was you who wrote the letters, wasn't it?' said Owen.

'Yes.'

'Letters?' said Mahmoud.

'To me. To other British. How did you find their names and places?' he asked.

'There is a book. The letter-writer told me about it. It is in all the government offices; I asked Habashi to steal one. And then I took it to the letter-writer.'

'Outside the Post Office?'

'You know?' she said, surprised.

'He said it was a girl.'

'Well, I thought it was clever, and that it would make Kamal look at me. But then I learned about the guns and I thought it was not so clever after all, that what Kamal was doing was so much greater. And then I despaired. But then I thought: why do I despair? For cannot I do two things with one throw? For if I kill the Signor, that will both save Kamal and show him that I am worthy to stand beside him.'

'But, Amina,' said Abd al Jawad reproachfully, 'this was a human being that you were killing!'

'I know, Abd al Jawad.'

Suddenly she knelt before him.

'I kneel before you,' she said, 'because he was your friend. I should not have done what I did. I ask for your forgiveness.'

'You foolish child!' said Abd al Jawad.

'I know. I know that now. I know what I have done. And that is why although I can kneel before you, I cannot kneel before the Signora, although I would like to. For I have taken away the man she loved and if anyone had done that to me, I would never, never be able to forgive them. But, signora, what I have done to you, I have done to myself also, for now I know that I will never be able to have Kamal.'

Kamal turned to Mahmoud.

'You are right, Mahmoud, although I did not know it. I am to blame. Come, take me.'

'I do not understand this,' said Suleiman, bewildered. 'I am the one. Not he, although I hate him; and not she. I killed the Signor. I seized him as he passed the end of the alleyway and pulled him in and strangled him. That is all. It was wrong and now I must pay the price. As for him,' he said, looking at Kamal, 'you can do what you like with him. But she is not to blame. Only I.'

'Suleiman, I have wronged you greatly!' sobbed Amina.

The message that Owen had been waiting for came the next morning from Assuan. Lieutenant Fuad, said Lofthouse, the Bimbashi at Assuan, had done what he had said he would. He had waited until he had received word from Georgiades that the guns had been stowed inside the bales of the Morellis' caravan and had then raced into the desert after the main caravan, which had by that time resumed its journey westwards. The Camel Corps had come up with it at Wadi Fashar. There had been a brief confrontation which had ended in Fuad seizing the entire caravan. The loads had consisted almost entirely of arms, bound, one of the men had told Fuad, for Tripolitania. Fuad had brought them all back to Assuan: guns, camels and men.

Not quite all the men, however. One rider had escaped, riding very fast, on a racing camel. The soldiers had described the camel in loving detail. Not so the rider, however. In fact, Fuad had been quite angry, calling them *magnoun*, crazy, when they had suggested that it had been a woman.

Owen was rather relieved.

The Camel Corps detachment at Assuan was strengthened and Bimbashi Lofthouse given a wider responsibility for intercepting illegitimate caravans that might be passing from east to west. Few, in fact, succeeded in passing, thanks to the indefatigable efforts of Lieutenant Fuad.

Kitchener was so pleased by what was regarded as Owen's success, and the opportunity it gave him to put one over on the Turks and obstruct the Italians, that he quite forgot, for the time being, his quarrel with Owen. Indeed, with the simultaneous end to the threatening letters, Owen's stock rose to dizzying heights in the British community generally; although that was only temporary.

The Khedive did, indeed, withdraw, in a huff, to Constantinople, but Nuri did not go with him. This was Paul's doing. He had run across Nuri at a Consulate reception and done his best to dissuade him.

'But, my dear Nuri,' he had said, 'it is a reforming government!'

'Reform? Excellent!' said Nuri.

'But is it? They believe in redistributing wealth, you know. Including yours.'

'But I haven't got any!' cried Nuri.

'And will have still less,' said Paul.

On reflection, Nuri thought it prudent to stick with the devil he knew.

The war between Turkey and Italy came to an uneasy end soon after. It was replaced almost at once, however, by war between Turkey and various Balkan countries. This was all right with Owen, who thought that since they would be bound to be fighting anyway, the important thing was that they should do it far away from him.

Zeinab, however, announced that she was volunteering to serve as a nurse on the Balkan front.

'After all,' she pointed out, 'that was where Florence Nightingale won her reputation. Roughly.'

'They won't have you,' said Owen. 'They've got the wrong idea about women.'

'They're not the only ones,' said Zeinab pointedly.

Owen decided that Zeinab was trying to tell him something. Perhaps it was time to take action.

'We can't go on letting things drift,' he said.

'Quite so,' said Zeinab.

'There's a police inspectorship in the Seychelles –'

Zeinab did not warm to a police inspectorship in the Seychelles.

They consulted the appointments columns together. As a result of his reading of the foreign newspapers Owen began to take rather more seriously the possibility that there could be another, more major, war over the horizon.

'You know,' he said worriedly, 'perhaps I ought to rejoin the army.'

'And get killed!' said Zeinab, losing her temper completely this time. 'What bloody use as a husband would you be then?'

# KILLER READS

## DISCOVER THE BEST
## IN CRIME AND THRILLER

Follow us on social media to
get to know the team behind
the books, enter exclusive
giveaways, learn about the
latest competitions, hear from
our authors, and lots more:

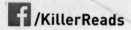 /KillerReads     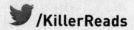 /KillerReads

Printed by RR Donnelley at Glasgow, UK